"YOU'VE GOT A WAR ON YOUR HANDS!"

Texan Tom Gillette strode into the saloon, his clothes gray with trail dust, his face an angry mask. The men he hunted were at the bar.

"Grist," he said, "you sent your gunslicks to steal my cattle and break me. In Texas we kill rustlers!"

Grist's foreman went for his gun, his arm blurring in the lamplight. A table crashed to the floor. Gillete swayed on his heels and his hand went to his hip. The exchange of gunfire shook the saloon.

The foreman suddenly lurched forward and sank to his knees. He was dead before his Colt dropped from his fingers.

"You wanted war," Gillette told Grist, his smoking gun still clenched in his hand. "Now you've got one!"

ERNEST HAYCOX

FREE GRASS

PINNACLE BOOKS
WINDSOR PUBLISHING CORP.

PINNACLE BOOKS

are published by

Windsor Publishing Corp.
475 Park Avenue South
New York, NY 10016

First Pinnacle Books printing: April, 1989

Printed in the United States of America

1 THE PRODIGAL'S RETURN

The Circle G herd, twenty-five hundred long-horned cattle out of Menard County, Texas, had passed the Arkansas and were bedded down off the trail two miles from Dodge City. The chuck-wagon fire traced an orange spiral in the night, at occasions fitfully illumining a puncher's face. There were eighteen in the outfit, counting the colored cook whose giant figure slid to and from the circle of light with the supper dishes. From the near distance floated the night rider's lament:

"Sam Bass was borned in Injianna, it wus his native
home,
And at the age uh seventeen, young Sam began to
roam—"

Cigarette tips gleamed; a dry voice broke the spell of silence.

"Had music wings that song would fall an' bust its neck."

The remark stirred the fluid of speech; a lazy rejoinder passed over the flame tips. "Yo' ain't no Jenny Lind yo'se'f, Quagmire. Fella can't tell they is a tune when yo' soothe the bulls."

Quagmire rose on an elbow and brought himself into the light; a skinny man, the colour of butternut, with drawn features and a spray of crowfoot wrinkles around each eye; a sadly sober man whose words seemed to escape from some deep pit of despair. "Who, me? I sing bass."

5

"It's God's mercy then they ain't more bass singers in this outfit."

Quagmire elevated his thin shoulders and turned his palms upward, Indian fashion. "I was borned durin' the War o' Secession when corn pone got all-fired skase. Not havin' any provender to support my voice it fell into the pit o' my stummick and it ain't come back sence. Go 'way 'long, yo' East Texas oat munchers. It takes starvation to make a genius"

"Well, by—"

Horse and rider moved into the light. Astride the horse, a stocking-legged bay with a shad belly, was Major Bob Gillette, owner of the herd. The firelight played on his face, strongly outlining the granitic ruggedness of chin and brow. He wore no beard, nor so much as a goatee—itself a sign of unconformity in a land where nearly every adult male went whiskered. In his fifties, this stormy petrel was indelibly stamped with the effects of a rough border career. Beneath the brim of his felt hat his hair showed an iron-gray in keeping with the uneven transverse lines of his face and the bold modeling of his cheek bones. His eyes were set far apart and considerably back in the sockets; thus hidden they deprived his features of the ordinary light and mobility and made them appear both harsh and uncompromising. It was a legend back in Menard County that a Gillette rider was the best in the state, not only excelling with horse and rope, but also with the gun. He worked his men hard, kept almost military discipline, and played no favourites. It was quite significant that talk ceased when he rode among the group.

"San Saba."

A brittle, slow answer came from the rear of the circle, "Yes, suh."

"I'm going to town. Keep about while I'm away."

"Yes, suh."

Major Gillette rode off. For some time the silence held, then Quagmire's rumbling, drear tones broke it. "Well, I'm perishin' for a little fluid. They say Dodge is a wicked, sinful city. Who am I to deprive it o' lawful trade? If they's anybody else wants to liquefy, le's go swell the population."

San Saba was still immersed in the shadows—a place he

6

always liked to be. But he challenged Quagmire with just two words, these seeming to crack over the fire like a lash. "Stay put."

Quagmire stared at the fire a long while, features coming to a point. Replying, he threw his words over one shoulder. "Now, who said so?"

"Orders," droned San Suba. "Trouble on the trail. They's others drivin' north asides us."

"Man—few o' years and full o' trouble," murmured Quagmire. "A wise hombre issued that remark." Conversation lagged. The early to bed rolled in their blankets and slept. Quagmire edged nearer the fire and began poking at it with a stem of sage. Once, when his eyes met those of another across the blaze, there was a point of flame in them. Just for a moment it was so; his chin dropped, and he traced an endless pattern in the glowing ashes.

The moon, full and bright, swung down from the sky as a silver pendulum. Major Bob Gillette trotted across the swelling prairie with the carriage of a cavalryman on patrol. To his right hand the river lay against the shadows like a shining ribbon. Ahead winked the lights of Dodge; ahead was the stench of Dodge and its buffalo hides. Major Bob passed a scattering of corrals, followed a trail into the dim clutter of buildings on the south side of town, and crossed the tracks. Turning, he rode down a dusty street a-swirl with life, a street across which fell yellow patterns of light from the building windows. These buildings marched beside the street, sagging and rising with it as it took its ungraded course through the town; they were, for the most part, bolstered up with a peaked or square false front as if conscious that their rickety substance needed some prop of dignity. A board sidewalk, treacherous to the high boot heel, undulated between street and buildings. Hitching racks were crowded with drooping ponies. A freighter lumbered by the Major, bull whip snapping; saloon lights were bright and alluring, pianos jingled. A woman screamed, a gun cracked, yet the men passing and repassing on the walk paid no attention. Life flowed here in a narrow and boisterous stream.

Major Bob Gillette wheeled, nosed the pony to a hitching rack, and for a moment studied his surroundings with a kind of grim-lipped pleasure. Then, dropping to the ground, he threw over the reins and marched into the Dodge House, confronting the clerk there with a short and clipped question.

"Is my son, Tom Gillette, here?"

The clerk's thumb pointed upward. "Room two. Been here a week."

Major Bob climbed the stairs and walked down the bleak hall to where he saw a crack of light seeping through a keyhole. And here he stopped, for the moment seeming to hesitate. It was quite a queer proceeding for one who was so forward and abrupt of manner, yet he actually appeared to dislike his mission, and he stood in the darkness and scowled, breath coming a little hard. In the end he turned the knob without warning, walked into the room and faced his son.

Tom Gillette had been reading, feet hooked on the table top. The unannounced entry of his father caused him to look up swiftly—and thus they met each other after five years of separation, two men of the same flesh and blood who over so long a time had been nearly a continent apart. Obviously, they were cut in the same pattern, for upon Tom Gillette there was the tribal stamp—the same big-boned frame, the same wide, deeply set eyes, the same cast of gravity. Still, there was a difference: the difference of thirty years' rough and tumble against the difference of five years' Eastern training. To Major Bob there was a certain softness in his son. His sharp eyes saw it immediately, before a word had been passed, and the fear that had been in him through the day grew more oppressive.

He was a man short of speech, he had no way of expressing what rose in him. So he spoke crisply and casually, as if his son had been away but a week. "Got in ahead of me, I see."

Tom laid away the book, marking the page. And the old man's heart lightened a little when he recognized that methodical Gillette trait. "Yes," said Tom, "I've been here since last Sunday. Didn't want to hold up the herd."

"We travel slow," replied Major Bob. "Don't wish to run off any more tallow than I can help."

Tom stood up, and the Major inspected him top and bottom as he would have inspected a horse. Good heavy muscles, fine shoulders, and a neck that coupled short. The boy had a broad barrel on him too, and he planted his feet on the floor as if he meant to take root. All these points showed through the ridiculous worsted suit that passed as fashion in the East: that suit with its short lapels, its white collar, and four-in-hand tie. Nor did the Major's eyes miss the low, flat-heeled shoes. Impractical dam' things.

There was a trace of humour in Tom Gillette's eyes as he stood there. "Pass muster?"

"How do I know?" answered Major Bob. "Turn to the light. You've lost your accent."

"It will come back. A month with the boys and I'll have it again."

"Glad to hear it," grunted Major Bob, studying Tom's face by the lamplight. The boy had left him immature, unformed. Well, he was a man now. He had been shaken down, he had filled out. He had a bearing, an element men would recognize and obey. That was his birthright. But what was in his head? How sound was his mind, how clear his eye? What did he think? The Major was almost afraid to ask, and he felt relieved when Tom, seeming to catch these unspoken queries, broke the pause.

"What's up?"

"Moving north," replied Major Bob. "Dakota Territory's been opened farther west. Free grass. Indians put on the reservation. We can't flesh up a cow in Texas, and the fever's been bothering us. Better grazing north and a better access to the market. So we are going, the Circle G, lock, stock, and barrel."

"The old home no more, eh? Kind of hate to think what's being left behind."

Major Bob heard the slight accent of wistfulness, and his fears rose afresh. There was no place for softness in a Gillette. He said so, abruptly.

"Dam' sentiment. You will get no place with that in this land, my boy. I was afraid the East would soften you. I told your mother as much. But she would have you go. Might as well be honest with you—I'd have yanked you back as

9

quick as a flash when she died, but she took my promise to let you finish. Understand it—you have nothing to thank me for. Your freedom was her doing."

Tom sombrely studied the floor. "That I know. I'll give her credit for whatever I have learned."

"And what have you learned?" challenged the elder Gillette.

Again a flicker of humour. "Among other things that the West will do for me as long as I live."

Major Bob was too old a poker player to reveal the pleasure that remark gave him. He only nodded, and pressed his questioning. "What else?"

"Well, sir, I think I can say Eastern whisky is better than Western, and that the no-horn saddle makes a poor rocking-chair."

Trivialities. There was more than this, but the boy had not developed into a loose-jointed talker. He buried his thoughts, for which the Major was exceedingly thankful. Then and there a part of his doubt vanished. And yet, being a shrewd judge, he also understood the younger man had something on his mind. Something lay cloudy behind the eyes. And thereupon he came directly to the issue.

"You've had your woman affairs? Got your fingers burnt? Made the usual fool of yourself—like all men must?"

Tom squared his shoulders at this and spoke with laconic definiteness. "Reckon that's gospel."

"Over with now?"

"As much as anything on earth can be over with."

Still vague. Major Bob bristled. "You have left no broken promises behind you, my boy?"

Silence. Silence in which Major Bob's breathing could be heard plainly. Tom swung, one hand lying open. "I think not."

Major Bob came forward. "My son," said he, very solemn, "if I thought you had dishonoured any pledge of yours I would break you into bits and send you back."

"I made a promise," explained Tom, a kind of sudden fire in his eyes. "It was accepted. Later it was rejected. I'll say no more. Wouldn't have said this much except to satisfy you. Judge for yourself."

10

"Then your obligation is cancelled," decided the Major with something like eagerness. He turned half away, sighing like one whose breath had been held overlong. And to cover what was perilously close to sentiment he relapsed into casualness. "Expected I might have had to hunt through town for you."

"Thought maybe I'd be down with my paint bucket?"

The Major raised and lowered his broad shoulders. Unconsciously he exposed the main beam of his career—a career marked by turbulence. "You will never find life up in a hotel room, my boy. It's out there," and he pointed his fist toward the street.

"Shoulder to shoulder, fist to fist," mused Tom. "Play your own hand, ask no favours, ride straight, shoot fast. Keep all obligations."

The Major nodded; a stray beam of light caught his eyes and kindled. "You have learned to express yourself well. Glad to know that. What you have said is all I ever tried to teach you. That you still abide by the code is my greatest pleasure. I had feared you would forget—that you would absorb ideas less worthy of a Southern gentleman. I will not preach—God hates a smooth tongue—but you must see the distinction between sections. The East is settled, it is orderly, it is governed by women's ideas. This is still a man's country. Make no mistake about that."

Tom bent his head. His father had struck to the core of the whole matter; had touched, unwittingly, the fear and the uncertainty within him. For he had departed from Texas with one set of ideas; in a quieter and more staid Eastern land he had discovered another. They set a value on human life there, they guarded it with jealous laws. Softness, his father called it—and softness it might be. This country to which he returned was a prodigal land, and five years had almost made an alien of him. What would he do when the time came for him to choose between codes?

His father's summary phrases recalled him. "We roll out in the morning. This will be your last night on a bed."

He shook his head. "Might as well sleep on the ground to-night." He moved to his Gladstone and took out a roll of clothes. Stripping off his suit he got into an ancient wool

11

shirt, faded trousers, boots, vest and a battered felt hat. It was the apparel he had worn out of Texas five years before. The Major, recognizing this, blew a great blast of air from his nose.

"Saved 'em, I see. Small for you now." Then he moved forward and unbuckled his revolver belt, holding it out to his son with an ill-concealed pride. "You'll be needing this again. It is your old gun. Brought it up for you."

Tom strapped the harness around him; his fingers touched the cold butt, and again he had the fleeting and unpleasant sensation of being alien. It seemed impossible he once had cherished the weapon with a fiery affection and shot pecan nuts off the trees in practice. He wondered suddenly whether he had lost the trick of swinging low and making a moving shield of his pony while firing under the animal's neck. Once he had been like an Indian.

He laid his new suit on the bed, smiling a little. "The next man may need it. I never will. Now, when I round up a maverick we'll be ready to travel."

The hallway resounded with some kind of a cry, the door flew open, and a burly young giant, larger than either of the Gillettes, rolled into the room shaking a shining yellow head. He was a pink and roly-poly Hercules, irrepressible and drunk. The love of life shone on his round, bold face, and exuberance babbled off his tongue. "Ha—wassis, Deer-slayer? Dam' awful liquor ever I drank! What a night! Tom, my rebel, now I know what made you such a screamin' savage. Whooey! Drop that gun, Jack Cade, or I'll pierce you with a needle! What was that song you taught me?

"But the dirty little coward that shot Mister Howard
    Laid poor Jesse in his grave."

"Sad—awful sad." Then, seeing Major Bob standing im-movable in his path he drew up and regained a measure of gravity. "Let's see. I haven't got to the double-sight stage yet, so you must be the old man. Pater, in other words. Well, you certainly sired a tough piece of beefsteak for a son. I'm delighted. Maybe you don't know it yet, but you've hired another cow hand. Love cows. Lord, yes! Love 'em still more if I could get another drink down without fryin' the linin' of my stomach. How, Pontiac, announce me!''

Tom Gillette nodded. "It's the Blond Giant," he explained to the elder Gillette. "True name is Claude Lispenard. Blondy, this is my father, Major Robert Gillette."

"Don't hold the first name against me," adjured the Blond Giant. His big hand struck the Major across one shoulder. It was fraternally meant, but Major Bob straightened like a ramrod. It was not the custom of the country to be over friendly at first, and the Major had all the Western dislike for loose-tongued liberties. His steely silence further sobered the Blond Giant. He stood his place, hands dangling helplessly.

"A friend of yours, Tom?" inquired Major Bob.

"One of my best," replied Tom. "But in certain respects he is as weak as water. I have brought him west to buck him up." And with the bluntness of long acquaintance he added, "He's made God's own fool of himself. Three months on the trail is the cure."

The Major extended his hand. "A friend of my son is a friend of mine. You are welcome to a place with us."

The Blond Giant took the hand somewhat sheepishly. Tom broke the silence. "Get your possibles. We are going to camp."

Lispenard found his bag, the meanwhile looking to his friend. "Not taking yours?"

Tom Gillette shook his head. "I'll never need it again. We pack our stuff inside the blanket roll."

"Well," grumbled the Blond Giant, "I'll stick to my Gladstone. Be some time before I can go without soap and water or part my hair with thumb and forefinger."

The Major thrust a single glance at his son—a somewhat grim glance—and he led the way out. Passing into the street, Tom pointed toward a saloon. "We'll christen the occasion, sir." Lispenard muttered a small oath and followed the Gillettes into the place. Together they elbowed to the bar and ordered drinks.

The place roared. Smoke eddied up from the crowd and hung like a storm signal against the ceiling. The gaming tables were crowded, chips rattled; a piano strove to carry its thin melody above the racket, and lights flashed brilliantly on the tinselled costumes of the girls. One of them was singing, and toward her the crowd restlessly eddied—cowboy and buffalo hunter, railroad hand, desperado and trapper. Lispenard's animation revived at the sight of it, and he lifted his glass with the Gillettes. "I give you Westerners credit. You do it well—dam' well."

Tom spoke across the rim of his pony. "The prodigal returns, sir."

Major Bob studied the red fluid. And it could only have been his relief that caused him to speak as he did.

"My boy, I didn't know whether I would find a son this night or not. I think I have. We will drink to the Circle G."

The screaming of a woman cut through the turmoil like a knife. Men swayed and backed against the walls. Tables went down, and across the smoky lane thus formed another tragedy of Dodge marched to its swift climax. Lispenard dropped his glass and gripped the bar. "My God!"

Two men faced each other, each bent, each weaving; their features seemed out of proportion. White teeth gleamed against an olive skin, sweat beaded across a narrow forehead, glistening like crystals. Somebody's breath rose and fell asthmatically. There was a grunted word and another swift and slashing word—and in the light the opposing duellists seemed to blur and merge. Again a scream shrilled throughout the house, striking Tom Gillette's heart cold. It rose to an unearthly pitch, then was drowned by the echo of a gun thundering and crashing against the four walls. Nobody moved, nobody seemed to breathe. But presently the man of the olive skin hiccoughed and fell. The lane began to close; through it the victor fought his way, hatless, wild of eye, waving his gun. In a moment he had passed out of the place, and the drumming of his pony's hoofs beat down the street and grew faint. Bedlam rose, like air rushing into a vacuum.

"Good God!" muttered Lispenard. He turned to the Gillettes, the ruddy colour quite drained from his cheeks. "That turns my stomach. Why don't they do something? Why don't they go after the fellow? Everybody standing around like a lot of stone images!"

Major Bob ignored him completely. He raised his unfinished glass, speaking to his son in the same grave and courteous manner. "To the Circle G." And while Lispenard stared, shaken to his depths, they drank. At that moment father and son never looked so much alike, both with a hard granite impassivity printed from cheek bone to cheek bone; the kind of an expression made with muscles tightly set. Meeting Tom's eyes, Lispenard was shocked to see the bleakness therein. It was as if he faced a complete stranger.

"We had better be going," said Major Bob.

The trio marched out and back to the Major's horse. He swung up and turned into the street. "I will go ahead. The camp is a mile beyond the corrals. Doubtless you will want to explain a few things to your friend."

This last sentence had no meaning to Lispenard, but Tom nodded soberly. "I will do it."

The two of them walked away from Dodge, past the corrals, and along the rolling prairie. To their left lay the river; above them swung the full disk of silver. Lispenard breathed heavily, and the scene in the saloon oppressed him until he could no longer hold his peace. "And you all took it so cursed cold! I begin to see the meaning of that flint and ice look you sometimes wear. The whole set of you put it on like a mask."

"Blondy, let me give you a single piece of advice. In this country, never give yourself away. Play poker with a blank face. Never tell a man anything about yourself, never ask him about himself. And no matter how you are hurt, never reveal it to a living creature."

"By the Lord, I'm not made of stone!" cried Lispenard.

"No," agreed Tom. "None of us are. But hereabouts men must carry themselves as if they were. Once a fellow started crying about his hurts he would never quit. This is a rough country. Nobody wants to hear about your feelings."

"Do you mean to tell me that that murder left you cold?" demanded the Blond Giant.

Tom travelled fifty yards without replying. Of course it hadn't left him cold. It had cut him to the very marrow and again made him seem an alien. And not long ago he would

15

have confessed it to Lispenard. But somehow he no longer felt inclined to the old exchange of confidences. He was going back to the old ways already, beginning to judge once more by the standards of the country. And according to those standards the Blond Giant had ill conducted himself.

"It makes no difference at all," said he, seeing the chuck-wagon fire ahead, "what a man feels. Somehow, when you get under the stars, it isn't important."

Lispenard fell to silence as they approached the light. Major Bob stood by the fire, around which the punchers were assembled. He had summoned them, and as his son came into view he spoke briefly, abruptly.

"This is Tom Gillette, my son. He rides with us. He asks no favours, he will receive none. If anybody wishes to challenge his mettle, that's not my affair. The other gentleman's name is Lispenard, a pilgrim and a guest of the outfit. San Saba!"

Tom swept the circle with a curious eye. None of these men had been with the Circle G in his time. It was a hard brand to work for, and the riders came and disappeared in quick succession. But he instantly recognized the calibre of the crew. His father picked only the best. Tall and short, lean and heavy—they were of all descriptions, yet they all fell into one type.

The Major's voice plunged into the darkness. "San Saba!"

"Comin', suh."

The Major meanwhile pointed to Lispenard. "I will tolerate no hazing with this gentleman. He is a guest. Remember that."

San Saba crawled reluctantly from the shadows, and Tom Gillette, seeing him for the first time, felt his muscles draw up. The man was as tall as any in the outfit and distinctly rawboned. His arms were gangling and hung to his sides as if useless to him; he slouched toward the group with his head tilted forward. It was a head too small for his body and indeed all his features seemed shrunken, from his narrow chin up to his sloping forehead which in turn slid back into sandy red hair. Tom Gillette thought he never had seen a more cruel mouth or such gimlet eyes. The colour of them

16

he could not tell, but a reddish pall seemed to hang over the surface, and the lids were likewise rimmed with the same colour.

"This," said Major Bob, "is my foreman, San Saba."

San Saba met Tom Gillette with a hurried, expressionless glance and dropped his head in scant recognition. Nor did he offer his hand until Tom first extended his own. Then there was only a slight pressure and a quick withdrawal.

"Han'somely pleased," drawled San Saba in flat, monotonous syllables. That was all; he backed away and was lost in the shadows. Major Bob disappeared from view and the most of the crew returned to their blankets. The introduction was over. Tom and Lispenard squatted before the flames, hearing Quagmire's rumbling voice take up some yarn he had been spinning.

"So them greasers staked me out on the ant hill an' let the bugs get a good feed. I was there twelve hours when the Rangers come up. We caught them renegades later, an' I skelped me the cuss what tied me down."

Lispenard was sober and morose. He stared at Quagmire, then spoke to Tom in a tone meant to carry across the fire.

"I suppose I'll be hearing all sorts of fool fish stories from now on. Do I look green?"

Quagmire appeared not to hear. But presently he swung his head a little, and the light played upon the left side of his face; it was nothing but a great pocket where some injury had scored him. Lispenard sprang to his feet, swearing. "Where do we sleep? My nerves certainly must be in a hell of a state."

The colored cook met them on the edge of the shadows, throwing two bedding rolls from his massive shoulders. He had no attention for Lispenard, but one fist gripped the younger Gillette's arm. "Marse Tom, yo' don' know me no mo'?"

Tom's voice sang upward. "Why, Old Mose! You ornery rascal—I've been wondering about you! Mose, remember the time we trapped the bear in the caves?"

The Negro's head bobbed like a cork in water. "Ya-as, ya-as. I been waitin' fo' yo', Marse Tom. Sho' seemed like

17

a mighty long spell. I'll sho' see yo' coffee cup am allus full. Sho'!''

Quagmire watched and listened. And when the two new-comers had faded into the darkness he spoke cryptically, announcing his conviction as to them. "One range hoss come back to the old stampin' grounds. Once a man gets the smell o' fire smoke in his nose it's hard to stay away. But as fo' sugar-fed pets, half broke, half wild, I nev' had any likin'. Man, short o' days an' full o' trouble."

The fire died to a golden glow. The camp settled to rest save for Quagmire, who was a notorious nighthawk. His thin and brooding face peered into the ashes as if seeking the mystery of creation there. Overhead the moon swung on its vast arc. Tom, once more sleeping under the stars, felt again the throb of the universe. It came to him out of the fathomless vault, it bore up on the night wind. He felt the presence of the herd, he made out the mutter and the snuffle of the animals on their bedding ground. The tuneless drone of the punchers on circle wavered up from the distance. A match flared, and he saw a face illumined for one moment. Again the drone:

"He was only a cowboy, gone on befo',
   He was only a cowboy we'll see no mo' . . .''

Lispenard turned on his blankets and muttered an irritable question. Tom never heard it. Five years he had been away from all this. Now he was back home. Back home! Why had he expected to be a stranger in his own land? The old life, the old sounds and smells, the old mystery of it returned to him as if he never had been away. The current picked him up and carried him on. Near the border of sleep he seemed to see San Saba's little red eyes staring at him out of the shadows.

2 ON THE TRAIL

It was yet starlight when Old Mose, drumming his knuckles against a wash pan, sang out reveille. "Arise, yo' sons o' sin! Mo'nin' comes, the sun will shine, an' the little dogies am ready fo' to go! Rise to beans an' biscuits!"

One by one the Circle G riders shook out their blankets, rolled bedding, and helped themselves to breakfast. Fog hung low over the ground; the damp sage rendered up its pungent smell. Already the cattle were stirring and the nighthawk was in with the cavvy. It was no time for lagging, no time for talk. Men drank their coffee in morose silence and went to the improvised rope corral for their ponies. Sharp profanity crackled in the cold air, loops whistled, dust rose; saddle gear jingled and squeaked, the horses crow-hopped under their riders—and the day's work began.

Tom found his old saddle in the supply wagon and lugged it to the corral, shaking out his rope. Major Bob, already mounted, came up. "I brought an extra string for you, Tom. Catfish, there.—Slit Ears—the Lawyer—the buckskin with the straight belly—that leggy roan. We had no time to do more than to break 'em rough. They'll carry you if you haven't forgotten how to ride."

Tom picked the buckskin with the straight belly, roped him and led him aside. The crew had scattered, but Tom, tightening his cinches, saw them covertly watching, and he grinned wryly. He stepped a foot in one stirrup, flipped over the reins, and was in the saddle. The buckskin's muscles quivered, snapped together. Tom felt the pony's back hump; and as the animal's head dropped forward he was swept by the old emotion of wild, half-savage joy. "Pitch, you crowbait, pitch, or I'll rake hide!"

He was carried fifty yards in a series of weaving, neck-snapping jumps. Dust obscured him, the earth disappeared, leaving him high and lonesome in his seat. He weaved like a drunken man, hearing himself yell. That yell came back to him—it was Quagmire's bullfrog croak. The buckskin wound itself into a last wicked bundle of knots, lurching sidewise, always sidewise to loosen and throw the rider off balance. Trip hammers pounded on Tom's skull, the pit of his stomach was a ball of fire. Then it was over and the buckskin swept across the prairie like the wind. Tom shook himself together and assembled his grin. "What a man learns, he never forgets. You old sidewinder, you're going to be a spunky horse. Swing around now."

When he got back to the chuck wagon Major Bob had only a silent nod for him. Tom spoke laconically, unconsciously falling into the old way of speech with its slurring softness. "Reckon he'll be tole'ble."

Lispenard had switched into more appropriate clothes— bought in Dodge—and stood watching Quagmire saddling another horse. The aftermath of his celebration in town was a fretful humour. He shook his shoulders, grumbling, "Here I am, dressed like Simon Legree. Now I suppose I'll have to board that vicious rack of bones and get my neck shook off."

Major Bob looked sharply at Lispenard, yet spoke with unusual courtesy—always a sign that he struggled with his temper. "You are a guest of the outfit, sir. Be assured. Quagmire is saddling the gentlest beast. If you were a rider, like my son, you would have to take your chances. In this country we don't break horses for other men. I will permit no hazing with you."

Lispenard walked slowly toward Quagmire. "I'd feel better about it if I had a drink. It's a hell of an animal to be called gentle."

The pony was an undersized brute, coloured like grandmother's blanket. It turned a scrawny neck and looked at Lispenard from two expressionless glass-green eyes, dropping one ear. The man rubbed his hands along his pants. "Never think a horse has no brain. That creature is openly sneering at me."

Quagmire cast a glance back at the Gillettes. As he gave over the reins he whispered sibilantly, "Don't like the way he holds his ears. Plumb bad sign. If he starts groanin' like a los' soul, you pile off hell bent fo' election. It means he's des'prit."

Lispenard scanned Quagmire's face. Nothing but solicitude and benevolence appeared on the puncher's warped features. The Blond Giant said, "Oh, well, here goes," and stepped gingerly into the saddle, holding the reins with one hand and clutching the horn with the other. Quagmire backed hurriedly off as if expecting trouble. The glass-eyed calico stood with his eyes to the earth like a bemused philosopher for a moment, then gave vent to a long, dreary sigh. His rider clawed at the saddle horn and struck the ground on all fours. The horse turned a puzzled face, moving not an inch.

Quagmire's countenance was as bland as a summer sky. In the distance one of the crew bent over, seemingly having trouble with his stomach. Major Bob spoke in a silken voice. "Quagmire, get out of here! Mister Lispenard, that horse stopped pitching twelve years back."

Lispenard muttered something and mounted again. Riding past Quagmire he gave the man a cold look. "Dam' funny, wasn't it?"

But Quagmire only shook his head. "Nev' trust a hoss— nev' trust a stranger's word," was his answer. And he rode away.

Tom galloped toward the herd with the Blond Giant in pursuit. The Circle G riders had spread out, making a long line on either side of the herd; the wagons were moving on. Major Bob, far to one flank, raised his hat and dipped it. Swing and drag riders pressed against the fringes of the herd. It moved, imperceptibly at first, but with gaining momentum, stretching into a long, irregular, formless mass. The drive was on.

Tom stood aside until the tail end of the procession passed, then fell in with the drag—those riders who ranged to the rear and kept the slower or more stubborn animals from straying. The sun rose out of the east all in splendour, the prairie stood forth in the clear morning's light, rolling league after league to the horizons. Dust curled against the sky, dust choked the drag. Bandanas were raised over faces; the day grew warm.

"Now watch, Blondy," said Tom. "Watch all this. It's a sight you never saw the like of before. By Godfrey, it's a picture."

"I wish I had a drink," replied Lispenard fretfully.

It was a picture—a picture flung prodigally across a sweeping canvas. Twenty-five hundred Texas cattle stretched in a long, sinuous line, dipping and rising with the ground, flowing onward at a steady yet apparently aimless pace; gaunt kine with big eyes and enormous horns that clacked tip to tip as they collided; here and there pausing to find a clump of grass; now and then bunching up and widening until the swing men closed in and pinched the line narrow again. Moving thus onward across a Kansas prairie green with grass newly born of the warm April rains and the warm April sun, across a prairie seemingly as boundless, as vast as the sea.

Quagmire sidled up, nothing showing above the bandana but his shrewd eyes. "They was spooky brutes when we lef' Menard. Tell a man. We walked 'em plum' hard till they got out o' the idee. Now ain't they trailbroke?"

Tom pointed to a brick-red steer that travelled as far out on the flank as it could get, tossing enormous horns into the air at every step. "There's a trouble maker."

"It's Jedge Lynch," said Quamire. "He ain't got but one eye, so he keeps out where he can see the rest o' the herd. Shore he's a trouble maker. Spooky to boot. He'll raise hell sometime. Ort to be shot." Then, spacing his words farther apart and looking directly into Tom's eyes, he added, "You'll find more'n one trouble maker on this drive." He swung about and dropped to the rear, leaving Tom thoughtful. Quagmire was an old head, a wise head. And after the custom of the country he often cloaked shrewd sentiments in seemingly guileless words.

"Funny face," grunted Lispenard. "He's certainly got a stale sense of humour."

Tom pointed his pony out of the dust and motioned to the Blond Giant. Together they rode past the swing men and galloped toward the head of the column which was now dipping from view. In the remote distance squatted a sod shanty; elsewhere the land seemed tenantless, left to the wild creatures that crawled or ran. The smiling sun struck the earth with the first hot rays of the season, the sky was azure, and afar to the left a string of hills stood clearly silhouetted.

"So this is the country you've bragged about for five years," muttered Lispenard. "Well, if I had to live in it I'd go crazy."

"Not unless you were crazy to begin with," said Tom. "Buck up, amigo. You'll feel better when the headache wears away. Didn't I tell you Western whiskey was poison for the uninitiated?"

"Mean to tell me," demanded Lispenard, "you actually like this desolation?"

Tom turned, vehement phrases forming on his tongue. But he could not express them. This man, once his bosom friend, was becoming strange to him. The barriers were up. So he contented himself with saying, "I'm just beginning to live," and put his horse to a faster pace. A jack shot out of their path as they fell over a roll of land and came upon Major Bob and San Saba riding side by side. Point men were ahead, not directly in front of the herd, but flanking it. Thus being unknowingly guided, the bovine vanguard ambled along. At the fore was an ancient and scarred steer with a broken horn who seemed to understand he led the parade. Major Bob pointed him out to Tom.

"Roman Nose. He took charge of this drive the third day out. That steer is as valuable to us as three top hands."

Tom fell in with his father. San Saba dropped back a little and thus paired with Lispenard. By daylight the foreman seemed even more taciturn and ill-proportioned; Tom was again struck with the incongruity of so small a head on so tall a body. It reminded him of a ball set atop a flagpole. Looking back, he met San Saba's eyes and nodded. But there was no response other than a short, impassive glance

23

from those little red-rimmed eyes. No more than that, and the foreman had turned, ignoring him. Tom heard the man's dry voice questioning Lispenard beside him.

"Hope, suh, yo' are findin' it pleasant?"

"Me?" grunted Lispenard. "I feel like an empty wine vat. When did prohibition hit Kansas?"

Again the foreman's laconic drawl. "Don't let the boys fool yo' with their antics. Any time I can he'p yo', let me know."

It was apparent that San Saba made an effort to be friendly. Tom thought about it awhile, then turned to a more important matter.

"Any particular spot in Dakota we are heading for? Or is it just a matter of discovery?"

The Major shook his head. "Last year news reached us that some territory around the headwaters of the Little Missouri was opening. I may say I got first word of it and immediately sent San Saba and Big Ruddy up to locate suitable range. Owing to our promptness, we have got the best of the ground. San Saba came back, leaving Big Ruddy to hold it. Since then other outfits have likewise sent scouts out and are driving north. But ours is the choice of the picking."

San Saba, hearing his name mentioned, swept the pair of Gillettes with a quick, wry glance.

"Can Big Ruddy hold it?" questioned Tom.

"Squatter's right," answered the Major. "It's free grass, but I shall file on the water. Meanwhile Big Ruddy has ample cartridges and a good gun. I have faith no one will try to jump the claim on him. However, I started early to avoid trouble in the matter. I believe we are the first outfit north this season."

Satisfied, Tom reined about and walked his horse down the line. Lispenard was talking to San Saba and didn't follow.

Onward they travelled. North, always north. Sunrise and sunset. Beans and coffee in the starlight. Night after night with the infinite heavens for a canopy and the yellow firelight playing upon Quagmire's twisted, solemn visage. Twenty-five hundred cattle trampling a broad trail across

24

the lush earth, Roman Nose plodding to the fore, wise with years. Hot sun beating down; swift spring rains pouring out of the sky, flooding the coulees and vanishing as quickly as they came. And again the hot sun playing on the wet prairie and the steam rising up. Five miles a day, eight miles a day, sometimes fifteen miles a day. They crossed the ford of the Smoky Hill, they crossed the Saline and the Solomon. Kansas was behind, and the plains of Nebraska beckoned them north—level, limitless.

Lispenard settled into the life with a kind of resignation. Riding pulled some of the flesh off him, the dust and hot winds erased his ruddiness. And since shaving in alkali water was no less than torture he let the stubble flourish on his face. When well kept he was nothing short of handsome; now he seemed all at once slack and untidy. The long hours in the saddle, the short sleep, the never-ending monotony of the food bore heavily on his spirit. Now and again a flash of his humour bubbled up, but rubbing elbows day by day with the tight-lipped stoics of the Circle G frayed his nerves and left him grumbling. He had not learned to lock his lips as others did.

"How long is it going to take us to reach Dakota?" he asked, one night.

Tom spread his palms upward. "Twenty days—forty days—sixty days."

"And not a drop to drink," murmured Lispenard. He scanned the circle with gloomy eyes. "I begin to understand what makes you fellows look like mummies. A drop of liquid would bloat the whole crew."

Quagmire stirred the fire. "Once was a fella down on the Brazos by name of Dode Leener who bragged he nev' had tasted water. Nothin' but whisky. One o' the boys goes out, ketches a rattlesnake, an' squirts a little venom into a cup, mixin' it with a thimbleful o' water. Takes it to Dode an' says it's the purest water in the state. Dode, he drinks it. By'n'by he sorter perks up. 'Men,' says he, 'if that's water I shore been missin' somethin' good all these years.' Nex' day he happens to ride acrost the Brazos, an' rememberin' what a treat he'd had the day before he squats down an' drinks his stummick full. Plain water."

25

Silence pervaded the circle. Quagmire continued to prod the ashes with his twig.

"Well," demanded Lispenard impatiently, "what happened then?"

"He died," said Quagmire, voice breaking.

Lispenard threw up his head. Grave faces looked back at him. San Saba stood on the edge of darkness, and San Saba's head jerked a trifle. Lispenard waited a little while before rising and going into the shadows. The assembled punchers sank back into the blankets one by one. Presently he came back, a transformed man. He was smiling broadly and his eyes rolled. Nobody paid him attention as he went to the chuck wagon and drew the gun from a suspended holster there. Of a sudden his voice yipped across the silence, the gun crashed twice.

"All dam' lies! Anyhow, I know Kansas ain't dry yet! Whoooopeeee!"

Tom sprang to his feet and knocked the gun out of Lispenard's hand. Blankets flew through the air as every cowpuncher raced for his horse. Out of the distance came an ominous rustle, a sound of horns clicking and feet stamping. Major Bob ran into the light, words lashing them all.

"Who drew that gun?"

"Well, I did," grumbled Lispenard, quickly sobered. "Wass trouble?"

A steady stream of profanity droned and sputtered beyond the fire. But a clear call stopped the feverish saddling. "All right—all right. It's God's mercy they ain't spooky tonight. Somebody give that gent a firecracker to play with."

Major Bob said never another word, but his glance went through and through Lispenard. He swung on his heel and disappeared.

"It only takes the snap of a finger to stampede a herd when they're restless," explained Tom briefly.

The crew returned. Lispenard went over and dropped the gun in its holster. Tom, watching him, saw his arms wobble and knew then what had caused the trouble. He raised his eyes to find San Saba peering through the darkness, taciturn, unwinking, and at that moment a chill shot down

26

Tom Gillette's back and he felt the hackles rise. San Saba disappeared.

It was on the following morning that Tom, high on a ridge, saw a small herd of buffalo feeding quietly in the plain. Turning, he raced down upon the outfit.

"Fresh meat," he called. "Buffalo boudins."

Major Bob slackened pace. "San Saba—Quagmire, go along. Tom, better take Mr. Lispenard for the excitement."

The quartette assembled and galloped back up the ridge. "Hold on," said Tom. "The wind's quartering away from us. We'll swing into that ravine."

Doubling back, they crossed the ridge farther down and got below the surface of the plain. Rifles came out of their boots. Lispenard's eyes snapped. "What now?"

"Stick with me," adjured Tom. "We could bring down meat by squatting here and taking a long shot. But it's your party, so we'll ride among 'em. Stick with me. Pick a bull and follow him down. Ready?"

The cavalcade gathered reins and shot out of the depression. Three hundred yards off the buffalo grazed peacefully. But as the hunters came to view their heads came up and immediately they raced away. Quagmire's horse forged ahead. San Saba veered slightly and lost some ground. Tom and Lispenard pounded on, gathering up the interval. Quagmire was riding like an Indian, and his pony flung itself directly into a breach of the herd. The puncher's bull-frog voice roared across the prairie, and his lithe body bent far in the saddle.

Lispenard seemed to find a road for himself, and Tom, aiming at a piece of open ground, shot alongside a shaggy bull. He was, of a sudden, in the mist of confusion, dust all about him. A rifle cracked at his side, and he heard Quagmire yelling again. Giving his pony loose rein, he brought up his gun and took a fleeting aim. But he never pulled the trigger. Another shot sang through the pounding, bellowing mêlée; his horse stumbled, went down, heels over head. Tom, wrenching himself clear, fell ten yards away. The herd roared by, sand sprayed in his face, and though the wind was out of him, he tried to find his gun. In a moment it

27

was all over. Crawling to his feet, he saw the herd galloping westward, Lispenard still in pursuit and losing ground. Quagmire was coming back; San Saba had already dismounted and was using his knife on a carcass.

"Gopher hole?" asked Quagmire, dropping from the saddle.

Tom stood by the dead horse. Blood welled out of a bullet hole just above the shoulder, and Quagmire studied it with an absolutely impassive countenance. After a time his shrewd eyes rose, and it seemed to Tom that the heat of some internal fire warmed them.

"Call it a stray shot," said Tom briefly. "The dust was high."

"Yeah—call it that," agreed Quagmire. In a lower tone he added, "I allus did say that one-eyed steer ort to be killed. They's trouble makers enough in this outfit without him." And he turned to skin his game. San Saba had nothing to say. Silently they packed the choice meat in the hides and rode back to camp, Tom doubling up behind Quagmire.

Five days later the Circle G lay on the north side of the South Platte, camped outside of Ogallala. They were seventeen days from Dodge, they had suffered no disaster, and now the lights of a far-famed rendezvous beckoned. Half of the crew rode in to see the sights, and foremost went San Saba and Lispenard. Friendship of a kind had sprung up between them, and straight to the first saloon they aimed. The Blond Giant, seizing the bottle from the barkeep with swift eagerness, poured, saluting San Saba.

"Now, my lad, do you remember the way to camp?"

San Saba nodded. "Reckon."

"Then don't forget it. When I finish here you'll have to carry me back. Happy days! I'm blotting out two weeks of dry misery!"

San Saba drank slowly, rolling the liquor around his tongue. And with each subsequent glass his gravity increased and the red pall in his eyes grew the more pronounced. He threw his shoulders back, went through every motion with preciseness. As for Lispenard, he was lost to these niceties. He swallowed the whisky, pony after pony;

his fist pounded the bar, his eyes rolled and flashed wildly. San Saba studied him like a judge. After a long interval he leaned forward, speaking impressively.

"My mammy was a Kentucky belle. My pappy was a Virginny kunnel."

"Let their bones rest," said the Blond Giant.

"Suh," proceeded San Saba, "I am the son of quality. And I know quality when I see it. Yo' are like me, damnably like me."

"We will christen that statement. San Saba, I see the devil hidin' in your eyes. You're an unregenerate piece of humanity. I'll bet you're the man that drank rattlesnake juice and liked it."

San Saba's face relaxed and he smiled, a sparing smile that never reached his eyes nor parted his thin lips. "I see yo' got a little more intelligence than ordinary." And when he saw Lispenard's head droop in weakness he said something more. "It takes a dam' rascal to know another dam' rascal."

"Wha' that?"

San Saba shrugged his narrow shoulders, seeming to weigh his partner. Casually, he looked about the room. Almost immediately his attention was affixed to a far corner where a paunchy, middle-aged man with dead white hair happened to be standing. Their eyes met; the elderly man nodded his head, and San Saba, glancing around to see if he was observed, returned the nod and walked out of the saloon. At the next alley he paused, retreating into the shadows. Presently the elder man marched out and followed. San Saba's arm reached out and arrested him.

"Where's yo' camp, Kunnel Wyatt?"

"West three miles. San Saba, why the devil are you here? I thought you agreed to keep Gillette back on the trail."

"Time enough yet. Go on, suh. My boys are in town. Don' want any to see me with yo'. I'll follow yo' to camp."

They separated. San Saba returned to the saloon door. Lispenard was in a poker game, in the process of being professionally trimmed. San Saba went to his horse and, keeping to the shadows, rode out of Ogallala westward.

3 LORENA WYATT

Twice during the short ride from town San Saba swung off his trail, back-tracked a hundred yards, and listened for the sound of pursuit; and when the chuck-wagon fire of the Wyatt outfit winked across the prairie he again hesitated, seeming to weigh his inclinations. Whatever this man's actions and thoughts, he consistently surrounded himself with a wall of caution. He liked to stay in the shadows; he never rode boldly into a camp, but, as at present, stalked and circled until he was sure of what he was to find. He possessed all the caginess of an animal that once had been trapped—he perpetually looked back over his trail, no matter where or when he rode. By nature he was a taciturn, isolated creature, seldom speaking a blunt or decisive word. He talked as he moved, warily, never giving another man more than a hint of what went on in that little nutshell head.

Thus, when a few paces from the firelight, he paused to scan the faces he saw. He knew those fellows, he recognized Wyatt's paunchy figure standing by the flame. But not until he had thus covered the group did he expose himself to the light. Wyatt threw up his grizzled mane, speaking impatiently. "What took you so long?" A scattered greeting rose from the recumbent punchers.

"It's San Saba, by Joe. Comin' back fer to work this brand again, Red?"

"Well, if it ain't the same smilin', sunny gent. Ain't yo' pritty far no'th?"

There was little enough warmth in the reception. These

men had worked with San Saba, and they knew him. San Saba nodded his head; a brief, sparing smile flitted across his lips. "Howdy, boys. Diamond W looks both f'miliar an' prosp'rous. Kunnel Wyatt, suh, if yo' will step away a minute—"

San Saba retreated beyond earshot of the crew and slipped from the saddle. Wyatt followed, still impatient. "God's Kingdom, man, will you ever quit burrowin' like a groundhog?"

San Saba's reply was flat, singsong. "A man playin' two hands ain't in no position to march at the head o' the parade, suh."

"Let it go—let it go. Hell's pit—what brings Gillette along so fast? I had a hundred miles less to go, I started a full week earlier. Yet here he is—here you are. What about it?"

"Suh, Major Bob is a fast traveller."

"Meaning, I suppose, I let my cattle drag all over Satan's half acre? By the beard o' Judas—"

"No, suh—no, suh. I meant nothin' like that. It's just that he makes us march like a troop o' cavalry."

"It's his cursed military style! I've heard of it before. Well, what are you doing? What about all those ideas you had? San Saba, did I not know you better I would say you broke no eggs. But I know you. Now, get busy. At this rate he'll beat me two weeks to the Little Missouri. That won't do. By the gates of Paradise, it won't do!"

"Yo'-all sent yo' men no'th to perfo'm a certain chore, Kunnel?"

"I did!"

"Is that chore done?"

"How am I to know? Neither man can write a letter. I presume they did. They understood exactly what I meant, and they're old hands. Even so, supposing Gillette beats me to the spot and finds my men on it where his man should be? Think he'll take it like a Sunday-school preacher? I'll be eternally fried in mutton grease if he will! He'll shoot my men and—there you are! I have got to get there first! You start your part."

31

"Oh, I'll delay the Circle G, suh. Don't worry. Plenty of time yet. You know Major Bob, pers'n'lly, Kunnel?"

"Met him once in Austin."

"He's a hard man, suh. He has a son, suh." Here San Saba's words grew drier. "A son like the name."

Wyatt grunted. "I recognize the qualities of the name. But once I get my outfit established on that particular piece of range St. Peter's own crowbar won't pry me loose!" The Colonel slapped his hands together, and by that token San Saba knew the interview was over. Climbing into the saddle, he followed Wyatt back to the circle of light. Somebody had been telling a yarn, but it stopped as the Circle G foreman came within hearing, and nothing more was said. San Saba appeared on the point of speaking. Whatever the sentiment, it fell back from the barrier of his thin, tight-pressed lips. Gathering his reins, he turned about.

Hoofs thudded across the prairie. San Saba's head came up quickly and he put a spur into the flanks of his animal. But before he could get again into the concealment of the night a rider slid in front of him, blocked his path, and he had to pull aside. Colonel Wyatt planted his feet apart, grumbling.

"Lorena, where in the name of the Twelve Apostles have you been?"

It was a girl—a girl on that vague border across which lies womanhood. Her face, revealed by the reluctant firelight, formed a small oval; her cheeks were pink where the night air had touched them, her eyes sparkled, catching flame from the chuck-wagon blaze. And that was about all of the feminine about her, for her small body was encased in the clothing of a man, she wore a man's boots and a man's broad-brimmed hat, beneath which strayed a wisp of black hair. The bright beads of her gauntlets glittered as she sprang from the saddle.

"Why, I've been to Ogallala. Do you think I'd go through Nebraska and not see Ogallala?" Then her eyes discovered and recognized San Saba, and all the gay exuberance vanished. Standing between her father and the Circle G foreman she turned first to one and then the other.

"Now what's the trouble?"

"Trouble?" echoed her father. "There's no trouble."

"Then what's this man doing here?" she insisted.

"Why, San Saba, he dropped in to pay a friendly call."

Her boot heel sank into the sandy earth. "Friendly? What friends has he got here?" And, turning toward San Saba, she threw up her chin, crying, "Get out of here you—renegade."

Colonel Wyatt roared, "Lorena, you talk like a lady!"

"Pop, don't call me a lady. It sounds ridiculous. Get out, San Saba!"

San Saba looked over her head to Wyatt. "One more thing, suh," spoke he in a level voice, "you better stay west of the trail a few days. I reckon yo' understan' why." Removing his hat, he bowed to the girl, swung, and galloped off.

"Notion to tan your back," grumbled Wyatt.

But Lorena was smiling again, smiling and humming a tune. She turned out her horse, threw her saddle to the ground, and prepared to climb inside the wagon that was her home on the long trail. "Don't you try it, Pop," she called back. "You'd lose a good cow hand—and you can't afford that. Good-night. I've got some questions to ask in the morning."

By the light of the waning stars the Diamond W was under way. It was an earlier start than Colonel Wyatt usually made. He, despite his impatient spirit, had not the faculty of whipping his men through the preliminary chores or of overriding the unending series of petty obstacles always lying athwart a cattle drive. Nor, for that matter, did he have enough men. Counting himself and his daughter, there were but eight in the party. But the interview with San Saba had warned him to be up and doing; thus, sunrise found the herd well away from Ogallala and somewhat west of the main trail. Colonel Wyatt and Lorena rode to the fore, on point, while the rest of the crew were strung out behind. Nineteen hundred cattle wound northward to Dakota's greener, lusher grass.

From time to time Colonel Wyatt threw a covert glance

33

across the prairie toward his daughter. She was a splendid horsewoman, her slight and supple figure swaying easily in the saddle; now and then, when a steer broke from the herd, she swung her pony on its heels and hazed the steer back to the main body in swift, darting moves, dust rising around her, bandana whipping out. On these particular occasions Colonel Wyatt felt proud of his handiwork. He had raised her as he would have raised a boy, he had talked to her in the rough, shoulder-to-shoulder manner he would have talked to any other man, sparing few words. It was his boast that she equalled any puncher he had ever hired. And when he saw her streaking across the ground as if she were a part of the pony, or when he saw her drop her loop over a cow and send the animal to the earth a-bellowing, he understood her very well. She had his blood, his recklessness, she had his love of life; at such moments it blazed from her dark eyes, it betrayed itself in the manner she held her nether lip between her teeth.

But there were other times when she was utterly fathomless, when for hours she rode with her glance fixed on the horizon, never speaking, never changing expression. This mood made Colonel Wyatt quite uncomfortable and incompetent. Invariably it caused him to make excuses for the training he had given her. After all, it took a mother to raise a girl—and a mother she had owned only for her first four years. She was a woman now—the Colonel had discovered it only recently and with mixed emotions—and what did a woman think about, living and riding with men, day after day, year after year?

Glancing in her direction again he saw she was restless. And presently he pulled his wits together and prepared for a bad five minutes. Her gauntlet swung upward, beckoning a man to close in and take her place.

"Hell's pit!" muttered Wyatt. "By the body o' Judas!"

She made a wide circle around the head of the herd, charging upon the Colonel. Her pony sat on its haunches, pivoted; Lorena's voice stabbed through the dust, and the Colonel, hearing how crisply those words fell across the intervening space, knew she was on the warpath.

"What did San Saba want?"

"Want—want? Why, girl, I told you he come on a friendly visit!"

"Pop—don't lie. Keep your fish stories for business deals."

"Lorena—I got a mind to tan your britches! Are you saying I'm crooked with my tongue?"

The girl nodded vigorously. "You'd hemstitch the truth whenever it suited you. But I'm not deceived. What did San Saba want?"

"Girl, I raised you to be a lady! Now act like one!"

"Pop, if you call me a lady once more I'll shout. Bury it—burn it!"

Colonel Wyatt shrewdly saw a chance to shift the subject, and his voice fell to melancholy tones. "Your poor mamma. I promised her I'd raise you to be genteel."

"That's right—sing the sad songs. Blame my mother. Cut it out, Pop. If you wanted to make a lady of me why wean me with a horse and a rope? Say, I haven't worn but one dress in six years. I'd feel like a squaw in nice clothes."

The Colonel squinted at the sun and dropped his white mane. "I did the best I knew how, Lorena. I guess maybe it wasn't such a good job at that."

That roused her sympathy instantly, and her hand fell on his shoulder. "Now, Pop, I'm not blaming you a bit. Texas fever, I like the way you brought me up!"

The Colonel smiled his best. "All right, honey, that's a nice word for the old man."

And so the subject was closed and the dangerous topic avoided, as he thought. But five minutes later she turned upon him and the same crisp question startled him: "What did San Saba want?"

"Blisterin' liniment, can't you get that off your mind? Why do you keep askin'?"

"Because I want to know," replied Lorena placidly. "What's he after?"

The Colonel groaned. "None o' your business, girl. It was private an' personal."

"Then," said Lorena, "it must be awful dirty."

"Dirty! Use that word again and I'll tan your britches!"

35

She was not to be turned. "Why did he tell you to stay west of the trail?"

"Because the herds ahead of us are spreadin' the fever, an' he warned me to stay clear of the beaten track. Also, the water's better out this way."

The girl digested that, Colonel Wyatt meanwhile praying for peace. It was not to be; Lorena shook her head. "How could San Saba know about the country off here? He's a Southerner, like us. Pop, you're too clumsy at greasing the axle."

He assumed an air of mystery. "Well, since you're so all-fired smart, I guess I got to say there's apt to be trouble ahead of us."

"What trouble?"

The Colonel rose in his stirrup. "Beard o' Judas, get back to your place! I'm sayin' no more!"

She saw he would go no further and so abandoned her direct attack. Experience had taught Lorena that her father was an exceedingly dangerous man when fully aroused. There were pieces of his business she could never discover. Sometimes she heard stray reports, sometimes she made shrewd guesses and in each instance it left her troubled, uncertain. She was, above all else, loyal to the very core; but even loyalty could not subdue the distrust that occasionally—and more frequently of late—came to her heart. The Diamond W had not prospered these last six years or so. Why this should be she could not tell. All she knew was that the Colonel had grown more nervous, more secretive, and that there was an air about the outfit she liked little enough. San Saba, for example. Her father had kept the man season after season. . . .

"Trouble is what I guessed," she shot back. "Trouble always comes with San Saba."

"Seems like you have an undue distrust of him, Lorena. I never had a better foreman."

"Nor a more crooked one. He's got a bad face. Always made me feel like I was stepping on a snake. A renegade, that fellow. I never was so glad as when he quit. What's he doing now?"

"Don't know," grunted Colonel Wyatt.

The girl studied his face for quite a while. In the end she pressed her heels against the pony's flanks and sprang away. Wyatt had sight of open rebellion on her clear features. Nor did she resume her place on the left of the herd, but raced up and over a ridge and vanished from sight.

"She'll ride it off," murmured Wyatt, trying to convince himself. Yet he was not so sure. Lorena had stubborn blood; she had curiously straightforward ideas that on occasion confounded all his plausible explanations. "She'll ride it off. The girl has got to learn it's a tough world and maybe it takes fire to fight fire. By the stones o' Peter—yes, she will!"

Lorena's pony, given rein, fled over the rolling ground. The girl swayed in the saddle as if to relieve her muscles, and presently her doubts went away. Up the swelling folds of earth and down the coulee sides, with the sun pouring its heat out of the sky. Cloud castles floated across the blue. Afar she could see the frosted peaks of the Rockies. North, beyond that cloudy strip that was the horizon, lay Dakota. North was adventure—north was another world. Already she felt the difference in climate; the air was lighter, it brought up a sense of utter freedom, it had the power to make her giddy.

"Well, I wish I were a man. I'd never stop—I never would. Ho—what's over there, Mister Jefferson Davis?"

The horse, hearing its name, promptly applied weight to its front feet and came to a stop. Lorena was on a hump of land that curved across the prairie like a swell of the ocean. A mile distant horse and rider stood immovable on another rise of ground. Lorena stood in the stirrups, shaded her eyes, and studied this intrusion.

"Not an Indian. Well, let's go see."

She proceeded at a sedate pace, noting that the strange rider likewise advanced. A white man, all right; riding erect and free. But not a trapper. Good horse—puncher's clothing—young and no whiskers. Lorena stopped and waited. The newcomer trotted on, wheeled to approach on Lorena's gun side. That was manners. His rope, she saw, had one end tied to the horn, his saddle was double cinch. He had a familiar face, a rather blocky face with big features and wide-spaced eyes set rather far back. Not that the face bore

37

resemblance to any family she knew, but that it was of a stamp familiar in the South. And strangely bleached for a Western man. Lorena's curiosity leaped to immense proportions. The stranger stopped ten yards off and raised his right hand.

"How."

"Why—you're from Texas!"

"That's right." Then she saw him bend over the horn, eyes flashing surprise. "By George, a woman." And his hat came off.

"Of course" said she. Adding with a trace of wistfulness, "Just so you don't call me a lady it's all right"

"Ma'm, in Texas—as elsewhere—all women are ladies."

"Oh, fiddlesticks! You sound like Pop. However did you get so pale?"

"I've been East awhile."

"Sho' enough?" inquired Lorena eagerly. "I'd like to see Omaha some day, myself."

"Well, farther east than that. Say New York—or Boston."

Quite a long silence. Lorena gravely considered this, her features puckered, owlish. "That's different. Too far east. But I'd like to see Omaha or New Orleans. Where you bound?"

"North—let's ride that way."

So they fell in, side by side, and ambled leisurely across the broad prairie. Lorena still was occupied with the remoteness of New York and Boston, turning the matter over and over in her mind, weighing the sound of it, the possible truthfulness of it. The stranger seemed content to keep the silence, riding with his eyes sweeping the distance. Lorena tallied up a mark in favour of this silence. She had known Easterners, and they talked a heap too much. Piece by piece she checked his rig. Well, he was from Texas, no doubt. And maybe he was telling the truth about having been to New York, though she allowed herself a small reservation. There was many a grave-faced liar out of Texas. Suddenly she thrust a question at him.

"What kind of saddles do they use back there?"

"Mighty flat things with no horn and stirrups, something like a chicken's wishbone."

She nodded. "I've heard of 'em. Guess you've been there all right."

He smiled, and Lorena marvelled at the change it made. The difference between daylight and darkness. "No law against the truth west of the Mississippi, ma'm."

Her small, rounding shoulders lifted. "I was brought up on Texas lies. Some of the men in our outfit do it smooth enough to believe themselves."

He seemed to find fresh interest in her. "What is your name?"

"Lorena?"

"Lorena—what?"

And she, who had always been a candid, out-and-out girl, striving for masculine directness, suddenly discovered a contradiction in her heart. The first impulse was to satisfy his question. The second—and it puzzled her why she should feel so strangely about such a simple matter was to make him guess a little.

"Lorena's enough."

He shook his head, thoughtful. "Now, you don't look like a fugitive from justice with a past to conceal. I tell you— we'll say the last name is Smith. If anybody should ask me about a girl with a different name I wouldn't be lying when I said I didn't know her. Lorena Smith. Why, it's a pretty combination"

She rode in stiff, dignified silence. Nor did she unbend until he went back to the original subject. "Whoever told you not to be a lady? Or that you weren't a lady?"

"Hmf. What is *your* name?"

"Tom Gillette."

"Wait," she commanded, halting her pony. "That's familiar."

"Menard County."

"Knew I'd heard of it. As to being a lady—what is your idea of a lady, anyhow?"

This seemed to strike him unaccountably hard. Her watchful eyes saw him turn sombre; there was a metallic

39

ring in his words, a vibration that did queer things to her pulse.

"A lady? One square enough not to trade on her privileges—one straight enough not to disobey her mind—or her heart."

It seemed oddly at variance with all her own notions, and she said as much. "And she must sit straight in a chair, keep her hands white, and lie politely to all menfolks to keep 'em in good humour. Haven't I seen many a lady?"

"Unessentials," murmured Tom.

"Maybe—maybe not. Anyhow, I can't do those things."

"What can you do?"

"I can do a man's work without complaining, rain or sun. I can shoot. I can rope anything with four feet."

Once more that warming, transforming smile. It reminded Lorena of raising the curtains of a dark house and letting the sun stream in. Tom scanned the prairie. "We might locate an elephant and try out that ropin' proposition."

His definition she turned over and over, examining its various facets, testing it with preliminary acids of experience. "Where did you learn that much about ladies?" she demanded. All her questions were thus—sharp and short, striking fair at their target.

"History," said Tom. "Ancient history."

That time she paid no attention to the meaning of his words, but instead listened to the sound of them. Her head dropped a trifle, her eyes swept the prairie in one broad inspection, and she did something then she had never yet been guilty of. She showed her skill to please a man—to impress him. Her pony, under the reins' touch, sprang off, running a circle around the stationary Tom. Twenty yards away a crimson flower stood above the buffalo grass, nodding on its tall stem. Lorena threw her compact little body completely out of the saddle, plucked the flower as she swept by and came upright. When she had completed the circle and was back beside the man that flower was imbedded in her hair, a trace of that femininity of which she had never heretofore given thought.

She believed she had never seen so sharp a glance, so

40

penetrating a glance from any human being. And of a sudden she was afraid, both of him and of herself. The pony whirled and broke away. A few yards distant she brought up. Laughter bubbled brimful in her eyes, her cheeks were deep pink, and her nether lip, imprisoned between her teeth, was like a cherry. The exuberant, vivid current of life would not be concealed under the drab clothing, nor behind the poker expression she liked to maintain.

"Maybe I'll see you up North," said she.

"If I should meet the posse," he called back, "I'll tell 'em I only saw a fellow by the name of Smith—and that Smith was heading south."

She flung up a hand, tarried only to see him return the signal, and galloped over the ridge. The day was hot and still. She thought she had never seen it so beautiful. The rolling prairie, marching its countless miles into the blue strip of haze, surrounded her with the rising incense of things growing. How many centuries had it lain so, how many living creatures had passed across its fecund, smiling expanse? Feeling its warmth as she felt it, heady with bursting instincts as herself?

The Diamond W was twenty minutes west. When the long dusty lane of cattle came into view, a dun ribbon against the green carpet, she had overridden her gaiety. She was bitter with herself. "Why did I make a fool display? He'll think I wanted him to notice me! Oh, darn!"

Her father called, but she shook her head and passed to the left flank. For the rest of that day she rode with her eyes ahead, her lips pressed together; by turns pensive and turbulent.

One thing stuck to her mind, its meaning enlarging with each dusty mile. "A lady is square—a lady is honest. Mister Jefferson Davis, is that *all* it needs to make a lady? Oh, I don't believe it is that simple. Still, he's been East. He *ought* to know. Darn it, Mister Jefferson Davis, sometimes it would be a great help if I knew how to cry a little! No, that's awfully foolish."

The red flower in her hair bobbed with the pace of the pony, a vivid signal.

4 SAN SABA STRIKES

Firelight threw its orange arc against the night's steel-black pall. Dark banners whipped across the silvered half-moon. The stars were shrouded, the ceiling of heaven had dropped earthward, and thus imprisoned the gaining wind swept over the earth with a hollow, droning reverberation. At sunset it had been both clear and warm. Now a raw dampness touched men and beasts. Sand sprayed across the prairie, a stem of sage sailed into the light and dropped by Quagmire's crossed boots. Eerie voice beat through space—like that of a rifle shot. The canvas on the chuck wagon slatted against its ribs. One solitary drop of rain fell hissing into the coals.

Quagmire turned his wizened face and nosed the air. "Trouble comin' hell bent out o' the east. Why has they got to be an east, anyhow? Ain't south an' west ample? I think I'll tie my ears down afo' they float away."

A rider cruised around the near side of the herd, and the echo of his improvised song reached the fire. "Lie down, you brutes, lie down. Oh, a Texas gal is the gal for me— Lie down, you measly, locoed receptacles o' sin. The wind is risin' an' so are the dogies' tails—lie doooowwn."

"It takes a good bass voice to soothe 'em," opined Quagmire sagely.

"If this keeps up," murmured his near neighbor, "yo'll be singin' soprano outen the corner o' yo' mouth befo' mo'nin'."

Quagmire crushed this innuendo impressively. "Billy, yo'

42

ort to know I nev' sing soprano lessen I'm vaccinated to the eyebrows with that filthy mescal." A burst of rain struck the fire, frying in the flames. Quagmire reached around and squirmed into his slicker. "Guess I'm goin' to get that bath I fo'got to take las' winter. Dakota, howdedo."

The flat Nebraskan plain stood behind. Both forks of the Platte, that river a mile wide and an inch deep, had baptized the herd. The Niobrara had seen their camp fire; they had passed one stretch of the bad lands and put the Belle Fourche to the rear. Due west lay the dark, granitic folds of the Black Hills; due west lay Deadwood, born of gold fever and now thundering along on the flood tide of prosperity. Indian country. Once they had sighted a brave on a parallel ridge, sitting like a statue on his horse, watching them; and since they were schooled in the red man's thievery they loosened the flaps of rifle boots and doubly guarded the horse herd.

Sand and rain swirled about the group. Tom heard the tempo of the wind rising. Thunder rumbled away off. Things movable began to shiver and strain, and the old cook slid around his wagon, battening down the canvas. Quagmire, true to his ingrained habit, hovered by the fire and nursed it jealously.

"Talk about soprano," mused Quagmire, "that wind will shore be singin' it in a minute. I hope them cow critters have got a clear conscience this night."

"Stampede?"

It was Lispenard speaking. He had come out of darkness and squatted across from Quagmire. Tom Gillette, studying the man, had difficulty in realizing it was the same gay and debonair classmate he had once so freely confided in. In the flickering light the Blond Giant looked as ragged and unkempt as any other of the party. The soft protecting flesh had quite disappeared; under the stubble of his whiskers his jaw bones ran grimly to the jutting button of his chin. And since the night San Saba had brought him back from Ogallala, both drunk and viciously angry, he had adopted a kind of brooding reserve. The man was in splendid shape. At every gesture he made Tom saw the muscles rippling and flexing. Otherwise, Tom was not so certain. It occurred to him that Blondy's big and rolling eyes no longer attracted him, nor did he like the way Blondy's lips now and then slid back from his teeth. In school, his friend had cut quite a swath; sundered from that atmosphere, he seemed never yet to have shaken himself together.

"Stampede?" echoed Quagmire. "Well, I ain't wishin' to draw down any lightnin' by speakin' that word too loud. Who knows what goes on inside a critter's mind? I've seen 'em stand through weather so plumb bad yo' couldn't draw breath. Turn right around on a ca'm peaceful night an' they'd roll tails if a leaf budged. Critters ain't reasonable— no more'n a man."

The crew, unable to sleep, had drawn near the fire. San Saba, a mere silhouette in his gleaming slicker, stood in the background while all the others squatted on their haunches. Tom, himself a little removed from the fire, saw the foreman's small red eyes dart from man to man. Billy, the skeptic who adjoined Quagmire, thrust a sidling glance at Lispenard and of a sudden he chuckled, slapping one hand across his knee.

"Quagmire, yo'-all remember that twister we bucked down by the Nueces? I wouldn't ever have believed sech a thing could happen if I hadn't seen it with my own two eyes."

The rest of the crew, almost in unison, nodded confirmation. Quagmire studied Billy with a long, mild glance before replying. "Mean the time it picked up Anse Loving's herd an' carried it across the river?"

"Wasn't Loving's herd atall," denied Billy. "It was a bunch o' Hogpen stock."

"No such thing. It was Loving's outfit we worked for that year."

"Why, by—"

Lispenard threw in his contribution. "You trying to fool me again? Some dam' fish story about wind picking up cattle bodily—"

Profound silence. Quagmire vainly stirred the fire. "Ever hear of a twister? Don't they teach it in Eastern gee-og-ruffies?"

"Certainly, but—"

44

"Ever hear of 'em liftin' buildin's offen the ground?"

Lispenard raised his shoulders. "Well, go on, then. That's straight enough. But a whole herd doesn't sound possible."

Quagmire pointed into the darkness. "It's only blowin' mild right now. But yo' go out there, an' try to stand up in it. Then imagine a twister."

There was no answer. Quagmire brooded over the remnant of flame, water sluicing down his hat. He appeared to have forgotten the story, yet ever and anon he lifted his thin and wrinkled face to listen to what the wind told him. Slight uneasiness rode the shoulders of the crew.

"Anyhow, it was the Hogpen outfit," muttered Billy somberly.

That roused Quagmire. "Why, man, don't yo' recollect that wall-eyed buckskin I rode with the blaze?"

"Mebbe so," assented Billy, now dubious.

"Sho'," proceeded Quagmire. "I'm tellin' yo' I rode him that night. Black? Say, it was blacker'n the inside o' a crow's windpipe. Never saw a twister come up faster. We was on the east bank of the Nueces—"

"West bank," corrected Billy.

"That's right—west bank. On the west bank when it come. Right by that barn, yo' remember? No time to shove the herd aside. Funnel bearin' down on us hell bent. Every man for himself. Me, I lights out on that buckskin. Hadn't gone fifty feet when it struck. Heard an awful crash— must've been the barn—and then I sorter feels like yo'd feel after too much mescal. Yo' understan'—kinda feather-headed. I digs in my spurs, but I wasn't on no horse atall. I was fifty feet offen the ground, goin' over the river. The buckskin had vamoosed. Thought I'd lost him. Figgered I was dead when that twister let me go an' I dropped. Sho', but it's a queer feelin' to get up with the birds."

There was a rumble in the outer darkness, and the crew, to a man, straightened. A puncher rode in, dripping wet. "Still peaceable," he announced briefly, and disappeared. Tom relaxed, grinning when he saw how Lispenard's attention fastened to Quagmire's tale.

"Must've been a mile farther along," continued Quagmire, "with me gettin' higher all the times when I hears a sound like an express train comin' by. It was that dam' barn, with the top ripped off. They was ten ton o' hay in that shebang, yet it sailed by me like a shot. Then I hears a mos' piteous nicker, an' it's the buckskin, right behin' the barn. I remember I sorter prayed the saddle wouldn't fall offen him. Silver inlay saddle, an' it cost a heap.

"Well, we was a good six miles east o' the river by then, an' the twister begins to slide away from me. Me, I falls faster'n a shot duck. Had a watch on me, an' I recalls I takes it out an' throws it clear, not wantin' to light on glass. I knowed I was as good as extinct right then, an' I figgered I'd better pray. But how's a man to pray what ain't never learned the Commandments? Anyhow, I was worryin' about that silver inlay saddle. Down I went, head first. Saw the ground smack below. But that barn had lit befo' me, an' me, I struck the top o' them ten tons o' hay, bounced a couple times, an' slid right down into a manger. An' you may chalk me up as a bald-faced liar if I didn't find—"

He stopped, shaking his head from side to side. Lispenard leaned across the fire. "Well?"

Quagmire spread his hands, palms upward. "The buckskin had ketched up with the barn while both was in the air. The cuss had walked inside to get a free ride. When I slides down to the manger there he was, munchin' oats."

Billy collapsed first, moaning. The crouching punchers swayed back and forth, arms flailing, like priests performing strange rites. Wild laughter ricochetted up and against the whirling air. Lispenard jumped to his feet. "I told you it'd be another cursed fish story!"

He had to shout to make himself heard above the shrilling tempest. Quagmire still sat cushioned on his heels, water pouring down his slicker and pooling at his feet; still a sober, bemused figure. Alone of the Circle G crew, San Saba had not joined the hilarity, and now he stepped into the waning arc of light, unfriendly, brittle-voiced.

"It's an old, stale yarn to tell a gent."

Laughter died. Quagmire looked up. "Old? What's new in this ancient universe? But seein' as yo' speak of old things, I reckon I could relate a few."

46

"Personal allusions, suh?"

Quagmire got to his feet, but the foreman's height made him tilt his wizened face; it was a face upon which solemnity loved to dwell, yet on occasion it could be as hard as granite, as bleak as death. So it was now. "Once upon a time, San Saba—"

Lispenard stepped ahead. "Thanks, San Saba, but this is my quarrel."

Quagmire snapped at him. "It only takes two oars to row a boat! Yo' ain't got no quarrel!"

The Blond Giant fell silent, full lips twitching. Quagmire's thin chest laboured to shove his words against the wind. "Once they was a bad night—like this one. Looked as if they might be trouble—like it does now. Boss comes up to the boys and says, 'Boys, we are apt to have a stampede. Somebody's like to get killed afo' mo'nin'. Now yo'-all better write yo' true names on a piece o' paper an' tuck in yo' shirts.' That's what he said. Mebbe *we'll* have trouble. But they's only one man here which needs to write his true name on a paper. An' that's yo'— San Saba!"

"Quagmire—yo' lie!"

"I pay no attention to a dawg when it barks at me," replied Quagmire somberly. "Yo' past history may be unfamiliar to others, But *I* know it!"

"Yo' lie!" droned San Saba. "Eat those words, hear me?"

Tom Gillette stepped in between the men. "Drop it! There'll be no fights in this outfit. We're on the drive."

Quagmire turned away. But San Saba craned his nutshell head forward. "This ain't yo' affair. What yo' hornin' in for?"

"I'll make it my quarrel, San Saba." The wind swept Tom Gillette's words high up, and he had to throw all his power into them. "As for quarrels—you ought to know whether I've got one with you. Wait until the drive is finished if it's in your mind to settle."

The Major rode out of the dark pit, followed by the cavvy herder. "Saddle up! Everybody ride! Lightning striking half a mile off!"

The last flame guttered and was extinguished. Tom reached Lispenard shouting. "Stick with me! If there's trouble, keep away from the herd!"

He felt Lispenard's hand knock his arm away. "Don't worry about that. I'll look out for myself."

Confusion in the horse herd. Tom threw the dripping saddle on his pony, cinched it tight against the knowledge he might have to depend utterly on the solidity of those double bands, and swung out of the mêlée. A hundred yards off he struck the flank of the herd. The brutes were up, moving uneasily, heads tossing. The force of the wind was shifting them; they were turning spooky—in that frame of mind where any unaccountable sound or sight might set them running. Tom walked his pony along the rim of the straggling circle, rain driving against his slicker and pounding on his skin. He was in no humour to sing, but sing he must; anything to give those uneasy, forboding kine the reassurance of his presence.

"Oh, Buffalo girls, are you comin' out to-night.
    Comin' out to-night, comin' out to-night,
    Oh, Buffalo girls, are you comin' out to-night . . ."

The drums and trumpets of the storm rolled out a prolonged fanfaronade. Thunder rocked the heavens, and an instant later a sinuous, wavering bolt of lightning cracked the pit-black sky and hung suspended one long second. In the pale blue twilight thus cast over the earth Tom saw the herd massed together, tails and horns and bony backs moving like the wind-whipped surface of the sea. Stray members of the crew were silhouetted ahead, bent against the lashing rain. Then it was dark, abysmally dark, with a phosphorescent glow running across the thousands of horn tips. Thunder again, coming closer; wind and rain struck down against the earth with tenfold force. Tom's pony stood still, bracing its feet on the slippery soil.

"Oh, Buffalo girls, are you comin' out to-night,
    To dance by the light of the moon . . ."

College—law and order—elm trees shading green lawns. What was all that but a dream, a faint echo of life? Here on this tempest-torn prairie animate creatures struggled to survive. And some would not.

Lispenard had not left the chuck wagon, though he, like the others, had saddled his pony. The time might come when he would want to get away in a hurry. San Saba warned him of that after the rest had ridden off. The foreman had waited until he was alone with Lispenard, and even then he spoke as softly as he could manage.

"You stick here, amigo. If they should be a sound like hell bein' pulled up by the roots, skin out."

"Thanks"

And then San Saba grinned, though it was too dark for Lispenard to see this cheerless contraction of lips. "Ain't no call fo' thanks, friend. Mebbe I will be askin' yo' to return the favour some day."

He vanished, trampling the last dull ember of the fire. Nor did he fall into the usual drone as he skirted the herd. He went silently, with the picture of the herd as he had seen them at sunset in his mind. Judge Lynch, the one-eyed hermit, was over on the west side somewhat near the rear. Judge Lynch usually bedded down a little removed from his companions and seldom moved far from the original spot during the night. The critters were all up now, but the foreman was betting strongly that this morose and distrustful animal would be standing in his tracks. Barring earlier developments, he had business with Judge Lynch.

The first streamer of lightning found him half around the circle. Two riders were directly in front, but they were travelling in the same direction and thus didn't see San Saba. The foreman quickened his pace and on the ensuing flash looked behind him. Nobody within fifty yards. At the same time he located Judge Lynch, marking the spot in his mind as the darkness closed down. He bent forward, slipping his quirt; Judge Lynch's vague outline fell athwart his path. The quirt flailed out, struck the steer's rump. San Saba's voice teetered shrilly on the driving wind. "Hyaaaa!" Judge Lynch snorted, whirled from the blow, and lumbered off.

San Saba turned the pony and galloped recklessly into

the open prairie. Through the wild beat and roar of the storm came the distinct echo of the herd breaking away. A rumble of those thousands of hoofs, a clamour of bawling and bellowing, a clicking of horns. The reverberation of all this trembled along the earth and up through his pony's pounding feet. San Saba grinned his humourless grin and aimed away from the path of the stampeding brutes. For that path was one of destruction.

Tom Gillette had rounded the windward side of the herd when he felt a shock pass across the darkness. Once experienced, it was a sensation never to be forgotten. He had often been told by old hands that the fright of a single steer could strike through five thousand cattle with all the speed of an electrical impulse. He never had quite believed it until this moment. It came from he knew not where, the cause was equally obscure. Nevertheless, he felt the impact of that surging, milling mass of brutes as they swung, collided, and then struck off with the wind behind them. The babble of their throats drowned even the storm; and when the next flash of lightning played its smoke-blue gleam upon the prairie he saw them running, tails up, horns weaving; here and there they had become trapped by their blind fright—piled together like logs jammed up in the eddy of a river. But they were running away, and Tom saw Quagmire and Billy outlined just for an instant in the glare, trying to circle around to the front of the mass. Darkness dropped; he sank his spurs and raced after them.

Guns cracked. Somebody in front was trying to turn the flight. He heard a shrill yell beside him, and he wondered which one of the crew it happened to be. Not that it made any difference; yet his mind played queer tricks as he found himself on one ragged flank of the racing brutes. Queer tricks; for all the while this night and its fury hammered at his senses he kept remembering the last dance. Even the music of it came back to his memory. There had been a summerhouse out in that green and peaceful yard; a summerhouse open to all the fragrance of a June night. And where was she now, and what dumb man—for it seemed all men were humble and helpless at her hands—was receiving the favour of her provoking and elusive smile? Oh, she knew the game she was playing. What else could it be with her when every gesture and every word had so led him astray? And in the end it was her cool, scornful dismissal. "Tom, you Texan savage, why must you be so ridiculously serious? You ought to command your heart better. Thank you, my dear man, but I'll be no chatelaine out in the wilderness."

It was over, thank God! He found himself shouting the very words into space. He'd had enough. Enough of play acting and fine manners and—falsity. He had been a gentleman. What good was that? Why, those people never knew what living was. And they had infected him with their code, with the specious reasoning of their commandments. Good enough for them, but what would any of them do if they saw San Saba's little red eyes staring through the shadows, like the eyes of a reptile ready to strike? Curse that code, it had tainted his blood. It had made him feel cold fear on matching San Saba's dead, lusterless glance.

The muffled echo of a shot. The racing pony drew well toward the head of the stampede. He felt the steady surge of its muscles, and he thought of the cinches he had drawn so tight. Well enough, so long as the horse kept its feet out of a gopher hole.

The storm maintained its fury. They had gone miles from camp. Of a sudden Tom saw a jagged fragment of the herd break off, then he was surrounded and riding neck and neck with a racing shadow, feeling the touch of a horn against his stirrup. He drew his gun and fired point-blank, shouting at the top of his lungs.

"Pile up, you brutes, pile up!"

Oh and on he raced. It seemed many hours, it may have been many hours. But he was well ahead and he had company. Quagmire's bullfrog croak came to him at intervals, like the sounding of a foghorn. More shots, more wild incantations. His pony raced down a hollow, up the farther side; the rhythmic jolting of its hoofs lost a beat, the animal stumbled, caught the stride, and pounded on.

"Good boy. This is no place to die."

Gradually, as the time passed, Tom detected a lessening of speed, a kind of faltering among the cattle, a raggedness in their hitherto compact formation. Instantly, he slackened

51

his own pace until he rode abreast of the lead steers. The other punchers along the vanguard likewise had discovered this and were crowding together. Guns flashed in the blackness, voices rose shrill and profane. Tom ranged abreast a steer and pressed against it, sheering it off from a straight course. He heard Quagmire's rumbling cry of encouragement.

"Now she goes! Swing 'em—swing 'em!"

They swung, brute following brute in a giant circle. More men rode in, shoving against the swirling wall of flesh. The circle dwindled, the herd milled around and around; they fell from a gallop to a shambling trot and presently that trot declined to a walk. Mischief still swayed the more unregenerate, but the fright had worn off, the flight was checked. The stampede was over.

It was a smaller herd by half. Cattle were strung out the many intervening miles, but there was nothing to do but wait the miserable night through. Thus the crew wearily stood guard, wet and tired and uneasy. Rider came abreast rider, establishing identity.

"Where's Mex?"

"Dunno. Last I knew he was 'way back. Had a slow horse. Don't 'spect he could keep up with this hell on wheels. That Carolina over yonder?"

"Yeh, him an' me stuck together."

One by one they mustered. The names of the absentees were repeated in gruffer accents. "That you, Billy?"

"Nope. Billy was last man from camp."

"No, sir, he was right aside me up until ten minutes ago."

"Well, he's all right."

"Shore—shore. Prob'ly trailin' some strays. Show up by daylight."

Somebody began to sing:

"Oh, bury me not on the lone prairie,
    In a grave six foot by three—"

It was protested instantly. They were jaded, and an uneasy fear rode each of them. "What fool is that? Lord a'mighty, shut up! Cow critters don't deserve no melody tonight."

The crest of the storm had passed some little while ago; the rain lessened. Thunder echoed from a remote distance, and it seemed to be getting lighter. And so the hours dragged by, the Circle G crew sodden to the skin, riding weary paths in the trampled earth, and every now and then one of them would announce discovery of another member, only to be contradicted. Talk came in shorter spurts. Silence grew the more prolonged, though on occasion there was a crackling rapid-fire exchange of comment. Anything to relieve the tedium.

"What started this cussed party, anyhow?"

"Somebody spit over the wrong shoulder, I reckon."

"Yo' ain't funny, Baldy. Say, did anybody hear a sorter yippy-yip about ten seconds before it happened?"

"Ask Joe Priest. He was on circle then."

"I oughter been out there singin' bass," opined Quagmire, riding into the conversation. "It never would of happened. Tom—hey, Tom."

"Present and accounted for," drawled Tom.

Quagmire drew alongside and his arm rested on Tom's shoulder. "Knew yo' was ridin' with me. But I kinda lost yo' fo' a piece and I——" But he was not given over to sentiment. That was as far as he would go.

Tom swore at him. "You galoot, I'm riding a good horse."

"Sho'. An' the good Lord was watchin' yo' too. Else yo' pony wouldn't he'ped none."

The squealing of the chuck-wagon wheels announced Old Mose's approach. He had smelled them out somehow and was coming on the dead run. How or where he had found his horses no one knew. His falsetto voice assailed them.

"Ain't you boys got nuthin' else to do but run offen the earth? Gittin' sho'ly tough when doctor has to foller with the grub."

The rain still fell, and there wasn't a dry twig within twenty miles. But the cook knew his business. Presently a fire twinkled directly under the wagon bed, shielded from the downpour. When it had grown enough to threaten the vehicle, Old Mose drove clear of it, threw on the coffee pot,

53

and in ten minutes hailed them. "Come an' wa'm yo' giz-zards."

The first gray beam of false dawn crept out of the east. In a half hour it was light enough to take stock and recount noses. Nothing was said for a good five minutes, and in the end it was Major Bob who brusquely broke the silence. "Guess Billy's out followin' a stray bunch. We'll look. Quagmire, Tom, Joe Priest—you—Carolina—light out that way. Rest of you spread."

They strung to the four corners of the gray and sodden morning. Tom galloped directly back upon the trail—the broad trail flailed by the stampeding herd. The mark of ruin was on the earth, the grass churned into the mud, here and there a cow that had gone down in the rush. Tom rode steadily, tired clear to his bones. Drab tendrils of rain hung raggedly from the dark sky; it would be a sullen day.

Of a sudden he came to a coulee half awash with water. And he stopped dead, his eyes fastened there. Then he turned, pulled his revolver and shot thrice, spacing each shot. The extended riders swung and converged toward him. Those tarrying at the chuck wagon sprang to saddle and came on the dead run. Tom waited until they had assembled before pointing to the coulee.

"Pony threw him, I'd guess. Must've been tangled in the herd. Never had a Chinaman's chance."

Billy—the skeptic Billy who forever liked to contradict Quagmire—was sprawled in the coulee's bottom, half covered with water and mud, arms outflung, face down. And it was Quagmire who first got from his horse and descended. Somebody broke back for the chuck wagon, returning with a pair of shovels. And while the rain sluiced over the earth the crew stood grimly about as the grave was dug and Billy lifted into it. It was a hard silence to break, a difficult place to say what had to be said. When the last shovel of earth had been tamped down, Major Bob took off his hat.

"If anybody wants to say a prayer, let him do it. I reckon nobody wants to, though. Well, men have got to die, and men have got to be buried. Where is a better place than here? We'll see the boy again, make no doubt of that. It's the same story for us all. The candle burns strongly, but the candle burns fast.''

Quagmire's voice rose angrily. ''Well, Billy was a good gent—a good gent! Put another shovel o' dirt on that grave, Red. He shore was a good gent. He'll ride in marble halls! Dammit, Red, put another shovel o' earth on that grave! It's awful cold this mornin'!''

5 MURDER IN THE CIRCLE G

The Circle G herd was flung to the four corners of the compass. Fifteen hundred of them were with the leaders; the other thousand had scattered over an area of ten miles, and for three days the outfit camped, rounding up the strays. In they came, by pairs and squads and fifties; gaunt-eyed kine that had left Texas with no flesh on their ribs and now were nothing but bone and skin. They grazed on the open prairie, they were off in the pockets of the broken land. From starlight to dusk the men of the Circle G rode a widening arc, following the plain prints in the soft and sandy soil. Tom counted a dozen dead animals along the path of the stampede, and later, when he rode into the rugged country to the west, he came upon a cutbank where a hundred of them had gone over and piled up, tier on tier, all dead. But on the morning of the fourth day Major Bob called a halt and flung his arm ahead, signal to be on with the drive.

"We're still shy a hundred or more," said Tom. "Give us to-day and we'll find most of 'em off there in the coulees and cedar brakes."

Major Bob shook his head. "I'll take the loss. No more time to be wasted. Riding north this morning I found the tracks of another herd. Somebody's before us, cutting west. San Saba!"

The foreman rode slowly to the fore, eyeing the Gillettes warily. "Yes, suh."

"Time for us to be watching our direction," said Major

Bob. "Seems to me we ought to swing westerly somewhere round here. You remember the country from last year?"

San Saba swept the horizon. "Yes, suh, tole'bly well."

"Lead out, then. There's a party ahead, of us. Steer as straight a line as you can"

The foreman nodded. The swing and drag pressed against the herd. It moved forward, on the last leg of the journey. The sullen skies gave way, the sun beat down day after day, the prairie steamed and grew dry, the coulees were bereft of water once more. North they travelled, arrow straight, with San Saba in the lead, never saying a word, never revealing what thoughts stirred behind his small red eyes. They crossed the trail of the other herd and lost it at a point where it swung directly into the dark and timbered land westward. Tom kept his peace. Yet all the while a vague suspicion stirred in the back of his head. And one day he came alongside his father and spoke quietly.

"You said you were bound for the country around the head waters of the Little Missouri, didn't you?"

"Yes."

"Then it seems to me we're going too far north. We've passed the Grand and it sticks to my mind the Little Missouri makes an ox bow and sweeps south. I think I remember it from a map I've seen."

Major Bob rode for a mile without speaking. But his eyes were fixed on the back of San Saba, who was a hundred yards in front. "San Saba has been there. He's been a capable foreman to me. I have trusted him." He turned to his son. "You don't rub well with the man, do you?"

"I'll say nothing against him," replied Tom.

"No, of course you wouldn't. Matter of principle. East didn't wholly convert you. I hope, Son, you have never lost your eye for the centre of a target."

Tom held his silence, and Major Bob shook his head, just a little sadly. "Men must be as they are. God knows there is little enough softness in this world. Not that I would have it otherwise. San Saba!"

The foreman checked his horse and waited until the Gillettes came along. "Is it not time to swing west?" asked Major Bob, studying the foreman keenly.

San Saba appeared to verify his surrounding from the visible landmarks. "Not yet, suh, fo' a day. I am lookin' fo' a table-top butte with red streaks through it."

"Well, you know best. Remember, we can't afford to lose ground. That trail we passed makes me very uneasy—very uneasy."

San Saba raised his shoulders, saying nothing. His inscrutable eyes rested momentarily on Tom and the latter thought he saw a point of light break through the red pall. A point of light that gleamed and was suppressed. Then the foreman dropped his narrow chin, murmuring, "I'm doin' the best I can, suh. If yo' aim to turn west I'll say nothin'."

"Go ahead," replied Major Bob.

Tom dropped to the rear where Quagwire rode. Upon the wizened face was imprinted the sorrow of the universe. But he grinned at Tom and threw a leg around the saddle horn.

"Was a fortune teller once what told me I'd take a long trip. Paid him a dollar. Well, look what I got for my dollar. He said I was a gent that liked life. Hell, I got to like it! He tol' me I'd meet up with a dark lady an' she'd be a great influence to me. That gipsy sho' read my periscope."

"Met the lady, did you?" inquired Tom.

Quagmire squinted at the sun, the earth, and the remote horizon. "Rode a pitchin' hoss down by El Paso one year. Broke both collar bones, sprained a leg, an' bit myse'f in the middle o' the back. Laid up three months."

"What's that got to do with a dark lady?"

Quagmire spread his palms upward. "It was a black lady hoss."

Tom smiled. "Well, we live and we learn."

"Sometimes," amended Quagmire lugubriously, "we only live."

"It's the only life we've got," mused Tom.

Quagmire shifted his weight. "Now you spoke like my own son."

"If you'd had a son. Ever tried the institution of marriage for a reasonable length of time, Quagmire?"

"Shucks, no. I'm too stingy to divide my affections."

But much later, after a brooding study of the matter, he

58

amplified this. " 'Tain't exactly that, either, Tom. But, I tell you—I can sleep on grass and I can eat navy beans until said navy quits makin' 'em. Sorter hate to make a woman share that. My mamma was death on havin' me comb my hair. Mebbe that got me shy. Company ahead."

The herd came to a straggling halt. Over an adjacent ridge came a solitary rider clad in fringed buckskin. Tom trotted to the fore to join the ensuing parley. Major Bob rode out to meet the stranger. The man's skin was like so much parfleche, and a beard draped itself from cheek bone to collar, out of which glittered two intensely black and exploring eyes. He raised a hand, Indian fashion, and kept his peace.

"Know this country?" asked Major Bob.

"Ort to," responded the man. "Yallerstone Bill be my name."

Major Bob signalled to San Saba, meanwhile pursuing his point. "Then you'll know in what direction is the junction of Red Willow Creek with the Little Missouri."

"If you be goin' thar," replied the plainsman, "ye sh'd of turned due west couple days back."

San Saba arrived in time to overhear this and immediately spoke up. "They's a table-topped butte with red streaks hereabouts, ain't they, suh?"

The plainsman spent one very short and noncommittal glance on the foreman. "Dunno of any."

Major Bob's face turned unexpectedly harsh. "Will you guide us?"

The man nodded after a little reflection. San Saba again broke in, a trace of heat in his words, "Major, suh, it strikes me oth'wise," but Major Bob shook his head.

"We'll depend on this man. Forward, now. By Godfrey, we have lost time! Forward."

San Saba held himself very straight. "Suh, if yo' mean to doubt my—"

The Major cut him short "Never mind—never mind! Get back with the herd!"

The long line of cattle formed a dun-coloured crescent across the prairie. The speed increased, dust rose higher. And still Major Bob was unsatisfied, ranging back impatiently. Tom saw the mood of angry recklessness riding his father then, and it was with something akin to a shock that he discovered the same stirring impulse in himself. And when Lispenard, who seemed to hold himself aloof these days from all men but the foreman, came up with a subdued warning—"I'd trust San Saba sooner than I would that tough-looking fellow"—Tom broke in with unusual curtness.

"I wouldn't trust San Saba out of my sight, Blondy."

"Oh, look here! He's my friend, and I don't like to hear that said behind his back."

"Then," said Tom, "you are at liberty to tell him I made the statement."

They left the level prairie behind, wound in and out of what seemed to be an old buffalo trail through the black, tree-studded hills. The guide kept almost out of sight, never stopping. Hour after hour, on the trail long before light until long after dusk. It even wrung a dismal groan from Quagmire.

"They say death is a long sleep. Mebbe that's why we ain't doin' none of it now."

But the day at last came when the guide poised himself on a ridge and waited for them to catch up. Major Bob galloped ahead, beckoning to the men nearest him. When Tom arrived, the guide was pointing to the west. "Thar she is."

The rugged land formed a kind of bowl, the bottom of which made an isolated valley. In the distance, one side of the bowl gave way to the banks of the Little Missouri. Directly across the grassy plain ran a creek, sparkling under the sun. Cottonwoods fringed the edge of the distant river, and above the trees wavered a spiral of smoke. That caught and held their attention. Major Bob studied it long and intently. "Must be Big Ruddy's fire."

"I'm afraid it won't be that," muttered Tom. "Look over to the right—right where the ridge breaks into small pockets."

Cattle! Cattle browsing peacefully along the slopes. And by their number and the compactness of their position it seemed to indicate they had only been thrown on the land a little while before. Major Bob rose in his stirrups, shaded his eyes. When he swung to the others there was danger in his eyes. In passing, his glance fell upon the foreman and rested there one long, grim moment. San Saba appeared to catch up his muscles, to draw off; his features became pinched. But the Major had nothing to say to him at that time. "Quagmire," he cried, "get back and bring the crew! Bring them with their guns! By Godfrey, if anyone's jumped this valley from me they'll have to fight! Come on!"

It was not the guide's fight, and he let them go. Three together—the Major, Tom, and San Saba—they galloped down and across the little valley. Grass stood high along the ponies' legs, the creek was crystal clear; Tom surveyed this little paradise, acknowledging to himself in a wistful moment that it was worth driving a thousand miles to possess. All that man could want was right here, and though the land to either side might be equally fertile, it didn't seem to him possible there would be another site as ideal as this. The Major seemed to think so, too, for his eyes kept roving across the ground, and his head jerked from side to side as he flung out his few bitter words.

"I was uneasy about those tracks we saw! Very uneasy! Well, it's mine by squatter's right. Mine, by Godfrey! If they've shoved Big Ruddy off they'll have to fight! They'll have to fight me!"

San Saba lagged, saying nothing at all; his face was quite set, quite unusually devoid of expression.

They came to a thicket and followed single file through it and on into the cottonwoods. The path broadened. Tom's eyes saw fresh ax marks and, as they went onward through the trees, his eyes discovered a lane leading into a clearing. There were wagons ahead, the smoke of a fire—and men standing in a group with rifles cradled. His father was to the fore and seemed not to see, so he called out.

"Watch close there. I think they've got a reception committee."

"They'll have to fight, I tell you!"

A moment later the three of them had left the trees. Sharp warning fell athwart their path.

"Stop where you are!"

61

They reined in. In the moment of silence ensuing Tom took in the whole scene at one sweep. Eight men stood in a semicircle, each armed. To the front of the group was one who seemed to be in command—a short, paunchy gentleman with grizzled whitish hair and an excitable face. They had not been here long, for a dozen freshly peeled logs were rolled in a pile, the beginning of a cabin. Beyond the clearing were the banks of the Little Missouri. Still farther beyond stretched the naked hills. It was all very peaceful—all save this crew who stood so stolidly by their guns.

Major Bob was in a thundering temper, yet he mustered a semblance of courtesy. "And why, sir, this exhibition of guns?"

The paunchy gentleman spoke in rapid-fire phrases. "Hell's pit! You come swarming in on me like renegades! Got to watch out for 'em. Country's full of that kind. If you're peaceable, I'll down guns."

"What outfit are you?" shot back Major Bob.

"Colonel Jefferson Wyatt—Diamond W. Migrated from Texas. Sir, I believe I hear the Southern accent in your speech. To whom am I indebted—"

Major Bob broke through this parley. "Don't you know you are jumping my grass?"

"Sir!" cried Wyatt, turning purple. "By the whiskers of St. Anthony, that's a fine come-ye all! Your grass? Why, curse me, it's free grass, not your grass! Territory of Dakota belong to you? Not by a bag full of shot!"

Major Bob seemed to grow calmer as the interview progressed, and Tom knew this to be an ominous sign. "I lay not claim to the territory of Dakota, Colonel Wyatt. But I most assuredly lay claim to this ground. I had my men locate it last year. I kept one man on it to hold my title. That man is here. He represents me. You will have to move, sir."

Colonel Wyatt barked out, "Where is your man, then, eh? Where is your man, if you had one here?"

"I do not see him, very true," admitted Major Bob, every syllable dripping formal politeness. "It may be, sir, you can produce him quicker than I could."

" 'Postles and prophets!" shouted Wyatt. "You are trespassing on my honour, sir! Now, look here. If you had any man on the ground, he ought to leave some mark. D'you see a blessed sign of improvement, a single scrap to indicate? Any cabin, any sheds? You know you don't. But I will tell you something more, sir. I will tell you I had *two* men here these three months, waiting for me. Now, let's see what they say. Anse—Rob, step up.''

Tom's attention never left Wyatt's face. That anger might be real. Probably it was real, for the man seemed to have little control of his temper. And yet it seemed to him there was a furtive watchfulness in those shifting black eyes. When he summoned his two punchers it smacked a little of stage play, as did his examination of them.

"Now, boys, did you see any man on this ground when you came here for me? Answer straight now. I'll have no lies out of *my* camp.''

One of the two took it upon himself to reply a surly, "Nope. Saw nary a soul.''

"There you are. I will not say, sir, that you had no man. But I will say that if you *did* have one here, he mos' assuredly skipped out. That's not my fault. I will remind you again it is free grass. First come, first served.''

He was on the point of adding more, but the appearance of the rest of the Circle G crew threw him into plain uneasiness. With one arm he motioned his own men to spread farther apart, at the same time warning Major Bob, "No more about it. I'll stand on my rights. Don't want no trouble, now. You had better withdraw your men.''

"I am going to have a look,'' decided Major Bob calmly. And suiting the action to the word he rode toward the river.

Wyatt moved over, spreading his arms. "You will do no such thing. My word is good enough for you. Get off my land.''

Major Bob leaned forward with just a piece of a smile on his face. "I will ride to that river, sir, or I will blow every man in your crew to pieces. Step aside!''

Tom had been watching the crew for the first open sign of hostility, and there was something on the remote corner of his vision that bothered him. Something to the left, beside a wagon. He ventured a swift glance in that direction, to discover the girl of the prairie, the girl who had called herself Lorena, standing with one hand grasping a pistol. And yet every line of her small and boyish figure seemed to reveal that she would never use the gun, that she hoped only to be unobserved. When she found that Tom was looking directly at her, the pistol sagged and dropped and the hand came upward by slow degrees until it rested against her bosom; her cheeks were bereft of their pinkness; all her features were preternaturally sharp and sober. She was rigid, like some small animal on the verge of flying for shelter if discovery came too close.

Challenge thrust upon challenge. Colonel Wyatt was shaking his grizzled locks; yet for all his determination he was quite pale. "I repeat, I will not permit you to come another step. My word as a Texan gentleman—we know nothing of your man. Not a thing! Stay back, sir!"

"I am not questioning your word, sir," replied Major Bob, more precise than ever. "I only expressed a wish to see the river. I shall see it."

"You'll do nothing of the kind. Men, see to your guns!"

"Ah," murmured Major Bob, and he turned to his own crew. "I am going to the river. The first one of them that raises weapon you will kill. After that, answer them bullet for bullet." And he rode forward.

"Take aim!" cried Wyatt, trembling visibly.

Tom moved in the saddle. "Stop it! There'll be no fight. Come back here, Dad. It's their argument."

The Major swung around. "And how is it their argument?"

"What if Big Ruddy did pull out on us? It's too small a prop to start a fight on. There's got to be more proof than that to kill men. Let it go. If it is free grass, it's their grass now."

"Is that all you have to offer, Son?"

Tom's arm raised toward the girl; and from the manner of the Major's glance it was plain he had not seen her before. Silence hung oppressively over the clearing, a silence in which Tom distinctly heard Colonel Wyatt's breath rise and fall. A stubborn man, yet made of shoddy material. As

64

for the crews, they sat quietly—faded and weatherbeaten figures ready to fight on the spot.

The silence was at last broken by Lispenard's murmured astonishment. "My word—a beauty! A beauty out in all this desolation!"

Major Bob lifted his hat to the girl and turned his horse. Not a word, not so much as a change of a single muscle to indicate the tremendous disappointment. At his gesture the Circle G swung about and took the path back toward the valley; and it would have been a wordless withdrawal had not the girl, suddenly coming to life, sprung away from the wagon, pointed her finger at San Saba, and cried out:

"San Saba—you're a renegade cur!"

To a man, the Circle G riders whirled. Wyatt cursed his daughter. "Shut your fool mouth or I'll knock your teeth down your throat!"

"I've got no use for a traitor," said she stubbornly. "That man never did a decent thing in his life!"

San Saba sat in his saddle like a sack of meal, not meeting the girl's accusing face; a trace of colour tinged the sallow, malarial cheeks, and once he swept his own crew with what seemed to be fear. All attention was upon him, and he appeared to find it necessary to speak. So, venturing one brief look at Major Bob, he defended himself.

"I've done my duty by this outfit. Nobody's got a call to give weight to anything *she* might say."

"Let's go," said Tom. And again they passed down the trail. Not until they were completely out of the valley and on the ridge overlooking their own cattle did Major Bob pull himself from his profound reverie. "My heart was set on that location. I studied this country from end to end. There'll never be another like it."

San Saba tried to soften the Major's attitude. "Well, it's tough. But they's plenty more land in Dakota, suh. Just as good."

"There'll never be another piece like it," reiterated Major Bob.

The guide filled his pipe and spoke emphatically. "That be right. But since ye was beat out, foller me and I'll show'ee another spot. It ain't the same, but I reckon it'll pass muster."

"Go ahead," directed Major Bob. He had nothing more to say, either that day or the half of the next that they were on the trail. It seemed he wrestled with some bitter problem, a problem that he worried over and over in his mind, trying to reach a conclusion. Whatever the nature of his thoughts, he displayed no outward signals, but Tom made a shrewd guess, and when sunset came he drew Quagmire aside and spoke a brief phrase. Between the two of them they saw the night through, and never for a moment was San Saba beyond the range of their attention.

It was noon of the following day when the guide halted some twenty miles distant from their original destination and pointed at the rugged land ahead. "Thar she be. Water an' grass. Little Mizzoo off yonder two miles."

Major Bob no more than glanced at it. "Very well. Tom, look after things. Throw off the herd. Better ride along a piece and find a place fit to throw up cabins." Then his attention turned to San Saba and his voice filled with tremendous energy. "San Saba, come with me."

San Saba threw up his little head, the tinge of red filming across his pupils. It appeared for a moment that he meant to refuse. But in the end he nodded briefly and followed Major Bob over the ridge. Tom watched them go, stirred by an almost irresistible impulse to pursue the pair. Quagmire must have felt the same emotion, for he crowded toward Tom, muttering, "I'd never trust that gent to my back. I never would."

"No," acquiesced Tom. "But it's Dad's play right now. I can't interfere."

There were other things to do, and he beckoned Quagmire to come with him across the rolling ground on a tour of inspection. It might have been twenty minutes later when they heard the single gunshot come rolling over the ridge, and at the sound of it both their horses turned and raced northward in the direction whence it came. Quagmire shouted at the top of his voice:

"By God, I told yo' I wouldn't trust—"

"Stay back, damn you!" cried Tom. "It's my quarrel now!"

Quagmire reined in, a figure of wrath. Tom raced on up the ridge and down the farther slope. He had less than a mile to go, and he knew the answer to that shot before he slipped from the saddle and went running toward the single figure sprawled on the ground. It was his father; his father trying to hold himself up on an elbow, the blood staining his shirt front and a dimming light flickering from his deeply set eyes. At that precise moment Tom never knew what words came rioting out of his throat, but they caused Major Bob to shake his head sorrowfully.

"He's out of sight now. Never mind going after him. The world is a short and narrow trail for a murderer. I'm done. Gave him a fair break, but he played crooked. Bend down, Son—"

"Which way did he ride? Oh, by God, I'll tear his black heart out of his ribs!"

"In due time, Son. In due time. But I want your promise on that. You'll get him?"

"You've got it!"

"Well, the old flame's in you, Tom. I thought maybe the East had about killed it. Some girl took the sap out of your heart. Watched you on the trail. Wasn't the same boy I'd sent East. Don't go back there any more. Stick to your country—good country for men of our kind. We've got to have air to breathe"

He had only a few words left, and he nursed them along carefully. "Get him. Not just out of spite, Tom. But the Lord hates a traitor, and there ain't any room in the world for his kind. I gave him a fair break. The fool—I knew some of his past history, but I didn't know he was hooked up with Wyatt on this deal. He's always been a good foreman—and I'll forgive a man anything if he does his work well. Trusted him too far. Listen, my boy, it's your Circle G now—" He stopped, peering at a sun that grew darker for him; a sun he would never see again. "Your Circle G. Good brand. I made it. Carry it on. Something tells me you'll have to fight to hold it. Never mind. Carry it on. That girl—she called the turn on San Saba. Spunky kid. Listen. When you go

67

after San Saba, watch for a trick. Pay no attention to the gun in his holster. He carries another—in his armpit. Got me that way.''

After that, the interval of silence was longer. "One of man's duties is to live so's he won't be afraid to die. I'm not afraid. But, by Godfrey, I hate to go! Takes a long time to understand it's a beautiful world. Better make Quagmire your foreman. Good man. Just give me another ten minutes—''

But the angel of death was already laying a cloak over him, leading his spirit down that infinite corridor whither all mortal creatures travel. He gripped Tom's hand, whispering out of the remote distance, "Takes a little bit of Texas blood to christen a new country. I'll—tell—your mamma—''

6 AN ADVOCATE OF TROUBLE

Major Bob was buried at sunset on a knoll just back from the river. And after the subdued moment of farewell, his name was completely erased from the lips of the crew. Nor would they ever again utter it until time had made a tradition of his memory. Grimly the men went about the infinite chores ahead of them; Tom walked into darkness and was not seen again that night by a living soul. For him there would be always the ring of his father's last words, the memory of the promise he had made. Yet, like the rest, he would give no sign of what that crashing moment of disaster had meant to him. This was a land of the living, a land wherein men displayed a firm countenance to the world and kept their emotions locked away in deep vaults. Not that they were unfeeling or unemotional, for, if the truth were told, the members of that outfit possessed beneath their rough exteriors a womanlike sense of delicacy. But to have openly showed it would have been a confession of weakness. And weakness was fatal.

Of all the outfit Lispenard was the only one to transgress the rule of silence. Possessing no sense of loyalty toward the Circle G, the whole affair left him unmoved. In fact it struck him as being grimly grotesque, a parody on a play he had once seen back East. And he utterly missed the significance of the crew's holding aloof from Tom that night. At supper he marked Tom's absence, and it made him suggest that the cook bang the pan a little louder. "Nobody likes cold beans and coffee."

Not a word was said in answer, and presently, irked by the unresponsiveness, he spoke again.

"I used to think a man was batty when he got to the stage of talking to himself. Now I know different. Either I talk to myself or I howl at the moon like a poisoned wolf. Ever hear that story—"

Quagmire flung his emptied tin plate on the ground so hard that it skipped into the fire. "Oh, shut up! Ain't you got a lick of sense?"

Lispenard reared his head, and the sudden access of fury within him made his heavy lips tremble. He would have called Quagmire to account on the spot save that every eye was bent upon him in cold disfavour; it was the same expression he had met with ever since the second day from Dodge. He had no friends in that outfit, and well he understood the fact. If San Saba were only here now . . . At the thought he called himself to account. The foreman was a murderer and a fugitive. No, that wasn't exactly so, according to Western standards. San Saba had only exercised his privilege of shooting first; the man had gotten good and tired of the oppressive Circle G atmosphere—just as he, Claude Lispenard, was beginning to tire of it. And San Saba had been man enough to give vent to his feelings. The Blond Giant mildly applauded him for the act. Rising, he walked into the shadows. According to the Western code, a man was responsible only to his conscience, and at the thought Lispenard grinned up to the sky. It was a comforting thought, especially to one whose conscience had always chafed a little under restraint. A comforting thought.

"By George," he muttered, "I like this country. Not all the cursed work and grit of a cattle herd, but I like the free-and-easy idea. Some of these days I'll drift away on my own hook. After I get better acquainted with that little spitfire. Wasn't she a beauty, though!"

Dawn and work. Let dead men rest; this land laid down its challenge—struggle or be defeated. And in the subsequent two days Tom Gillette recalled the ominous phrase his father had voiced. "Something tells me you'll have to fight to hold it." So it would be. To begin with, this little corner of Dakota seemed more barren than almost any piece of ground they had traversed. The water holes were few and already dry. The bluffs of the river admitted but two trails down to water level within a space of ten miles. So much for summer; when winter came he prophesied he would lose many cows in the boxlike draws that broke the rugged surface.

"I'll do no more exploring," he murmured. "Here we camped and here we stay."

Lispenard, riding glumly alongside, bent an ironic glance at his companion. "What was that subterranean threat?"

"Nothing."

"Aha! The abysmal silences of a strong man. Volcanic emotions beneath an iron mask. Really, Tom, I'm beginning to falter. A set of building blocks would afford me the thrill of a lifetime."

"You'll come out of it, Blondy."

The Blond Giant swore irritably. "Good Lord, don't talk as if I were a kid to be humoured. I'm twenty-one."

"Then act like it," replied Tom. But he followed this by laying a fraternal arm across the man's shoulder. "Just forget that, Blondy. We all get short tempered now and then. Best way is to keep a tight tongue."

Lispenard drew away from Tom's arm and rode along silently. Tom, sweeping the terrain, saw a dust cloud kicking up to the east, and for the next half hour he watched it trail up and down the ridges, coming nearer. Presently the figure of Lorena Wyatt became visible, riding like an Indian. The Blond Giant's whole attitude instantly changed.

"By gad, there's our prairie flower! Tom, for the Lord's sake introduce me—introduce me! Did you ever see so compact a little beauty?"

She drew up and waited until they had approached, her face maintaining a gravity that her black eyes were forever threatening to dispel. She had but one noncommittal glance for Lispenard's sweeping bow and his broad smile. It was to Tom she paid attention.

"I'd like to see you alone a moment," said she.

"Oh, come now" protested Lispenard "we're blood brothers. Cross my heart if that's not the literal truth. Am I to be denied the sunlight altogether?"

A swift glance flashed between the girl and Tom. She straightened in the saddle and waited; Lispenard tarried, still smiling. "Formal introductions seem to be *de trop* out in these broad stretches. Who am I to fret over the fact? My lady, you have one more humble servant. Fact—"

"Have you no manners?" interrupted the girl scornfully.

That stopped the Blond Giant and, for all his sunburnt colour, a flush spread over his cheeks. "Manners? Oh, come. Who is there to judge manners out here? This is no drawing room, is it?"

"Most Easterners make that mistake," said she. At which Tom turned to Lispenard and cut off further parley. "Stay here." He and the girl rode along the prairie a hundred yards or so before she came to a halt.

"I've heard. Oh, I'm sorry!"

"Thank you for that."

She hurried on. "I never knew until we got to the river that the two outfits were racing for the same spot. San Saba—he's crooked, he's a born traitor! If I'd had any idea he was with you I'd have warned you."

He turned that over in his head. "Would you have told me even against your father's will?"

Storm swept out of her small body. "I would! I hate crookedness, I won't stand for it. Dad hired him—I don't know why—some years ago. Kept him even after I wanted to fire the man off the ranch. If I had been a man I'd have used a gun on San Saba. He's a snake. There's been things lately that have made me suspect—"

But her sense of honesty came in conflict with an ingrained loyalty, and she stopped a moment, proceeding wistfully. "When I saw you near Ogallala and gave you just my first name, it wasn't—it wasn't because I was trying to conceal anything. I just wanted to tell you that."

Tom shook his head. "You couldn't be crooked."

"How do you know?" she demanded with that characteristic frank curiosity.

The sunlight made a playground of her face, sparkling against the black eyes, losing itself in the dark hair beneath the hat brim and in the hollow of her throat. Most women he knew, looked out of place in riding habits, no matter

72

how fashionable. But this girl, dressed in the roughest of men's clothes, couldn't hide the rounding freshness of her body or the upthrust of vitality that came with every gesture and word.

"I know it," said he.

She appeared suddenly confused and dropped her eyes, whipping her quirt across the saddle skirts. "A woman can ask some foolish things," said she. "That's why I'd like to be a man. Anyhow, I wasn't trying to rope any information out of you."

"We're going to be good neighbours," drawled Tom.

"Just you know it," she said with a lift of her chin. "It's a darn big country to be fighting in. Or—to be lonesome in." She nodded toward Lispenard, who sat moodily in the distance. "Who's that?"

"An old Eastern friend of mine."

She smiled, a frank, sweet smile that seemed to ask pardon. "Then I'm sorry for having been so abrupt with him. I thought at first he was just—just another specimen. There's plenty of them nowadays. Just tell him, though, that manners are always welcome."

"He's got much to learn."

"Haven't we all?" she asked. And the two of them looked at each other until the girl's horse moved restlessly. She raised her small compact shoulders, gathering in the reins. "If ever I hear of San Saba I'll let you know. So-long."

"So-long."

She fled across the uneven ground and disappeared. Tom returned thoughtfully to his companion, and they cruised homeward. Lispenard held his own counsel as long as he could, which was no great length of time:

"Well, what's it all about? What's the secret?"

"Nothing," drawled Tom.

"Oh, by gad! Tommy, I'm truthful when I say this Western taciturnity galls me like the devil! Have you forgotten all the old fraternal confidences?"

Tom Gillette had not meant to reveal the conviction that had matured in his head over the long northern drive. Nevertheless, it slipped out now. "Blondy, the time for that is all behind us. The time and the place as well. Men change—all things change."

"I have sensed as much," replied Lispenard drily. "A severance of diplomatic relations, as it were?"

"No, not at all?" said Tom. "Our past four years were years for talking. From now on it is the time to be doing. God knows there's plenty of that ahead."

Lispenard relapsed into one of his sullen spells; his big lips were splayed in a kind of a pout, and his whole face mirrored dissatisfaction. At the chuck wagon he abruptly left Tom and had nothing more to do with him all the day. As for Tom, he regretted speaking out as he had done, and he would have made amends—save that he couldn't make headway against the conviction that his one-time friend was in the process of a mighty transformation; that the man's impulses for good and bad—always hitherto more or less evenly matched—were being forged by some kind of internal fire. The dominant traits would triumph, the lesser ones would crumble. Tom was afraid of the result; he had more than once wished Lispenard were back East where the restraints of a more complex social order would take hold.

Quite promptly more important affairs put the man from his mind. Foremost was the matter of getting some legal claim to water rights along the river. Next was to get trace of San Saba. Then cabins and pens were yet to be built against fall and winter. Leaving Quagmire in charge of this last chore, Tom struck out for town, thirty miles north, early next morning. The route led him down the river until he was within Wyatt's new range, then across a ford and over the undulating prairie. By eleven he was at Nelson, seeking out a surveyor.

Nelson was a cattle town on the boom. Along the solitary street ranged a double row of buildings not yet old enough to have lost the sweet, aromatic pine smell, and at the same time old enough to have received a baptism of bullet holes through the battlemented fronts. But one structure boasted paint; and naturally enough this was the saloon. At the end of the street three or four tents were up; beyond marched the prairie. Railroad tracks skirted one side, and a depot squatted a hundred yards distant, a little removed from

74

which were rows of cattle-loading pens. Considering the size of the place, it seemed crowded this day as Tom Gillette laid his reins over a rack and cruised slowly through the street; crowded with every taciturn and picturesque type of the frontier. Cow hands, nesters, trappers, and Indians strayed from the adjoining reservations, each man wearing whatever suited his taste, from buckskins to fourpoint Hudson Bay blanket capotes.

Tom finally found a surveyor and described his location along the river. "What I want is the section, township, and range lines, so that I can find them on the land-office plats. After that I want you to come over to my place and lay off the corners."

The surveyor, whose skin was like a piece of yellow cloth long faded in the sun, explored his maps. "That ford you say is in front of your place must be Sixty Mile Crossing. And sure it is. Well, then"—writing a set of figures on the back of an envelope—"there will be your claim. 'Tis the fourth man you are who has come to me this week on the same business along that river. The country is settlin' up, make no mistake. You understand, of course, that this land all lies along the river. Back from it the country is open and unsurveyed. You've got only squatter's right there."

"That's all that's necessary just so I get legal claim to my water right. The rest is safe enough on squatter's right."

"To be sure—to be sure," replied the surveyor. There was a lingering note of doubt in his words, and Tom tried to pin him down.

"Well, where's the catch?"

"Ah," replied the surveyor, winking. "And where is the catch? I'd like to know it as well. I'm sayin' nothin', mind me. Uncle Sam is a grand uncle, but it happens sometimes he's short-sighted. Some o' his nephews an' adopted sons ain't above cheatin' him. Never mind. You want me to come out, then? All right—I'm all-fired busy, but I'll make it tomorrow."

"Good enough," said Tom, rising. But the surveyor gave him a sly glance, murmuring:

"D'you happen to know who might be your neighbour on the north side o' the river?"

75

"Directly across from me, you mean?"

"Directly across? I can see you ain't long in the country. Not only directly across from you, but in every direction your eye might happen to extend. Up and down the north side a good hundred miles. Mebbe fifty miles in depth. Dunno, eh? I will be tellin' you"

His mouth closed like a rusty trap. Tom fancied he could even hear the surveyor's jaw muscles squeak with the sudden action. Through the open door of the surveyor's office walked a compactly built fellow wearing Eastern clothes and a stiff-brimmed hat. His was a pleasant face—or one upon which pleasantness had been forcibly imprinted. There was nothing much about him to catch the eye, no singularities of habit or gesture. He looked at the pair with a faint smile, raising his arm.

"Hope I'm not intruding."

The surveyor's left eyelid, turned away from the newcomer, fluttered at Tom. "Now, it's the same old politeness, Mister Grist. I was just tellin' this man he'd be havin' you for a neighbour. Might as well be gettin' acquainted. Mister Gillette—another Texan—will be facin' you at Sixty Mile Ford from now on until—"

"Until what, you mysterious Irishman?" asked the newcomer, still amiable.

But the surveyor shook his head. "I'd better be mindin' my own business. Sure. Mister Gillette, this gentleman's name is Barron Grist. He's resident agent—ain't it a fancy name for a foreman?—of the P. R. N. Land Company. It's the P.R.N. your eyes will get weary with lookin' at on the north side of the Little Mizzoo."

Tom shook hands with Grist, the man offering him a limp grip. "You Texans certainly are swarming north this season. Here we were, a wild set in a wild land. And all of a sudden here comes the great migration. Oh, well, we couldn't expect to have it to ourselves forever. Who led you Texans out of Israel?"

"I'm afraid I can't tell you," said Tom. "Our Southern prophets have none to sing their songs."

"Singin', ha!" grunted the surveyor. "Little good singin' will do a livin' soul in this country."

Grist laughed. "Don't let this purveyor of scandal influence you too much, Mr. Gillette. I bear a bad name in this country, and he'll tell you many things. But as a neighbour I wish you luck. If at any time I can help you—" Without finishing the sentence he nodded and backed out. The surveyor winked portentously.

"Mark him well," said he. "Whether you want it or not, you'll have business with him. Oh, yes."

"I didn't know land was valuable enough to speculate in," offered Tom.

The surveyor passed him another knowing glance. "Land? Well, it ain't land the P. R. N. profits by. It's cattle. Eastern money back of it. They've got a beef contract with the gov'ment. Deliverin' all their stuff to the Indian agencies. The redskins have got to be fed now that we've licked 'em and corralled 'em on reservations."

"Sounds profitable," mused Tom.

"It's rotten with profit," broke in the surveyor with a trace of energy. "Now, you'll be thinkin' to try that scheme, eh? Forget it. Takes a pull to land a beef contract. No, it's cattle—not land. But they're hell on wheels to get all the range they can. I'm tellin' you. Beg, borrow, and steal. How they get title to all this unsurveyed stuff is beyon' me. But they do. An' moreover, they put dummy homesteaders on every piece they can north o' the river. See?"

"But not south of the river in my country?"

The surveyor shook his head. "Guess it's a policy o' theirs not to bother with that country. Not now at least. But the way they're spreadin' it looks as if they mean to corral half of Dakota."

"I'm obliged," said Tom, starting for the door. "I'll see you on the ranch tomorrow, then."

"So you will." And as a last word, the surveyor added a warning. "Don't tell the land-office fella any more o' your business than's necessary. See?"

Tom grinned and turned into the street. Every section had its gossip, and quite evidently the surveyor fulfilled that function here. He discounted the man's warning fifty per cent by the time he had gone a block and an additional twenty-five per cent when he reached the land office. But after he had seen the official therein and had wrangled twenty minutes over a host of minor regulations he dropped the last discount. Petty rulers have a way of standing on their book of instructions and exercising their little quota of authority; the land-office agent at Nelson was inclined to ruffle Tom's fur the wrong way. Later, in the street again, he swore mildly to relieve his anger, mailed a pocketful of eastbound letters, and came squarely against his next piece of business.

It was a grim business, this canvassing of saloon keepers and merchants. Each time he put the question to them he understood he sowed another seed of trouble. It would be public knowledge within the hour that he sought San Saba, and thus a public feud was developed and nurtured. Nevertheless, he pursued the search until the train whistled across the desert and the town abandoned its chores and went out to the depot. At that point he gave up, got on his horse, and left Nelson. The engine dragged its string of cars to the depot and stopped, panting like a dog after a long chase. Smoke billowed from its funnelling stack. A scattering of gunshots announced the civic greeting, and a bell clanged through the sultry air.

From a distance Tom watched the train disgorge its travellers, then went on. And not until he was halfway home did it strike him he had avoided putting the question to the likeliest of all people—the United States Marshal. Why not? According to Eastern standards it should have been his first move. Weren't the law and the officers of the law for the purpose of maintaining justice? Theirs was the right to seek and find—and perhaps to kill—San Saba. It wasn't his right.

Oh, yes, he knew the argument from end to end. And throughout four or five years it had become a part of his belief. Yet how swiftly the West had reclaimed him—how strong was the grip of the frontier code! A man must take care of his own quarrels, never delegate them. To shirk this was to confess weakness. And that weakness would follow him like an accusing finger wherever he went. He was the son of his father, a citizen of the land. For good or bad he had to live according to Western ethics. For good or bad.

The struggle was so strong in him that he stopped the

78

horse and turned about, facing Nelson again, wistfully eyeing the horizon; all very well was this complicated reasoning in a complicated society. Back there *they* were sheltered by that thing they chose to call the law. Out here it was the other way around—the law's mantle never quite reached far enough. Beyond its fringes each man rode as a judge and a jury.

"No," he muttered, "I can't do it. It's my quarrel. I've got to settle it with San Saba myself. Now or twenty years from now."

And he went on toward his ranch, well knowing he had at that point thrown overboard most of what the East had given him. Somehow he felt the better for it. Life became less difficult; the face of the wide prairie seemed to be fairer, seemed to say, "you are mine." The guideposts of his life were few, but they were distinct, immovable: never to go back on his word; to give all humans the right to live the way they wished to live in return for that same right to himself; to uphold this right with the last breath of his body.

The train from the East brought Nelson's mail. And among other letters was a long set of directions for Barron Grist. He got these things weekly from the Eastern owners of the P. R. N., and usually they were but reminders of old instructions or slight additions. Going to the hotel with his ranch boss, who had ridden in a little before, he settled into a chair for a half hour's hard reading.

"Soon as I get this digested I'll go out with you," he told the ranch boss. "Wonder they wouldn't quit this nonsense. I know every syllable before I break the seal."

But he found, from the very first paragraph, that the P. R. N. had arrived at a new fork in the road and were ordering him to go out and accomplish certain chores. As he ran into the carefully detailed pages his smile vanished. Once he glanced up to the ranch boss with genuine amazement, murmuring, "My God!" Upon finishing, he sat in a study and, not satisfied, reread the whole letter. Suddenly he jammed it in his pocket and rose. "Come on, let's get away from this mess." Together, the pair rode west from town, following the same path Gillette had taken for a good distance. The ranch boss kept his peace a good two miles before asking, "Well, what's the excitement now? More cows, more contracts?"

Grist answered indirectly. "Sometimes I think those fellows back East are stark, staring crazy."

The ranch boss, who himself never had owned anything more valuable than a sixty-dollar saddle, felt he understood capitalists better than that. "Crazy? Well, I guess not. Not more'n ten per cent crazy, which is the rate of interest they risk their dollars on."

Grist shook his head. "The P. R. N. has got to make it twenty per cent, or consider business very poor. Now, do you know what they calmly tell me to go and do? Not satisfied with the land they own or control on the north of the Little Missouri, they've decided to take in the south side of the river. In other words, I've got to squat on both banks."

"Just like that," mused the ranch boss. "Just reach out an' embrace it atween both arms. Don't they know they're about three months too late to buy or scare the existin' occupants?"

"As to that," replied Grist, "I've got full authority to deal with the Texans. To purchase or to threaten."

"Do they say 'threaten'?" inquired the ranch boss.

"Of course not. You never heard an illegal sound issue from that bunch. But I'm supposed to read between lines. That's what I draw my pay for. Why didn't they spring this a couple of months earlier? Now I've got to argue and bargain—and Lord knows what else."

"That what else part of yore speech is correct," asseverated the ranch boss, rolling a cigarette. "Lessee—they's six outfits south o' the river now. Eapley, Diggerts, Love, O'Morrell, Wyatt, and Gillette. You'll pay high, Grist."

"Oh, I don't worry about spending money," was Grist's irritable answer. "It's their money, and they don't mind spending it on land. But it's the definite way they tell me to get it. No ifs or buts about the matter. Just go and get it. That bunch is up to something. By Joe, I feel sometimes like pulling out and letting the other fellow do all this drudgery."

The ranch boss chuckled. "You'll think twice on that, Grist. The pay is plumb too good." He squinted at the sun. "It sure gets me. Now supposin' they pay the top price for every man's squatter right. Top prices for every man's herd, to boot. How do they expect to net a profit? I don't see it. Even sellin' rotten beef to the gov'ment won't pull 'em out of the red.

"It's not beef," said Grist.

"Then what is it?" demanded the ranch boss. "Gold? Shucks, no. What else is val'able?"

But Grist had no answer for the question. They had come to a lower ford of the river, and here he parted from his ranch boss. "I don't know the answer. All I know is that I've got to get it, one way or the other. If they won't sell—"

The foreman was very matter of fact about it. "Well, we've done it afore and we can do it again. Ain't we gettin' good wages?"

Grist nodded and turned into the ford. "Here goes. Might as well start early."

7   THE NET DRAWS TIGHTER

There met, in the city of Washington, one summer's night, three men whose names and fortunes stood behind the P. R. N. Land Company; to wit, Prague, Randall, and Noonan. The crystal chandelier sent down its refracted light upon the table by which they sat and across the centre of which was spread a map of the territory of Dakota. Description of these three is unnecessary; indeed, they would not have wanted to be described. For, in spite of the evident luxury of the quarters, the whisky glasses, and the tapering cigars, they had ventured the sodden heat of the capital city on business of considerable import and great privacy. None of these three gentlemen had any illusions to speak of, for they dealt in a traffic that demanded quite questionable practices. And this very night they were about to consummate something just a little more questionable than that which had gone before. At this precise moment, while awaiting a caller with a distinguished title, they were casting over the ground to be covered. And like the amiable gentlemen that they were, no overt word, no incriminating phrase sullied the staid dignity of their presence.

It was Prague, the florid and substantial and jovial Prague, who did most of the talking. And it was he whose index finger traced an imaginary boundary across a strip of western Dakota.

"You see it, I trust. Dammee, you can see it? Look at all that land—and here we have been overlooking the greatest of our opportunities. It is the venture of a lifetime."

"Entirely legitimate," chimed in Mr. Randall.

"Oh, entirely—entirely," corroborated Prague with considerable haste. "At the same time, caution must be observed. You understand how these things are."

They quite understood. Prague nipped the end from another cigar and chewed it with the relish that is born of expensive luxuries. "And it is for that reason, gentlemen, I have made contact with a—ah—er certain person who can materially aid us."

"Legitimately," quoth Randall.

"Indeed," said Prague. "There must be no smell or taint of illegality about the affair. You know how those things are. And this—er—person is in a position to render us that particular service which is utterly essential to the venture."

"Ah," was Mr. Noonan's contribution.

"Then," went on Prague, "we are quite agreed."

And amid the nodded approval the door of the room opened and a gentleman slipped through, taking care to close the portal behind him. At once the three rose to their feet with the courtesy due so illustrious a figure.

It was that gallant tribune, Senator Ignacius I. Invering, whose tones of patriotic devotion had more than once rung passionately through the land. They always rang passionately, these tones, and they were always patriotic. He was a herring-thin man, the colour of a pressed rose petal, and a stogy projected skyward from his lips. The stogy was unlighted, for the Senator had dedicated his health to the service of the nation and therefore nursed it assiduously. He took off his hat, bowed with a ceremonial politeness to the assembled three, and amid a scraping of chair legs and a muttered, "Pleased, Senator," "An honour from such a distinguished gentleman, Senator," the ice was broken and the Bourbon gleamed against the light of the chandelier and vanished on its appointed mission. Senator Ignacius I. Invering stood, as if poised to flee, while the others took their seats. One chary eye skittered across the outspread map and immediately forsook it, quite as if contaminating influence rested there. Then, in a dry wisp of a voice he said, "Now, gentlemen."

Prague rose, fingering some papers before him. "You

83

understand, sir, the nature of our company. That has been explained to you. Needless to enlarge upon it. All we wanted to accomplish at this meeting was to present to you formally your share of stock in the P. R. N. Land Company—as per previous agreement."

"Quite so," said the Senator, fiddling with his finger tips.

"Now, it so happens that we are about to declare a dividend. Quite a happy occasion for us, I'm sure. And we are more than pleased to announce that the dividend on your number of shares will amount to—ah—ten thousand dollars."

"Profitable investment," murmured the Senator.

"Yes. The dividend will be dispatched to you at your office in the morning."

"In cash," specified the Senator. "You understand. Not that there is any unscrupulous angle to this. Not at all, sir. But I have many enemies who would try to trump up a scandal if they could. A mastiff always has the lesser dogs baying at his heels."

Prague agreed that this was true and unfortunate, but that those fearless of duty and pure of spirit had to endure mud slinging. Then he paused a moment, glanced at his associates, and went on.

"Now, being a partner of our enterprise, so to speak—"

"A silent partner and quite unadvertised," broke in the Senator.

"Just so. Being a partner, there are certain affairs in which you can—ah—er—guide us."

"Precedent for it," said the Senator. "Precedent dating to the very foundation rock of our union, sir. Quite within a public official's right to have business interests on the side. Were it not so, I could hardly serve the nation. Proceed."

"Senator," proceeded Prague with emotion, "you see eye to eye with us. Now, our business has been the raising and disposing of cattle to the government for their Indians, in which business you have so kindly assisted us in the past. But lately we have conceived an enterprise which will be profitable to us and, we trust, of signal service to our country."

"Entirely legitimate," murmured Randall piously.

"What we have in mind is this," said Prague, pointing to the map. "Our holdings abut on the sides of a reservation. Now, as time goes on, it seems probable the government will need more lands in that reservation. Therefore, as a public service, we are willing to sell our holdings to the government at a fair and decent profit for that purpose. We are also acquiring other near-by lands in order that small ranchers and settlers will not rob the government when it wants to acquire additional land. You understand, sir, we are actuated by business considerations, but with a thread of altruism also involved. But, being unsurveyed land, title cannot be acquired to it in the—ah—ordinary way. It would take, say, an act of congress to give us this title."

Silence. The Senator pursed his lips and twiddled his fingers. The care of a nation rested heavily upon his frail shoulders. Heavily but securely. He nodded once—twice. "A bill attached as a rider to some appropriation would do the trick. Yes. I shall see about that."

"I have always said the nation underestimated your worth," breathed Prague.

"But," went on the Senator, "you must have possession of the lands you wish title to. Can't evict squatters. Legal, perhaps, but dangerous. Cause a stink—that's the bald word for it. Must be entirely in your possession. Then no attention would be focussed on the rider. The less attention the better."

"I think we can adjudicate the matter of squatters," said Prague. "We shall."

"And then," pursued the Senator, "when you have title, I can perhaps speed up the government's desire to appropriate your lands for Indian reservation use. That will be another bill, later."

There it was, pat and perfect. And since perfection cannot be improved upon, the four of them drank silently and in comfortable understanding. The Senator retrieved his hat, the three partners scrambled to their feet. At the door the Senator swung. "Remember, you must settle with any squatters on that territory you wish. See that you are alone in possession. Then send me the boundary lines and I shall incorporate it into a rider."

85

Three studious bows. The Senator had one more word. "Caution, gentlemen. There are those who would tear me limb from limb. Ravenous beasts, sir. All this is legitimate, legal. But a reformer will torture the truth to any length. I detest reformers."

And though he named no names, each of the other three silently thought of Senator William Costaine, whose beagle nose scented fraud and corruption at a tremendous distance—especially if that fraud and corruption were in the opposite party.

The Senator whisked himself out of the chamber; the three gentlemen drank with that mellow spirit that comes of deeds well done. And then Randall drew paper and ink to him and began to write in a copper-plate hand those directions which Barron Grist, the resident foreman of the P. R. N., was later to receive, while about him hovered Prague, adding fodder to those directions from time to time. "Be sure to make it plain enough that he must settle with all squatters now on the land we want. Remove 'em. Make it plain."

"Plain, but legal," agreed Randall. "He will understand."

8 EAST COMES WEST

A month passed, the year turned its apex and swung down the farther side of its arc. The broiling heat of a forenoon's sun blasted the land; all things withered beneath it, all things were turned to a dun and henna colouring. The hardy pines were coated with a dust that hid their natural greenery, and they appeared to suffer a suspension of life. Fog stretched across the horizon, the surface of the river was like glowing brass. Tom Gillette, from his vantage point a half mile removed, saw the new Circle G cabins shimmering and rising with the heat mirage. He turned to Lispenard.

"Nevertheless, Blondy, it's a fertile land, and we've got our footing. Let winter come. Let anything come. We can fight."

Lispenard shrugged his shoulders. He was clean shaven once more, and he had let his yellow hair grow until it fell below his hat brim, plainsman's style. "Winter? It's a devil of a time to be thinking of winter, my lad. And why should you be so cursed proud of a few clay-daubed huts?"

"It means—" began Tom, and then caught the words before they ran past his lips. After all, Lispenard wouldn't understand how much those few cabins and corrals meant in a raw country. Achievement—security—the onward march of a dream. So he murmured, "It means shelter," and let it go at that. He wondered of late why it was the man seemed to arouse in him a defensive mood. It appeared that his friend had shaken himself into a certain state of mind, a kind of taciturn aloofness and a veiled antagonism that couldn't be penetrated. The old smile and jest had returned to the Blond Giant, but there was no charity in either. He had quite distinctly hardened; and he had grown secretive.

Tom turned about. "I'm going to town. Coming along?"

"No. I want to explore the north side of the river," said Lispenard. And he grinned. "But give my regards to the prairie beauty, old man. Ah, touched! Of course I know you'll see her along the way. I could even tell you where she makes her stand. Don't you suppose I have ridden over there myself on occasion? She's a spitfire—but the time will come when she'll see me in a better light."

Tom returned the man's smile with a sharp glance, wondering at the flare of anger he felt. "Still the lady's man, Blondy?"

"It's a weakness," replied his companion. "Give her my regards and say to her that there are other desirable types of men in addition to the rockbound and frowning creature tramping across the footlights."

"What's the nubbin to that, Blondy?"

The Blond Giant raised his shoulders again and spurred off. Much later, when Tom had gone eastward, he swung to see the man outlined on the bluff north of the river a moment, then dip from view.

"What draws him over there so much?" The question stuck to his mind for several miles and then vanished before a kind of expectancy. Halfway to the Wyatt range he saw Lorena—Lorena loosely poised on her horse and watching him approach. Her hand swung upward, and of a sudden her pony sprang to life and raced across the prairie, the girl's compact body weaving from side to side. Without ceremony she wheeled alongside—and thus they rode for a good half mile, saying not a word. Neither of these people made conversation to order, neither of them seemed to feel the necessity of it. Presently she waved her arm around the compass points.

"Guess my dad's fixing to sell out."

"To Grist and the P. R. N.?"

"How did you know?" she demanded.

88

"He's been after me," replied Tom. "Seems to want this country pretty bad."

"Then that's why both Eapley and Diggerts have sold. And I guess we will too." She struck her gauntlet against the saddle, crying, "I don't want to leave—I don't *want* to!" With that same disconcerting swiftness she faced him. "Are you going to sell?"

Gillette shook his head. "No, I guess not. Where would I go? This is my land now. I'm stickin' to it."

"It's the way I feel," she explained wistfully. "But Grist offered Dad a lot of money—and where does he think to make a profit?—so I think Dad will take it. No idea just where we will go next. I don't want to leave."

"Corporation money," said Tom, "is cautious money. It may seem as if they are paying a fancy price, but don't you doubt they'll get it back twice over."

They came to the lower ford, across which lay the road to Nelson. The girl studied the sandy earth for a long interval, then swept Tom's face with a quick and shrewd glance. "I don't want to go. I won't. If Dad leaves here I'll go to Nelson and work in the restaurant."

"I'd hate to think of you doing that," protested Tom.

There was another short silence, in which Tom silently applauded. The girl in the East would have made a marvelous play of his sentiment. She would have coquetted with him, would have softly asked, "Would it make any difference to you, Tom, what I did?" But not Lorena Wyatt. This clear-featured girl—whose eyes now and then so arrested and troubled him—had nothing of the coquette about her.

She spread her hands apart; the white V of her throat slid beneath the bandana's knot. "I'm strong. I'm not afraid. What harm would there be? Oh, I know what you think. You've got all those queer ideas as to what a lady shouldn't do. But, you see, I'm not—"

"Don't say it, Lorena." He wasn't aware that he had used her given name for the first time; and perhaps that explained why he was so puzzled to find the quick glow in her black eyes. It bothered him so much that he turned into the ford, calling over his shoulder. "Blondy sent his regards."

He heard a sound of impatience. "How very kind of him. But you can tell the gentleman I don't need his company."

Tom's horse took the water, veering aside. And it was then the quiet of the land was broken by the crack of a rifle, and a jet of sand shot up on the bank, just behind horse and rider. The girl cried an abrupt warning. "Behind the bluff's rim. Above you—see the smoke? Come back!" Even before he drew his own gun she fired at the thin trail of powder smoke eddying from the summit of the bluff. A second shot ripped the water. Tom bent over and put the shelter of the pony between himself and the unseen marksman. The powder smoke was a poor mark, but he threw two bullets up that way and raced through the deep part of the ford to the farther bank. He was now in a bad trap, for the trail led sharply up between a cleft in the bluff, and he was exposed to whoever lay along that rim and watched him. Still, he galloped on, hearing the girl crying at him from behind, hearing her horse splash through the ford. He twisted in the saddle, half angry. "Don't follow me! Get to shelter!"

His pony took the steep grade at great irregular jumps and came out on high ground several hundred yards from the edge of the cliff. He stopped, seeing nothing. The land on this side of the river was tortured with pockets and folds of earth—excellent concealment for the ambusher. Moreover, this rugged terrain led away to the right into a series of ridges. Possibly by now the man was retreating. Tom slid from his horse and spent some time inspecting the ground. The sing of those bullets had come from the barrel of a rifle; here he stood, a blessed fine target. So he dropped to a knee as the girl raced out of the mouth of the cleft and flung herself down beside him. "Oh, that was foolish!" she lectured him. "He could have killed you out there in the river! I saw his hat rising up. Made him duck, too! Where are you going?"

"Think he's pulled back for shelter. I'm going over to find out."

She protested so sharply that he delayed the move. "Supposing he's still lying in those pockets? He'll kill you the first shot. Let me ride around to that ridge on the right and scout from the high ground while you close in. I can keep him entertained if he's still opposite us."

"No. My Lord, Lorena, this isn't your fight. What made you cross the river?"

"Oh, nonsense, this is a free country, isn't it? You talk like all the other men! I can take care of myself."

"It's not your quarrel," he repeated, irritable. "Now lie flat while I inch along."

"If you are going to be that foolish, then I'll circle toward the ridge."

"You'll do nothing of the kind," was his flat answer.

"I will so!"

That stopped him. Turning on his side he looked back to where she lay; her eyes were snapping and a rose colour filled her cheeks. He had never seen her so aroused—or so striking. And presently he crept back, reaching for a cigarette and broadly smiling.

That definitely took the edge from her temper. "Well," she demanded in a fainter voice, "what are you laughing at? It's a Chessy cat laugh."

"You'd think we'd been married ten years the way we scrap. Lorena, don't you reckon I can take care of my own skin?"

"You'd been shot down in the river if I hadn't made him duck," said she.

"I'm thanking you for it now."

He said it so gravely and so humbly that her resentment instantly evaporated. "Well, it was a rash thing to do—but I liked it. Tom, I'll apologize."

"For what?"

"When I saw you first I thought you didn't have too much sand. It's been bothering me—up till now." She hesitated. "Seemed to me you rode around sort of doubting yourself. I hated to see it—truly I did."

That sharp and certain penetration. He flipped the cigarette through the air, considerably disturbed. "All right, Lorena. Now, I've got to pay that gentleman a social visit. You can't cross the river again until I clear the landscape a little. Do you think I want to pack a dead girl back to the Diamond W?"

She avoided his face, writing lines in the sandy ground. When she lifted her eyes, it was with so troubled an expression in them that his amusement vanished. Her sturdy little shoulders rose, and her arm rested a moment on his wrist. "All right, Tom. I'll be good. But you watch carefully."

"Sure—sure."

He crawled across the rolling earth, scanning the rim of the hillocks for the mark of a hat brim or the gleam of a gun barrel. Nothing disturbed the profound stillness of the hot day; when he arrived at the first depression he slid into it for a brief moment and studied the flanking angles. The girl was prone on the ground, between the two horses, her chin cupped in her palms. But he noted that her revolver rested directly in front of her and even at the distance he clearly saw the pinched intentness of her oval face. Crawling up and down the contour he at last slid from her view, and at once commanded the whole sweep of ground as it marched to the bluff's edge. Nobody there. He relaxed his vigilance and circled the area until he found the gouged spots along the soil where the ambusher's boot heels left their prints; the fellow had swung from one point to another in his effort to get a fair shot, and then had fled toward the protecting ridges on the right. The deep set of the toe and the faint mark of the heel indicated the hurry he had been in. Probably he'd left a horse beyond that ridge and now was riding for distant shelter. Gillette thought about pursuing, but decided against it. That rough country was an effective cloak for the ambusher; the sun stood well up in the sky, and he had a long trip to town and back. No time right now for going on a hunt that might take him several days. He rose and waved his arm at Lorena. She jumped into the saddle and galloped toward him.

"He's skipped over there, then," said she, indicating the ridges. "Going to follow?"

He shook his head. "No time now. More important business on tap."

"Do you have an idea who it is?"

"Somebody trying to smoke me out, I reckon."

"San Saba?"

He thought not. "San Saba wouldn't stick to this country with a price on his head."

"Don't be too sure," she warned him. "That man is thoroughly bad. Snaky."

He grinned. "I'll wait right here till you cross the river. Friends again, ain't we?" And he extended his arm.

She took it, her hand slipping into his greater one and resting there a fleeting instant without pressure. The touch of it disturbed him, and he must have displayed it, for she drew away and turned to her horse. Five minutes later she rested on the opposite bank of the ford, her arm raised to him in salute; then the pony fled over the prairie, and Gillette walked to his own animal.

As for her, all the pent emotions of womanhood broke down the barriers she had so carefully preserved and gathered into one passionate cry. "Oh, if it were only so—if it only were! But it isn't! He doesn't see me that way! And I won't trick him! I hate that! He's got to see it with his own eyes—and he never will! Some dam' woman back East hurt him! I'd like to see her for a minute!"

She raced madly over the swelling earth, her teeth sunk into the nether lip.

After the girl had gone, Gillette swung away from the Nelson road and took the high ground along the ridge. He saw nothing to westward indicating the path of the ambusher. But, within five miles of town he found the dust rising off the main trail to the east and made out three horsemen and a buckboard traveling toward the ford. In town he went directly to the postoffice for his mail and then to the surveyor's. But before he reached that purveyor of gossip he came face to face with Barron Grist, the P. R. N. agent, and immediately that gentleman drew him aside.

"My proposition," Grist reminded him, "still holds."

"So does my answer," said Gillette. "I like Dakota."

"Man—there's plenty of Dakota left you. I'm offering a top price."

The foreman was so pleasant, so friendly that Tom betrayed himself more than he otherwise would have done.

"The price isn't a consideration," he explained. "Grist—there's a Gillette buried on my range. Do you see?"

Grist nodded, thoughtfully impressed. "I admire you for it. Really I do. But here—my company wants that strip of ground. Damnably bad. I'll not mince with you. They want it. Here I stand with an offer. I'll raise the ante a clear three thousand, pay you for the beef on your own count—on your own count, mind—and give you your own estimate on the improvements. You stand to gain from every angle. You're free to prospect Dakota to the four walls. Anyhow, you've got a poor piece of range. The poorest on the south side of the river. I'm only buying you out of a bad bargain."

"Then why should the P. R. N. want it so badly?" questioned Gillette.

Grist smiled—an unimpressive, unrevealing smile. "Say, you can search me. I don't know. I only work for 'em. But they want it."

"Well, just you write and tell the gentleman back East I'm not selling."

"Persuasion and money won't do it, eh?"

Gillette marked the added sharpness. "It won't," he agreed.

"Listen to me," broke in Grist. "I've got all the other five sewed up. Taking 'em over right down to the last can of beans. Eapley and Diggerts already gone. Rest going. Your nearest neighbour, Wyatt, will be gone before fall roundup."

"It will leave me the less crowded."

"There's where you are mistaken," said Grist emphatically. "I'm going to throw cows across the stream until the grass roots groan. You understand what that means?"

"I presume you're hinting that you'll overcrowd the range. All right, my boy. But remember, when it comes to starving out beef you'll lose more cows than I—because you've got more to lose."

"And can afford to lose 'em more than you," countered Grist. He had ceased to smile. "Maybe I'll lose ten to your one. All right. When you're out three thousand head you're ruined."

"Now you're talking war," said Gillette, taking a grip

94

on his temper. "Talking war to a Texan. I'll call it. Don't ever think I won't."

"Up to your limit," agreed Grist. "Then you're wiped out. Listen, I like you and I hate to see you buck a corporation. Better take your profit. It's a big one."

"I reckon not."

"Why, damnation, but you're stubborn," muttered Grist, half in anger, half in surprise.

"Do you mean to make it war?" asked Gillette soberly.

Grist studied his man a long while. "It's got to be done," he finally replied. "I'll obey orders. Else I lose my job. There's the cards on the table. Yes, by George, it'll be war. You're foolish. Why force me?"

"I won't. I'll let you fire the first shot. And then, God pity you, Grist. You never have seen Texans fight. It's not a pleasant experience."

"I can muster a hundred men," snapped Grist, face muscles drawing tight.

"Eighty-five more than I've got. I'm repeating—you don't know a Texas crew. I'm sorry for you and your job."

"You needn't be." Grist stood a moment, an uncolourful figure who even at a moment like this could not achieve dignity. "Let it be so," he murmured, and walked away.

Tom watched the resident agent vanish into a saloon. Forgetting about the surveyor, he bought a sack of stuff at the store and started home, following the trail of the buckboard and the horsemen to the ford. Here, he skirted the high ground before going into the water. Once across it the buckboard tracks still kept ahead of him. And when he reached the yard of the Circle G houses he knew he had visitors. Quagmire rose up from a corral and ambled toward him. Almost furtively he motioned toward the main cabin. "She's in there."

"Who?"

Quagmire stared dreamily at the sky. "Well, if it ain't an angel then my ideas o' heaven sure are scandalous wrong."

Tom ducked through the door, almost at the same time muttering, "Christine—Kit—my lord—!"

She was seated in a chair with her hands folded sedately

in her lap and the shadows of the room adding to the soft allure of her face. As always, she seemed to have taken possession of her surroundings, to have put herself at ease. She smiled—that provocative, enigmatic smile that had haunted him for so many, many months on the trail, and her cool, half-humorous words, so gentle and yet so certain, reminded him that he was now what he had always been, an unsuccessful suitor ill at ease in the presence of a reigning beauty.

"Well, Tommy, here I am. And you shall pay for neglecting me so cruelly. No letters, no word. Oh, well, I have swallowed my pride. . . ." A graceful gesture of a hand finished the sentence. How subtly she conveyed meaning with those small movements, how many shades of expression she could weave into the dullest word. He went forward, took the slim hand that stretched up to him. There was the slightest pressure in it; it drew him down. "Tommy, you are the same Western barbarian. But I like you in this setting. Indeed!"

Lispenard, upon fording the river, travelled in a direct line toward the most rugged piece of land within five miles as if making for a place well known to him. But once lost in the weblike tangle of pockets and ridges, he proceeded with an unusual amount of caution; and when the echo of a shot floated faintly over his shoulder from the rear he instinctively ducked. Then he turned about, reached a commanding summit, and dismounted. Flat on the ground he shaded his eyes against the earth's glare and waited.

He had not long to wait. Presently he made out a figure spurring toward him, travelling as fast as horseflesh would allow. From time to time the man fell below a ridge and momentarily was out of sight, each time reappearing at a different corner of the compass. Only a man in flight, or a man extraordinarily cagey would act like that. The Blond Giant traced him for a good twenty minutes, or until the tall and lank body had come within hailing distance. And then, though not without a certain reluctance of movement and a reassuring pat on the butt of his gun, he crawled to his knees. If the meeting was to take place it must be before San Saba got within good revolver range. Up stood Lispenard, one arm hailing the renegade ex-foreman.

San Saba's horse sat abruptly on its haunches. San Saba's thin, dust-powdered face screwed into a series of ragged lines. He made no particular move toward his gun, but his voice, sharp as the edge of a skinning knife, slit across the interval. "Well?"

"Oh, drop that," muttered Lispenard. "Don't you know a friend when you see one?"

The ex-foreman thought on this for a spell, his free arm akimbo. Lispenard had never before realized just how searching and cruel one man's glance could be. It touched his nerves.

"How'd yo' know I'd be here?" demanded San Saba.

Lispenard grinned, though his lips were dry and slightly trembling. "Trailed you for a week. Didn't catch wind of me? Well, then, I guess I'm not so poor at this sort of thing. Come on, be neighbourly. I'm not out for your hide. You haven't taken any of my toys."

For all his treachery, San Saba had grit in his make-up, or perhaps he read Lispenard well enough to understand. At any rate, he walked his horse to the top of the ridge and a little down the farther side before dismounting. Even then he was careless of the other's presence, his first attention being spent on the skyline eastward. His hard face relaxed, he squatted and rolled a brown-paper cigarette, meanwhile studying this unexpected visitor.

"Well?"

"Well," mimicked Lispenard. "Hell, San Saba, but you're a hard fellow to locate. Anyhow, you didn't catch on I was ramblin' across your trail."

"Don't fool yo'self," murmured San Saba.

Lispenard's satisfaction was destroyed. It made him irritable, a little sullen. "That being so, why didn't you meet up with me?"

"Wanted to see what yo' game was."

"Dam' queer you couldn't trust me," grumbled Lispenard.

"Do—so long as yo' near at hand. Remember what I once said in Ogallala?"

"Something—but I was too blessed drunk to catch it. Explain."

San Saba was not rash with his words. It took time to reach down and bring out the phrase that at once illumined his own character and his opinion of the other man's. "Said we was both rascals an' that it paid rascals to stick together."

Lispenard grinned. "Admirable powers of perception—and deception."

"Both good items to have," was San Saba's laconic answer. "How'd yo' know I was still in the country?"

It was Lispenard's turn to be shrewd. "There's something sticking in your craw, my boy. And I thought you'd hang around till you swallowed it."

San Saba's little red eyes were partially curtained behind a screen of cigarette smoke, but the Blond Giant was startled to see a film of colour moving across those pupils. The cigarette suffered destruction; the foreman sighed. "Yo' not such a poor hand, yo'self, friend. We wouldn't make a bad pair."

"I've thought about that. This sedentary life palls on me. Not to mention the puritanical atmosphere surrounding the Circle G. I had enough of that sort of thing back East. Don't appreciate it out here. My forte is something different."

"Big words," mused San Saba.

"When are you pulling freight?"

"Direct questions ain't stylish," was the man's dry rejoinder.

"Oh, come out of it!" grumbled Lispenard. "If I'm going to trail with you—"

He felt again the weight of that hard, unfriendly glance. The light of day was directly in San Saba's eyes, yet it was queer how little of that light reflected back from the ex-foreman's face. Something cold and deadly lay coiled behind the brittle, impassive features; Lispenard had a sudden doubt. The foreman looked at the Eastern horizon once more; he seemed to be calculating, his nutlike head bent forward. He rose.

"I'll wait here fo' yo', friend. When yo' come we'll go. They's still a bone to pick, understan'? But it can wait. Ain't no hurry. It's a long life."

"Bully. United we stand—divided we doubt. You'll be wanting grub, old-timer. Hiding in the hills on an empty belly is a cursed poor vacation."

San Saba permitted the wisp of a smile to pass his colourless lips. "Yo' learn fast, friend. I give yo' credit. Where'll yo' get it?"

"I'll drop into Nelson in the morning and load up. See you here to-morrow at dark. Providing you're not afraid of my bringing the posse."

San Sabe rose. "It's a bet. As to the posse—" He raised and lowered his thin shoulders, and Lispenard had an uncomfortable sensation of fitting too snugly with the man's purposes. There was now and then the hint of death about this character. It popped out, unsuspected, in those catlike gestures, in the occasional sidewise flashes of eye. He dismissed the thought. He outweighed San Saba a full fifty pounds; he had learned something of the rough and tumble himself. Let San Saba walk the narrow path with him. He, too, had his plans. San Saba spoke again. "Then we pull freight, eh, friend?"

"Not to-morrow. Give me a couple more days."

"She's a pretty wench," ventured the ex-foreman.

"Damn your sly tongue, she is," grunted Lispenard. He extended his arm. "Bargain signed, sealed, and notaried." San Saba's hand was clammy, there was no pressure to the grip. Lispenard felt the reservations in that bargain, but he dismissed his fears, got to his horse, and rode off, flinging back a casual arm. Beyond sight of the renegade he wiped a drop of sweat from his temple and grinned.

"By the Lord, I'll have my cake and I'll eat it too. That gentleman will be good to me. I can be sly as well. And he's an old enough head to teach me a few things."

He crossed the ford and unsaddled, throwing the horse into a corral. And when he came inside the door of the main cabin and saw the girl he threw up both arms in pleased surprise.

"Kit Ballard—of all the beautiful happenings!"

She had a brilliant smile for him as he crossed the room and took both her arms. "Still the same gallant Apollo," said she gaily. And then, seeing how quiet Tom had turned, she disengaged her hands. "How like the old times. If we only had another lady we might put on one of those cotillions."

Lispenard threw his hat across the room. "There is another, by George! Thomas, I command you to ride over and get the prairie beauty."

Christine Ballard's smile tightened, though it was wholly imperceptible to Tom. She threw a swift glance at Lispenard—a glance that he perfectly understood—and murmured:

"Yes? Tell us about her, Tom. You have been keeping something from me."

9 CONFLICT

Tom roused himself from a study; and though he was still a little under the spell of this girl's brilliant, elusive beauty, he felt a strong irritation at having Lorena Wyatt's name introduced into the conversation. It put him on the defensive, and he answered almost curtly, "There is nothing to tell."

"Ah," murmured Christine, and with her feminine instincts perceiving the danger signals she turned the subject gracefully. "It's good to see you, Claudie. The same impetuous hero. Did you ever know how many hearts you broke with that conquering air of yours? The figure of romance! Oh, yes!"

Lispenard grinned. "Happy days. Wouldn't it be great sport to spend that time all over again?"

"No," said she, each word bearing its full burden of thoughtfulness, "I'm not sure I'd care to." Tom, blunt man as he was, caught the lingering wistfulness, and it made him the more uncomfortable.

"Each day unto itself. Why look backward?"

"I—I hope so," she agreed. Her hand made a slow gesture. "Claudie, wasn't Tom always the contemplative figure, though? What was it you men called him—the barbarian? Why was that?"

Lispenard rolled a cigarette. "Well, he was always ready to fight. That overweening Texas honour of his put us all on nettles. He also had an extremely matter-of-fact way in speaking of murder and sudden death. A hair-raising calm, so to speak. Some of those wild, weird yarns I used to disbelieve—until I came West."

"Well," said she, appraising Gillette between half-closed lids, "he hasn't changed a whit. Except to grow more sober. His native heath agrees well with him."

"Oh, he's built for ruling his kingdom," murmured Lispenard. His smile grew somewhat shorter. "I could always whip him—until I touched him too hard. Had more weight, more science, a cooler head than he ever dreamed of having. But when I stung him a few times—"

"The specimen being thus dissected, we will now pass to other things," drawled Tom. "Render your verdict on Blondy."

"Quite fit—quite the same debonair heart disturber."

"Thanks," said the Blond Giant; he rose, made a profound bow, and started out. "But you see only the surface calm. On my honour, Kit, I'm a rough and tough character; a seething furnace roars beneath this placid mug. Oh, you have no idea."

She waited until he was outside before raising her palms in plain distaste. "Ugh! How he has hardened."

"Pay no attention to what he tells you, Kit," said Tom.

"I see it!" she flashed back. "Once that boldness fascinated me. Now it's actually repulsive. How thick his chin is—how heavy his eyes!"

Gillette doubled his hands, looking sombrely at her. "Why did you come?"

"I like that, sir! If I am not welcome—"

"Don't fence with me, Kit. You do it too easily."

She seemed half inclined to be sober, yet not for a moment did she allow the tantalizing smile to desert her. "I told my father I needed a change of climate. He was shocked—oh, very much so. But I have a little Ballard stubbornness in me, you know. That was my professed reason. But one day I ran across Jimmy Train, and he showed me a letter you had written him. So I came to plead."

"Kit!"

"Oh, I have no modesty left. My suitors are all married—I grow old and lonely."

The colored cook stepped inside the place and cast one

102

comprehensive glance at the pair, vanishing with a twist of his body. "Boss sho' looks 'sif he got a mizry," he murmured. Quagmire, loitering by the corral, motioned him to stay away from the house; Old Mose's white teeth flashed.

Gillette's fingers were laced together; he sat forward in his chair, studying the floor, and the girl noted how his hair curled back from the temples as well as the dogged and resolute set of his lips. And for the first time in her life she lost faith in her ability to command men. No hint of that doubt, however, crept into her half-bantering words. She was relaxed, her head thrown back, looking across the interval with a slanting gaze—such a look as he had once said distinguished her from all other women. How was it he did not notice it now? And, fearing his silence, she broke through it. "I would give more than a penny for your thoughts, Tommy."

"It's good to see you again, Kit. But, my dear, you must not drag any more string across the floor for me to grasp at."

"Meaning—I have played with you?"

The answer was so sudden, so vehement that it startled her. "Can you doubt it—can you consider it anything else?"

"We all make mistakes, Tommy. Perhaps I—"

"No, don't say it that way, Kit. You are fencing again. Listen, my dear, I have thought of you all along the trail. Every day, every night. Never a sunset or a sunrise but what your picture wasn't somewhere in it. Once there was a stampede, a man was killed, and even when I saw the boys throwing mud over him, I thought of you. Do you see? Lord, I couldn't help myself. I wanted you. Up until the moment I stepped inside this cabin I wanted you."

"But, Tommy, here I am."

He broke through with a swift move of his hand, and to her that was another mark of the change in him. Once he would have been quieted at her least whisper; and now he commanded her not to interrupt.

"Let me finish. What have I said? That I wanted you until the very moment I saw you sitting there. But, Kit, you come just as I've finished the battle. You bring all that—that damnable misery with you. Misery! Well, you must

103

not torture me any more. I've put myself beyond it. I've licked the wounds dry. They're still in here, understand, my dear. But they're dry. And I won't have 'em opened again.''

Her smile was brilliant, a little as if the light of her eyes passed through a film. ''You are blunt, Tommy!''

''I've gone back to the blanket,'' he muttered, lowering his head once more.

''What does that mean?''

''It means when an Indian has gotten his white man education he goes back to the reservation, throws away all his civilized clothes, and takes up the old ways.''

''You are no Indian, Tommy.''

''No? They called me the barbarian once. It still sticks. I'm in my own land. I've thrown away every blessed thing the East gave me. Chucked it overboard. The old gods are mine. And, by the Lord, Kit, I'm beginning to live once more.''

''Have you chucked away everything, Tommy?'' she asked quite softly. ''Everything?''

He looked up to her; his eyes betrayed the uncertainty in him, and the girl, at this unconscious revelation, let her whole body go limp; laughter tinkled in her throat. She bent forward, hands making little motions in her lap, and the laughter died. ''Tommy, supposing I haven't come to torture you? Supposing—''

''You gave me my answer once,'' said he stubbornly. ''You've had your sport.''

''Oh, why did you have to be so deadly serious about it all the while? My dear, did you think to pursue and win in a day? Don't you suppose a woman has to be shown—to be convinced?''

''And to be amused,'' he added. ''Remember, Kit, I'm not open to torture any longer.''

But she was wise with Eve's wisdom; she had seen him falter. So she turned the conversation in her own inimitable way. ''Tom, I heard about your father. Did they ever catch the man?''

''Not yet.''

''But they will,'' she reassured him. ''The law will get

him." There was something so grimly sardonic on his face that she asked, "What is it?"

"The law out here expects a man to take care of his own troubles. I shall get him—I shall kill him."

"Why, Tom, isn't that—isn't it murder?"

"I told you I had gone back to the old gods, didn't I?"

She bit into her lip; a tinge of colour stood against the soft whiteness of her flesh. "I thought it was only woman's privilege to be unfathomable, Tommy. I'm sorry I mentioned it."

The colored cook's shadow fell athwart the door again, and Tom nodded at him. Presently the grub pans and the dishes were on the table. One by one the men of the outfit came dismally, sheepishly in. Tom put Christine at the head of the table and amid a dead silence introduced her.

"Boys, this is Christine Ballard of New York. She has come on a visit. Now, behave yourselves. I have already pointed out to her which of you are the lady killers. So beware."

The charge was so manifestly outrageous that the agitation only increased; not a man raised his eyes from the dead centre of his plate. Lispenard came in and took his seat. Tom, quite cheerful, began to relate the salient points of the more outstanding members. "That's Quagmire. Yes, the one with the extremely guilty look. Oh, they all look guilty, but he seems to look guiltier than the rest. He has a wife in each state and territory between here and Texas, Montana excepted. The reason he has no wife in Montana is because he has never been to Montana. Whitey Almo, the one with the bad sunburn—or is that sunburn Whitey?— collects interiors. Jail interiors. I have never known Whitey to pass a new jail without entering to see the wall decorations. Usually he doesn't pay much attention to these walls until the next morning, when his eyes begin to function again. Why did they cease to function, did you ask? Well, it has been rumoured that Whitey drinks water with his whisky. I'd shoot him like a dog if I thought it were the truth."

There was the sound of somebody strangling in his coffee. Thirteen heads bent nearer the table; a knife dropped, and thirteen bodies started. Tom grinned affectionately. "I have probably the most completely assorted bunch of liars and scoundrels ever gathered under one roof. Quite possibly I shall be neatly shot in the back before break of day. Slim, if you stoop any lower you'll dye your moustache in that coffee cup. Oh, don't mention it. You're quite obliged."

The proximity of a woman utterly ruined the meal; Tom Gillette's frank lies and pointing finger served to reduce them to a state from which air and solitude only could effect a recovery. The first to finish eating slunk out of the cabin with the countenance of one who hoped he wasn't watched but was sure the spotlight played upon him. Thus they departed; and presently from the corral came a high skirling of words from a man whose soul was in labour. Lispenard, who had been wrapped in his own thoughts throughout the affair, quietly left.

Tom grinned. "It has taken me a long time to get even."

"But what have they done to you?"

"Nothing," he answered, rolling a cigarette. "No finer outfit ever rode. I love 'em like brothers. That's why I'm abusing 'em."

The old cook slipped away with his pans; the lamplight strayed against the girl's soft face, accenting her utter femininity; she sat quite still, hands folded and seemingly placid. Yet beneath the surface a hundred cross-currents of thought ran free. The puzzle of this familiar yet so startlingly unfamiliar man was being attacked from a dozen different angles. She loved a conventional world, as all women do; even so, she could on occasion be both reckless and daring. Daring enough to tell Tom she had come west to plead her case—and then to hide the stark truth of it beneath those quick and subtle changes of spirit that were so much a part of her. It didn't matter what had changed her mind regarding him. She wasn't sure she knew why, or if she did know she refused to be truthful with herself. It didn't matter. What mattered was that, once having changed her mind, she meant to see the affair to the very end; to play the game with all the skill, all the shrewdness and impetuousness she owned. The shrewdness had always been a part of her, but the impetuousness was new, and born, perhaps, of the

106

knowledge that she had made a mistake concerning Tom Gillette and that she grew no younger. It was even new enough to disturb her whole outlook upon life and to set her off on a trip half across the continent unchaperoned. And it was disturbing enough to have created in her one irrevocable decision: she would win back Tom Gillette if she could, surrendering as little as she must, but if parsimony failed then she was willing to throw every last coin and possession upon the table and say, "There it is, I will not haggle. Take it." That was the story of Christine Ballard, as much as it was given anyone, even herself, to know.

The room grew cold with the coming of night. Gillette touched the kindling with a match, and she relaxed to the heat, one hand idly trailing over the chair arm. "That one—Quagmire—I thought was quaint."

He shook his head. "Wrong word, Kit. Quagmire's been hurt so bad he couldn't cry. He's loyal down to the last drop of blood. A more scorching pessimism never came from the lips of a mortal, but that's only a false front to cover a heart as soft as a woman's."

Silence a moment; the girl made another long dētour and came to rest on a distant topic. "Tom, I remember once something you told me about what your father had said. When you left for the East. I've often wondered, often thought—something about a man's word."

Gillette dropped the cigarette. Fine lines sprang along his face—a rugged face and handsome in a purely masculine fashion. There was a flash down in the deep wells of his eyes. And it took just such a shrewd observer as Christine Ballard to detect how he held back the upthrust of feeling; held it back so rigidly that his words were dry, almost bleak.

"He told me always to remember that a man's word was a piece of the man himself and never to betray it."

Of a sudden she rose. "I'm tired, Tommy. Do I sleep in front of the fire or up in the attic?"

"Doctor's already put your possibles in my room." He went over and opened the bedroom door. Passing through, she turned and hesitated. The perfume of her clothing clung to his nostrils, and for one long moment he was carried back to the days of his schooling. Her arm fell against his shoulder. He kissed her; and then as the door closed, her tinkling, elusive laugh escaped through. *"Au 'voir,* Tommy. Are you quite sure you've buried all the old bones?"

It was not for some time that he realized why she had brought up his father's remark about the word of a man. His fist struck the table resoundingly. "By God, I will not be stripped for torture again!"

The cabin became too small to hold Kit Ballard and himself at the same time; he passed out, glancing up to the full, lemon-silver surface of the moon. The bunkhouse light cut a clear path across the river. Quagmire stepped athwart that pathway, advancing.

"Hey, Tom. Yo' been ridin' to'rds that black butte today or yestidy?"

"No. Why?"

"Tracks," answered Quagmire succinctly. The tip of his cigarette made a crimson trail in the darkness. "Somebody's been havin' a look at our stuff. Question is, what for do they want to look?"

"There's a fight coming up, Quagmire. We'll be one man against ten."

Quagmire digested the remark. "Man is mortal. An' numbers don't mean nothin'. What yo' aimin' to do about it?"

"Why, I told Grist I wasn't selling out," said Tom. "Starting to-morrow, we'll keep a man hidden on top of that butte. Just to see what he can see. No use in being played for a sucker."

"It was my idear, likewise," murmured Quagmire. "Then, of course, it might've been the tracks o' yo' friend."

"Blondy? Yes, it might. He circles the country quite a bit. I'd better ask him."

But Quagmire only brought up the supposition to introduce a new fact. "It mighta been him but it wasn't. Last three days runnin' he's travelled across the river." And after another long silence, he added an entirely unrelated and cryptic thought. "I hate a talebearer."

Tom divined that Quagmire possessed information he wished to divulge and that it troubled both his habit of secrecy and his sense of loyalty. He could have made it no

108

plainer he stood willing to speak if pressed. Gillette watched a cloud sail across the face of the moon. "Well, Quagmire when the clothes are all washed the dirt will come up. Let it ride like that."

"Yeah," grunted Quagmire and turned toward the bunkhouse. Tom followed. Lispenard, he noted, already had rolled in.

Exercising her prerogative, Christine Ballard slept through breakfast. Gillette, having business over on a corner of his range, carefully instructed the cook to keep a hot meal simmering until she rose. On his way out he met Lispenard. "Tell Kit I'll be back within two or three hours and we'll go for a trip round the place."

"Good enough," agreed the man. He seemed extraordinarily quiet, on the borderland of one of his fits of sullen humour. Tom grinned. "What's the itch, Blondy? Does she remind you of the fleshpots you have left behind?"

"Oh, go to the devil," grunted Lispenard. He was about to add that he was infernally sick of his former comrade's tolerant amusement, but he checked this churlishness and scowled at Gillette's back until the latter was out of sight. Turning into the main cabin he settled himself by the table, his heavy, bulging eyes staring at nothing in particular. When Christine came from her room he appeared to be unaware of her presence until she spoke.

"Claudie, why the sulks?"

He raised himself from the chair—a trace of politeness that remained from his former training—and fell quickly back. "It bores me," said he, in all frankness. "Bores me to extinction."

The cook arrived with the girl's belated breakfast, rolling his eyes at Lispenard as he retreated. "The king has been gracious enough to command me to inform you," grunted Lispenard, "that he would be back in a couple of hours and take you for a ride."

"How very nice of him—how unpleasant of you. Claude, you don't display your talents in such a temper. Why do you call him that?"

109

"I mean it quite literally, Kit. Don't for a moment doubt his power over this ranch and the yokels on it. It's a blessed feudal estate. He is the law. Oh, quite so! Quaint Western manner. He drives 'em like a pack of dogs. Why they stand it I don't understand. Observe, when you ride with him, how he'll stop on a ridge and look over the country. A king could do it no better. As much as to say, 'This is mine. I command.' "

She made a wry face at the coffee and observed the heavy slabs of bacon with evident resignation. "I must be a Spartan," she murmured, and then smiled at the man. "Well, Claudie, why not the grand manner if it is all his own?"

"Rot! It irks me. I detest self-sufficiency. They shout about equality out here—every man as good as another. More tosh. I've been an alien every blessed minute—made to feel like one. They dislike me as much as I dislike them."

She moved her hand slightly. "Do you know something about yourself, Claudie? You played the conquering hero once, and now you hate to see another go above you."

"Above me!" cried Lispenard. "Don't be ridiculous."

She put down her coffee cup and turned toward him, serious. "Let me tell you. Tom Gillette has grown head and shoulders above you. Unpleasant, isn't it, my dear boy? Then you shouldn't be discourteous to a woman before breakfast."

"So you come to be another herald at his court?" He rose. "What did *you* come here for, anyway?"

"I answer no direct questions before ten o'clock," said she, gay again.

"Work fast," he muttered, grimly amused, "or you'll lose him."

"Claude!"

"Oh, don't assume your airs with me, my dear Kit. I know you quite well. Much better, in fact, than friend Tom knows you."

Colour stained her cheeks. "Once that manner became you. It doesn't now."

He brushed it aside, bold eyes looking down at her. "In fact, you are much like I am. So much so that I can tell you what's below those fine gestures and that charming smile."

110

She bit her lip, anger glowing in her eyes. "You deserve to be whipped, Claude!"

He laughed at her; a high, mirthless laugh that rang against the poles and died. "Let anyone hereabouts try it. I'd welcome the exercise. Well, my dear Kit, wish me luck. I'm going to rid you of my unwelcome presence before the week is out. Fact. I imagine you'll feel easier to have me gone."

"Going back East to cadge off your friends again, Claudie?"

"Quite a cruel thrust. I said we were much alike, didn't I? No, I'm not going East. They'll never see me again back there. I'm going—God knows where." The fresh sun flamed through the window and struck his long yellow hair. The girl had a full view of his profile—its hard jaw bones, its over-heavy outline of eyes and forehead. He disappeared without a backward glance, and she heard him ride away.

"If I were a man," she murmured to herself, "I'd give him a fine whipping."

But all marks of anger were erased by the time Gillette returned. She had got into a riding habit, and when she trailed across the yard to the horse that was to be hers she was quite gay and beautiful. Together they cantered east, rising and falling with the swell of the earth; the sun was a blood disk beneath the threat of which the land quivered. The river, sucked into the sands, showed only a rivulet of water. It seemed wholly impossible that man or beast could find sustenance in the expanse of tortured prairie stretching its endless leagues into the smoky horizon; and for all her determination to be a good Spartan, Christine Ballard felt the weight of that searing, oppressive day. It was as if some unseen giant crushed her and blew his breath into her face. Her pleasantries became harder to manage, and at the end of several miles, when he stopped her on a commanding ridge and began to point out the extent of the range, she interrupted. "Tom, it's magnificent. Really it is. But—do you ever feel that you are wasting the best of yourself out here?"

"What's the best of me, Kit?"

"Oh, putting your talents in a place where they'll make

you great. Why, Tom, back East you could be splendidly successful. How many of our friends have told me you were able to break through any kind of opposition. You could be in high places.''

He drew his arm around the horizon. "I'm humbler than that, Kit. You can't live under this sky, having it as a sort of next-door neighbour all the time, and not lose a lot of pretensions. What good are high places to a man if he's not satisfied? Why fight for something you've got no heart in? And what more could any man want than this? Look at the prairie sweeping off there. It's mine to ride on. I sleep sound at night. I go out in the morning and look at the sun coming up and I feel as if the day was made for me and nobody else. A fellow loses himself and his troubles. Time doesn't count. Everything marches along slow and a man lives slow—which is the way folks ought to live. What's better?''

"Sometimes," said she, "I think it's criminal in a man not to achieve all he is able to achieve.''

"For instance?''

"Why, you could go up politically, you could make a fortune of your own choice. Look at my father.''

He shook his head. She thought she had never heard him say a more solemn word. "I've gone back to the blanket, Kit. Don't drag out the torture machines again.''

It was so definite, so final that she forbore to press him further. And in one of those swift flashes of wisdom she sometimes permitted herself, she saw events marching along to that last gamble when she would be putting herself up and saying, "Take me on your own terms." The thought should have dispirited her. Yet it was otherwise. A current of emotion bore her along on a flood tide, and with it came a strange pleasure. She who stepped so carefully around the crater of life was on the point of throwing herself willingly into it. She, Christine Ballard!

He had discovered something on the ground that interested him, and they followed it a hundred yards before he spoke again. "Trail. I think it's Blondy's horse. But we'll just have a look.''

No more was said for a good while. The hoof prints led them into coulees, over ridges, and through extremely broken pieces of ground. The girl, obedient to his humour, kept her peace, wondering at the watchfulness that came over his face. More than once they galloped away from the trail and into the recesses of a box cañon, or détoured below the horizon and crawled slowly to the ridge tops again. Somewhat to the right of them stood a butte, black and forbidding, at which Gillette constantly glanced. And at last Christine ventured a question. "What is it?"

He drew himself from his study. "I'm trying to make up the story in this. There's always some kind of a yarn in a set of hoof prints. And when you see hoof prints mixed with boot prints that story usually promises a surprise ending."

Quite of a sudden his head came up, turning sidewise. She thought she heard a faint sound floating through the morning drone. And again she marked the strange shift of his expression. "Come on," he muttered. His horse raced up a slope, Kit lagging. He stopped an instant on the backbone of the ridge; then she saw him rise in his stirrups and fling the quirt down on the pony's rump. When she rode to the crest he was a hundred yards away.

Directly in his path and another fifty yards to the fore a pair of horses stood idle. Her eyes caught them first; then, as Gillette swerved, she saw two figures locked together, struggling. Gillette was off his horse, sand spurting up beneath his boots, and racing onward. The pair had split; two men in a fight. One of them was Lispenard. Kit galloped ahead.

The other was not a man, but a girl dressed in man's clothing; quite striking of features and at this moment trembling with exhaustion. Certainly it wasn't fear, for her black eyes sparkled with outraged emotion, and she was crying, "You dam' dog! I could kill you! I could!" Then Christine Ballard heard Gillette break in; and there was such a suppressed fury in his words that she felt the stab of an emotion hitherto quite alien—jealousy.

"I am going to whip you, Blondy," he was saying. "It ought to be a gun, but I'll give you your own weapons. Put up your hands, you damned yellow cur! You are going to get a lesson you have needed all your life."

Lispenard's heavy lips pulled back from his teeth; a

spotty, purplish colour stood along his cheeks. He was sullen, vindictive. "You fool!" he cried. "I've had enough of your fine manners! I'm weary of 'em, hear me! By heavens, I've sickened on your cursed air of superiority!"

"Put up your hands."

"Don't get on a pedestal for the women!" shouted Lispenard; he flung back his shoulders and the knotted muscles rippled through his shirt. He had never bulked so immense, so destructively powerful as at that moment; he stood half a head over Gillette, he was thicker, more massive in every respect; and as he took a step forward, knees suddenly springing a little under the weight of his body, he seemed like a wild animal from the jungle. "I have always whipped you, my lad! And I'll smash your ribs until you won't walk so upright and almighty—And then I'll take my leave! I'm cursed tired of your ways!"

"Save your breath, Blondy."

The great body went across the interval as if shot from a catapult. Fists struck so swiftly that Christine Ballard couldn't follow them. She screamed, but above the shrillness of it she heard the impact of bodies, the expelling of great breaths, the shuffling of feet in the sand. It was quite impossible that large men could move with that agility; Lispenard's yellow head made a complete circle under the sun; arms feinted, drew back, feinted again and smashed against their targets. Tom sagged, supporting himself on one knee; Lispenard's face blazed with the killer's instinct. "Get up and fight! Always did lack guts! Get up and fight before I kick you to pieces!" Gillette was up. Again Lispenard's great frame snapped across the space. Gillette was off his guard, and he was flung back by a single sledgelike blow. In falling he caught Lispenard's arm and together they sprawled on the ground, rolled, arm wrenching at arm, knees striking like pistons. Body crushed against body. They were on their feet once more and Tom Gillette's face was crimson and his shirt had been ripped from collar to belt.

Lispenard came on, crouching, a strangled cry in his throat. And the rip and smash of flesh so sickened Christine Ballard that she had to support herself in the saddle with both hands. They had gone mad, all reason and all sense of pain had deserted them. They fought as only the most brutal type of animals could fight, bent on the kill. And now and then, as Lispenard's choking yell broke the silence of the prairie, she recalled his remark. "Beneath, I'm a seething furnace. Oh, quite so." He had been truthful to her; hell could not distill a more insane fury than that which trembled on his smeared and distorted face.

She was not a man, or she would have noticed, as the fight drew out, that it was Lispenard whose head went down and whose charges grew the more aimless and broken; whose breath came out of him like a sob. Gillette was checking the other's attack. Through a dimming vision he found his mark easier to strike. He pressed, he saw his opponent's face at odd angles as his fists smashed it and rolled it back. Lispenard's bulging eyes lost their firmness, and at that point Gillette summoned whatever was left of his strength. He had been taught fine blows once, he had been instructed in sportsmanship. All that went overboard with the rest of the Eastern junk. He could not hit hard enough to satisfy the urge of his will. He could only follow on and on, past the blur of a woman on a horse, past the blur of a woman crouching to the ground; lashing out and feeling a numb reaction run through his arms. To strike again and follow in the endless circle until, through the red film, he saw only the glare of the horizon. His throbbing body felt no return blow; and he looked down in a hazy wonder. The Blond Giant lay senseless.

He turned, seeking his horse. He wanted something to lean against before his legs gave way, he wanted to see the prairie again before he went blind. There was a shadow in front of him; he thought it was Lispenard returning to fight. A girl's voice spoke in warning. "No—don't hit at me, Tom! No—Tom, it's all over. He's down. Put your arms around me! Your poor, poor face."

He sat on the ground, a cool hand pressed against his temple and a cloth skirted across his mouth. It was all over, and Lorena was on her knees trying to wipe away the blood. The ringing died out of his ears, he began to feel the ache of his body where terrific blows had punished him. But they were lesser things. Lesser things. It was Lorena who kept

115

doubling back the bandana to find a dry spot; and what was a woman thinking about and what was a woman feeling whose eyes were like this girl's? God alone knew, but that expression would trouble him from now on, sleeping or waking.

"I think," he mumbled, "I'd better smoke. I'm comin' back down the tunnel. For a time I went twenty feet away from myself."

Talking dispelled the mists. He rose uncertainly. "If he'd hit me a few more times I'd be knocking on the gates." He felt light-hearted, without a trace of resentment. The smoke of the cigarette stung the bruises of his lips, and he threw it away. Lispenard was reviving; as for Christine Ballard, she sat very still in the saddle, which reminded him of something.

"Kit, this is Lorena Wyatt, next neighbour to me. Christine Ballard, Lorena. She's a guest from the East."

It seemed a little queer that neither of them spoke—only bowed. He turned away and left them together while he confronted Lispenard. The latter pushed himself upright.

"I could always whip you—until you got stung," he muttered. "All right. No love lost, my boy. And we'll forget about shaking hands, too. I'm not through with this yet."

"I'll donate you the horse," replied Gillette. "Travel in any direction you want—but not back to the ranch. If I see you on my range again I'll use a gun. You're rotten fruit, Blondy. I've suspected it for some time."

He followed Lispenard and stood beside the latter's horse. "They say it's every man for himself out here," mused Lispenard. "Well, I'll be on my way. But just put this in your bonnet, old-timer: I don't consider it over with. I'll balance the ledger if it takes me a thousand years. Put it down in red ink."

The fight had drained them of animus; so they stood and looked at each other, a world apart in every respect, utter strangers. Then Lispenard got in the saddle and spurred away. Gillette turned to the women.

Neither had spoken a word; all that while they were exchanging glances, Lorena's clear face thoughtfully wrinkled, Christine Ballard sitting very straight on her horse. Lorena

116

made a small motion with her hand and turned to Tom; and it seemed to him she marked him then for whatever he was and stored it in her memory. Never before had she touched him, save to accept his hand, and though he had no reason for it he felt a distinct warning when she brushed his arm with the tips of her fingers. And smiled a crooked little smile. "Tom, heat some water for your face when you get home. And this is the girl?" Her voice sank to the barest whisper. "Oh, I knew it all the time. Even if you didn't tell me." His hat still lay on the ground; she stooped and retrieved it and with just a touch of possession in her gesture she put it on his head. "You've made another enemy and you've gotten more scars—because of me. A woman can cause so much trouble. That's why I wish I were a man."

She ran to her horse and stepped into the saddle. Dust rose up from the turning hoofs. Her hand came out to him and he heard a faint, "Be good, Tom," as she raced away.

Gillette swung up, ranged beside Christine Ballard, and started homeward.

"She's very pretty," observed Christine.

"Yes," said he, turning to look. She was far along the ridge and dipping from sight. His fingers tightened on the reins, and the pony stopped. That last phrase sounded like a farewell. Christine studied him with so queer an expression that he pressed forward, puzzled and depressed and not knowing why.

10   A KILLING

Lispenard fled away from the scene as fast as his pony could be spurred, nor was he anything less than cruel with those gouging rowels. Physically, he was done up, and the terrific jolting at Tom Gillette's hands left him momentarily sick; he felt as if there were iron hoops around his chest, and the muscles of his face had congealed until it seemed he wore a plaster mask. The power was out of him, he could scarce raise his arms. And over and over again he rehearsed the blows he had struck. His fists had landed; the dull ache that ran from wrist to shoulder told him he had reached his mark. He knew he never yet had hit any man as often and as hard as he had hit Tom Gillette. It hadn't been a boxing match; he meant to kill, he meant to slash and maim. Yet Gillette had beaten him, knocked him out—Gillette whose biceps were not much more than half the size of his own.

That shook him badly. It roused him anew to a dull, vindictive passion; and his horse suffered for it. The truth about Lispenard was quite apparent; he had gone bad—his was the stuff from which were made the border's greatest renegades. Back East, under restraint, he might never have crossed that line of lawlessness, but rather pursued his way with the aura of his athletic reputation paving a career for him; unscrupulous perhaps but not dangerous; a little dissolute, making feminine conquests with his bold eyes and his gay manner that would grow harder with the years— and more threadbare. Society tolerated his kind under that fanciful pseudonym of "the man about town."

Out here, with no restraints, the uncertain fibre of the man frayed through. The step across the line was but a short one and easily taken. He had not yet taken that step, for the opportunity was not yet come. But he was right for it, spoiling for it. And thus he rode into Nelson, tethered his horse, and made his purchases. A gunnysack of grub, cartridges, and a blanket. At the saloon he tarried some time. The man had an insatiable thirst; he filled himself full of the trader's whisky and bought a bottle to pack along. At noon he passed out of Nelson with his purchases and struck straight back on the trail until he arrived at the ford. Here, instead of crossing, he paralleled the river a matter of miles and gained the heart of the broken land. High on a ridge he took his bearings and advertised his own whereabouts; San Saba would be watching, that he well knew. So he pressed on, and within twenty minutes the renegade ex-foreman stood in front of him, sheltered by an outcrop of rock.

His tongue was a little thick, his perceptions were somewhat blurred. Yet his wits were enough about him to receive a warning; he squared himself defensively as he dropped to the ground, and he took care to keep his right arm free. San Saba's little round head dropped forward, and the lank face was speculatively grim; the man was studying Lispenard, turning Lispenard's usefulness over and over in the cautious recesses of his mind. Something tipped the balance on invisible scales, and San Saba relaxed.

"Grub?"

"Dam' you, boy," muttered Lispenard, "I'm playin' square. See you do the same by me. I may look green, but I'm not soft."

"Name yore own contract," murmured San Saba, eyes never shifting; here was one man whose gaze he could meet.

"Fifty-fifty, all the way around, all the way through," was the reply. "I'm on to you, San Saba. What was it you said?—'takes a scoundrel to know a scoundrel.' That's right, my son. And I know you. I'm not your cat's-paw. We ride equal in this firm."

"Agreed," was San Saba's laconic answer. Something

like sly humour flickered in the depths of his small eyes, too remote for Lispenard to see or understand. "Grub there?"

"Sure."

San Saba rifled the sack and brought out a side of bacon; he took his knife and cut a half pound slice from it as he would have pared himself a piece of chewing tobacco. Lispenard never had seen a man eat bacon raw, and the sight turned his stomach. San Saba grinned maliciously. "Ketch holt of yo'self, boy. Yore on the prairie from now on. I'll teach yo' things. Wait till we get a buff'lo—nothin' better'n liver raw."

"Don't prod me, San Saba," protested Lispenard. "I'm holdin' too much rotgut in my system."

San Saba took to studying the land with a certain wariness; he squatted on his heels and drew patterns in the sand, from time to time looking up at his uneasy companion. "Had a fight, did yo'? Gillette kind o' battered yo' features, I'd guess. No love lost atween the two of yo'?"

"I'll cut my initials in his hide yet!" exclaimed Lispenard. He threw back his head, and the thick lips trembled from the sudden upthrust of passion. "By God, I'll mark him! I can whip him—I can whip him any day in the week! It was a stroke of luck for that cursed Puritan—and there he must show himself before the grand stand of two fine ladies! No, I took too much from that damned flint face! I hate a man who sets himself to be an African potentate. Back East he walked humbler, and I'll see he walks humbler before I'm through. Next time—"

San Saba's saturnine eyes bored into the Blond Giant. Of a sudden he leaned forward, and his question snapped like a whip. "Next time, what?"

"I'll use a gun," muttered the Blond Giant.

San Saba rose. "Agreed. Fifty-fifty. Now come along."

"Where?" grumbled Lispenard. "Here, what are you running away from the man for? By God, has he bluffed you? Sitting out here in the hills like a whipped dog."

San Saba was in the saddle, his thin, repellent face devoid of expression. "Time for that. No hurry. Let him drop his guard before we try any rigs. Never stalk an animal in the wind—yo' won't never ketch him. Come on."

Lispenard followed. The outburst left him in a kind of lethargy. He felt San Saba's will taking hold, and it revived his uneasiness. The man was unbending, inflexible; behind that cheerless mask was a core of flame. Lispenard sensed it, and for a moment the chill of fear started along his body. He wanted to protest; San Saba turned and beckoned for him to draw alongside. So the Blond Giant obeyed, surly and half in rebellion.

San Saba struck straight into the west. Never a word was spoken. The sun went before them, and the land blazed like the very pit of hell; the sky was a brilliant brass shield, then the sun dipped and dusk came with a grateful touch of wind. San Saba wound in and out of the draws. He accelerated the pace, he slowed it. They passed a ridge and halted. Lispenard roused himself at the ex-foreman's whispers to see a point of fire glowing through the darkness below.

"What is it?" he grumbled.

"I spotted 'em this mornin'," replied San Saba. "Prospectors from Deadwood. Restin' up."

"What about it?"

"Loosen yo' gun, man. No prospector comes out o' Deadwood lessen he totes a full poke. We ride down casual-like. When I say 'now'—yo' understand?"

Lispenard pulled himself together, just short of an oath. If ever he were to draw away from this gaunt, sinister partner, now must be the time. San Saba's horse crowded nearer; the ex-foreman's shadow hovered over him. Words struck him sharply, imperiously. "By God, suh, if yo' yalla, go back to Nelson; I trail with no gumpless chicken hearts. What yo' deceivin' me fo'? It ain't strange Gillette whipped yo' offen the ranch!"

Lispenard's throat burned like fire. He fumbled into his roll and drew out the whisky bottle; he knocked out the cork and drank it like so much water. "All right—I'll match that, you rascal. I'm remembering those sweet words, my friend. All right."

"When I say 'now,' " was San Saba's cold murmur. His horse moved downward. The two of them quartered the slope, drawing near to the fire. A picketed horse whinnied and a rugged figure of a man passed the light swiftly. A challenge struck them.

"Who's thar?"

"Friends—friends," called San Saba. "We ain't struck a water hole all day. Yo' kin'ly oblige?"

A second voice, unfriendly, joined in. "Man's supposed to kerry his own fluid in this country, stranger. Ain't you knowin' the ways? Too many dam' pilgrims clutterin' the Territory. Git down—come to the fire."

San Saba dismounted. Lispenard dropped clumsily to the ground and walked abreast the ex-foreman. The prospectors stood on the edge of light, a pair of burly creatures full bearded and gimlet eyed. San Saba spread his hands over the flame points. "Gits cold almighty sudden after sundown. No, suh, we ain't pilgrims. Texans, suh. My pardner is a-lookin' for a man this way. Got a impo'tant letter. Blondy, yo' got that letter in yo' breeches pocket, ain't yo'?"

The Blond Giant stood uncertainly in his tracks. What was San Saba driving at now? He licked his lips, feeling the weight of the man's little red eyes. And of a sudden he understood San Saba was giving him a chance to drop his arms nearer his holster. He obeyed. San Saba muttered "now" in a husky, remote voice. Half blind, Lispenard clawed for his weapon. The two figures of the miners seemed to blur and weave aside. A carbine flew up in his face. There was a shot, and he felt his own kicking back in his hands, time and again. And still this scene was but a blur, and he was sick at his stomach, and the blood pounded in his head. Somebody still fired, but the miners had disappeared from his vision.

San Saba's brittle voice warned him. "That's enough. Yo' killed him. Pull up—don't he'p none to scatter bullets in a co'pse."

Lispenard dropped his gun, seeing one of the miners sprawled at his feet, face downward and dead. He stumbled around the fire trying to find something to lean against. But San Saba was bent over the men, and presently the ex-foreman stood up, grimly triumphant. "No prospector

122

comes from Deadwood lessen he totes a full poke. Here's yo' poke. Now, come away. We ride all night.''

Lispenard's mind grew clearer. The poke weighed considerable. He slipped it into his coat pocket and groped back toward his horse. If that was all to killing a man—San Saba already had passed beyond, and Lispenard spurred in pursuit.

"I'd protected yo' case it was nes'arry,'' murmured San Saba. ''But yo' did well. First fight is allus blind. Nex' time keep yo' wits. Aim straight an' don' use more'n one bullet. We ride fo' Deadwood.''

"What was the idea of this?'' muttered Lispenard. "Cold murder, man! We could have done it without that.''

"Sho', I told you I'd teach you tricks. First kill is allus hardest. I picked miners for yo' to try on. Miner's shoot pritty poor.''

Lispenard was stone sober and chilled to the bone. "Some day, my friend, I'll have to kill you. By God, I will have to do it or be killed myself.''

San Saba's dry chuckle reached him. "Mebbe—when yo' get too big fo' me. Meanwhile, we got a stake, and Deadwood is full o' chances. Fifty-fifty.''

"See you don't forget that'' growled Lispenard.

"We'll come back to Mister Gillette later, murmured San Saba. "Prick that pony.''

11 THE RAID

There was a windstorm brewing in the south; Tom Gillette, poised on a ridge, saw the gray screen of sand in the distance. Presently it would be on him, beating against him like so many needles, choking the wind down his throat. Reluctantly he turned ranchward; for a week the far edge of his daily ride had brought him to this high point separating his range from that of the Wyatts. And here he tarried, not sure why he waited, yet always looking eastward for a telltale fluffing of dust against the sky and the view of Lorena's lithe body swaying in the saddle like that of an Indian. She had formerly kept a casual rendezvous with him, and the sight of her clear, grave face had always made the day a little more pleasant, even though she had the trick of puzzling him with odd emotions now and then mirrored in her black eyes. But for a week, since the fight with Lispenard she had forsaken this ridge; and no news came from the Wyatt ranch.

He travelled back, uneasy and dissatisfied. In the distance he caught a glint of the river, a thin trickle above the porous sands; alkali dust stung his throat, the blazing, blistering sun beat against the dun earth until the eye wearied of the sight. The prairie quivered under shimmering heat waves; southwest the dark folds of the Black Hills reared against the brazen sky. Over there in the heart of the hills men dug yellow metal and a town was in the full tide of a boom.

News came slowly to his section of the territory; he heard that all the Texans along the river were gone, save Wyatt.

According to the P. R. N. resident agent Wyatt likewise had sold, but Tom Gillette only half believed the tale. Wyatt had been too anxious to acquire that strip, and Lorena, who swayed her father to some extent, bucked the idea of moving. Why was it she kept away from him? Whatever she thought of Christine Ballard and his relations with the girl was wrong. He wanted to tell her she was wrong.

"What difference does it make?" he muttered. "But couldn't she see for herself there's nothing between Kit and me?"

It left him irritable. He was a man; he didn't understand women, and he knew he never would be able to understand them. They muddied up the current of life, they cut across the established order of things, they acted out of impulse—or if it were not impulse then it was some obscure motive he couldn't grasp. Kit always had been elusive and enigmatic, but he thought Lorena moved more straightforwardly, that she had no contradictions in her nature. He had thought so until the fight. And then, when her cool hand slid over his face and those queer muffled words reached him he knew all women were essentially alike.

The van of the windstorm swept across the prairie, sage stalks rolling along before. "Mosey," said Gillette, and raised his bandana. At the moment of action he saw scuffed hoof prints on the ground, and he checked his horse, bending over to study them. They came out of the northeast and struck directly into his range. Slightly stale hoof prints. In another ten minutes the wind would erase them completely. Tom touched his spurs, and the pony bunched to a gallop. That made the second time he had found strange spoor on his territory; Circle G men didn't often travel in pairs, and they didn't cover this end of the range.

"Mosey!" The wind bore down of a sudden, and the word was whipped out of his mouth. There was a sound like canvas slatting; the perspective of the land changed, the horizon was wiped out. A gray driving pall slanted past him, the spraying sand sheered against his neck. Breathing became more difficult.

"Mosey!"

The horse raced on, pushed by the storm; up and down

the rolling prairie. A gray row of skeletons marched through the unnatural dusk, and he was in the heaven of his home buildings. He left the pony in a shed and himself quartered to the house. Christine Ballard stood in the middle of the room, one hand pressed against her breast, white of face. "What is it, Tom?"

He lowered his bandana and shook out the sand. "Dry storm. Nothing to get worried about."

She had been reading a book. One finger marked the page. Stirred by fretfulness, she threw it across the room and sank into a chair. She had a peculiar manner of drawing herself together, of tucking her legs beneath her; and thus she sat, chin cupped, staring at Gillette while the shadows weaved across her expressive eyes. Gillette loaded his pipe and smoked, sitting on the table.

"And this is your country, Tom?" Her slim shoulders rose. "Well, a man can find pleasure in odd places. I was frightened out of my mind until you came in. It's too raw, it's ungenerous. There's no sport to it. It's cruel. Listen to that wind—do you hear what it says, Tom?" Suddenly she threw back her head and the white triangle of her throat gleamed; one fist was clenched. Tom Gillette marked that picture well, for there was beauty in it. And Christine's eyes were sombre, a rare mood for this girl who seldom let herself be touched by too deep an emotion. "It's telling me I'm small, I'm nothing, and that I can be crushed. Hear it?"

Gillette nodded. "It's been in my ears all my life, except the time I spent East. You bet. But what's wrong with knowin' yourself to be a humble thing, walkin' under a canopy that's got no corners and no ceilin'?"

Her answer was almost aggressive. "I hate to be reminded of it. I like to think I amount to something."

"Sho'. In the East folks lose sight of the truth. Inside a house they're little tin gods—but the house makes a servant of 'em. Out here we walk abroad. We know we're small potatoes, but we're free."

"Do you really like it that well?" she asked, bending forward. "Or are you just talking?"

He knocked the ashes from his pipe, the old reticence

126

returning. After all, she was an outlander. She couldn't catch his point of view. No more than Lispenard did. "All I am belongs to it. It made me. It's in my system, and I couldn't get rid of it if I wanted to. If you lived here long enough you'd feel the same way."

She was gay and provocative instantly. "I haven't been invited to stay indefinitely, Tom. Are you meaning to invite me now?"

He met her glance stubbornly. "I'm reachin' for no strings, Kit. That's over."

"Oh, why must you be so stolid, so dense?" she cried. "Look at me!"

He shook his head. The wind ripped at the house savagely, a voice trailed past the eaves, weird and meaningless. It was growing darker.

Christine's laugh was like the touching of crystal pendants. Her question barely carried to him. "Am I, then, so undesirable?"

"It's apt to be the other way around," said Tom, turning. And after a moment he flung a hot phrase at her. "Do you think I'm made of wood, Kit? What have you come here for—under the same roof with me?"

"Oh, I have no pride left. I have come a-begging to make up for a mistake." Then she slipped away, in one of those characteristic changes, to another topic. "Back home at this time I would be going out. And there would be a dance at the Coopers. Do you remember those dances, Tom?"

He nodded. It was quite dark and he lighted the lamp. Christine lay back in her chair, relaxed, studying him. "Do you recall Harry Cooper? He stood for the assembly in the eighth district. My father backed him, and now Harry is at Albany and well on the way to political honours. My father always helps a good man, Tom."

"Every fellow to his liking."

"You could do anything you set your mind to do," was her quick answer. "Anything."

She stopped there. Tom was smiling at her, humour wrinkling around his eyes. She caught her breath, the colour rising to her cheeks. Still, she displayed a courage and a directness he had not suspected she owned. Her tapering fingers spread apart; a diamond flashed in the amber light. "Must I surrender everything, Tommy? Isn't it generous in the winner to allow a little?"

He stood up, tall and rugged against the lamp's glow. "Kit, I have always said you were more beautiful than any woman I knew. I begin to think you are brave as well. But you surrender nothing. Don't do it. You are only tormenting a man meant to be a cowpuncher the rest of his days."

She was out of her chair and before him, one hand striking his chest again and again. "You are a fool, Tom Gillette! You are a fool!"

The door rattled. Christine moved back to her chair as Quagmire let himself inside, coated with sand, red-eyed. "I rode over to where yo' stationed Baldy Laggett, Tom. He met tracks this mo'nin'—two hosses tailin' around the broken top buttes. It's the second time a-running'. Night work, Baldy says."

"I saw those tracks away east of the buttes not more than an hour ago," replied Gillette. "Looked as if the parties were travelling fast. You get the idea, don't you, Quagmire?"

Quagmire nodded; his homely face pinched together. "I comprehend plenty, as the parson would say."

"How many cows have we got over that way now, Quagmire?"

"Three-four hun'red." After a pause the foreman added, "They's sorter bunched up the last few days. Driftin'. Baldy Laggett says they shifted overnight to'rds them arroyos that fork."

"Tracks there?"

"Yeah—tracks. 'Sif somebody was scoutin'!."

Kit Ballard stood in a corner and watched them. She sensed the undercurrent of conflict behind the words, the slow gathering of a decision; and she admired the casualness with which the two covered themselves. Tom's head dropped forward, there was a tightening of his features and a harder glow down in the wells of his eyes. She saw him in a fighting mood, and this new point of character left her with mixed emotions. He was beyond her power to sway, beyond her ability to cajole. Quagmire's hand described an Indian sign that meant nothing to her but seemed to impress Gillette. "P. R. N. cattle crossin' the river four days ago. Saw a travellin' puncher this mo'nin' headin' to'rds Deadwood. He told me. All Tejanners gone from the south bank. Wyatt lef' las' week."

Gillette's head came up. "Where to?"

The girl caught the bite of that question; she stirred, wanting to speak yet not able to break in. How much aside they placed a woman out here—how much of a man's world it was! No time for philosophy, no time for that exchange of wit she was so accustomed to. No time for playing at all. They moved slowly, they seemed to drift with the elements. But she began to see they were not drifting but fighting. Always fighting the treachery of nature and the treachery of man. Struggle was the warp of their lives, it left its stamp on every one of them.

"Dunno," murmured Quagmire; "puncher didn't remark. All gone, though. An', like I say, they's P. R. N. stock with P. R. N. punchers on all them ranches now"

Gillette's pipe disappeared in his pocket. He was drawling, "Tell Whitey Almo he's to stick on the ranch. Rest of us ride."

Quagmire's eyes strayed toward the girl and bashfully dropped. "Yo' hunch runs with mine," he murmured and went out.

The wind was dying, it was dark, and the day's heat had gone. Tom Gillette touched a match to the kindling in the fireplace; the colored cook entered like a shadow and stood questioningly on the threshold.

"Get it on the table, doctor. We pull out early."

The black man left. "Where to, Tom?" asked Christine.

"Out along the range, Kit."

"Trouble?"

"Just a little night riding, Kit."

They stood at opposite corners, looking at each other across the interval while the old cook slid in and out with his dishes and his platters; they seemed to be unconscious of him. Christine had a trick of putting her hand up to her breast when disturbed. She did it now, and the yellow light revealed the trouble in her eyes. Once, when the black man

129

was out of the room, she half whispered to him, "You are not the same man I knew back East."

"Clay to clay," muttered Tom Gillette, cheek muscles snapping.

"No—you are bigger. I am sorry—you will never know how much—that I made you dance to my tune. Tom—isn't it Western to forget and forgive a mistake?"

The crew came filling in and there was no more between them. Christine took the head of the table, and even her wit was damped; they disregarded her this night, they ate with intolerant haste and they were gone again; twelve homely faces grim set, twelve sets of eyes burning in the lamplight; rough men, illiterate men—men whose lives made queer and sometimes shameful patterns along the past. Intuition told her that. Yet they were brave. The wind had gone, and outside she heard a slapping of saddles and a murmuring—a soft murmuring and now and then a slashing oath in the darkness. Quagmire's face appeared a moment in the doorway, his head dropped and he was gone. Tom's cigarette sailed into the fireplace; he squared toward her.

"Be back before midnight, I'm thinkin'. Whitey Almo and doctor will be camped outside this door."

"I am not deceived," said Christine, coming forward. "You are going out to fight."

"I'll not be denying it," said he, soberly. "We've got no constables to summon hereabouts, Kit, when the law is broken. Maybe a fight—maybe only a false alarm. My back's to the wall. I'm not crying about it, understand. I'm only doing what my dad would have done, or any other man would do. That's the law of the range."

"To kill or be killed!" she cried. "I don't understand it! Here in America in this century—I don't believe it! You are not cold enough to take a life, Tom!"

"The fellow that rustles another fellow's cattle dies. I'm telling you it is range law. You're a long, long ways from New York, Kit. Do you know what the old fur trappers used to say? North of Leavenworth there is no law. Well, there's law now—but it never catches up with us folks running west."

"How many are they, Tom?"

He turned to the door, broad shoulders rising. "Ample, Kit. But they don't know the temper of Texans. They don't know—"

She was in front of him. Her hand fell across his arm. "God keep you, Tom! Oh, it's a brutal land! I hate it! Be careful!"

Again that pressure drawing him down toward her lips and the sweet smell of her hair and the gripping beauty of her face. It was like wine to him, it brought back every old memory, and some of the old desire. He pulled himself free and crossed the threshold, half blind. Quagmire murmured, "All set." He swung up to his saddle and reined around. The cavalcade led off, and the cold air cleared his brain. "Stretch out," he muttered; they galloped southward into the night, and the girl, supporting herself in the doorway, listened until the drum of their ponies' hoofs was absorbed in the vast vault. She turned inside then, oppressed by the stark blackness of the heavens; there was a power pressing her down, sapping the courage from her veins. Mystery swirled just beyond the threshold. Out beyond lay men waiting to kill other men. The colored cook entered, muscles rippling beneath his torn shirt; Whitey Almo's face appeared vaguely across the doorway, taciturn and watchful.

The Circle G riders swept steadily onward through the swirling shadows, silent save for the chafe and tinkle of their gear and the rhythmic pound of the horses. Arrow straight for an hour; Quagmire rode abreast Tom Gillette, stirrup touching stirrup, and it was the pressure or withdrawal of Quagmire's thigh that gave Gillette the course. He knew the land well; but Quagmire, who loved the night and who seemed to be able to see through the utter blackness of it, knew it even better. And it was Quagmire who gradually turned the cavalcade from south to southwest and then slowly eastward. The moon was a thin arc of silver, the ancient stars grew more and more remote. Onward they galloped, up and down the swells, the night breeze cold against their faces and the sound of the coyotes in their ears, howling out of the distance with the sadness of ages quivering in that lonely song. Ahead, the shadows piled thicker and the dim strip of the horizon was broken. They were falling downward, or the presence of the butte in front made it seem so. Gillette sat back in the saddle.

"Halt."

They stopped. He got to the ground and pressed his ear against the sand. The invisible telegraph carried no messages. Quagmire's voice croaked mournfully, "Not far now. At a walk, uh, Tom."

"At a walk."

They swung along a circle, the massed shadow turning their right flank. Twice they stopped to listen; and presently the shadow was behind and they were in the bed of an arroyo. Cattle moved directly to the front. They dismounted and stood silent.

"My shoulder aches," murmured Quagmire, following a long quiet. "It's a plumb bad sign. Was a man once in Tucson with a trick toothache. Trouble allus follered. He got to depend on it and sorter bragged about it. First time his mother-in-law died. Second time his wife died. Third time it ached nothin' happened and it sho'ly aggervated him. Looked like the dam' tooth wasn't nowise dependable. But they took him up an' hung him fo' murderin' said mother-in-law an' wife. On the scaffol' the gent says: 'I die happy. Didn't I tell yo' somethin' allus happened when it ached?' That's what yo'd call infallible." He moved nearer Gillette. "Reckon I overlooked a bet. Didn't know yo' wanted Wyatt's new location or I'd of asked."

"I'll find her, Quagmire."

"Woman—the star which leads up the hill. And sometimes down the other side. The gent which classed 'em with wine an' song must've been an old burnt fool like me. If a woman looked at me twice she'd faint. If she didn't faint I would."

"Which side of the slope is Baldy Laggett on?"

"He ain't more'n three hundred yards off at this moment, I'm bettin'."

Silence again, the silence of infinity pressing down. And then a whisper and a hint of things moving out beyond the arroyo's rim. Gillette's arm touched Quagmire in signal. Circle G mounted, the soft rubbing of leather running along the line. The moments trailed one upon the other, and a shadow appeared a moment and sank back into the screen of darkness. Presently riders moved along the earth in faint silhouette—a line of them—and passed to the right. One soft phrase exploded like a shell in the stillness. "Easy, boys."

Quagmire's murmur was in Tom Gillette's ear. "They're bunched now. Set?"

"Wait for evidence. Hold it, Quagmire."

And beyond, men spoke more freely. "What's the idea, Gib? How many of 'em? Which way?"

"Never mind all them questions. Save yore breath. Spook an' Ray—you circle and push. Easy—plenty of time."

Quagmire's arm touched Gillette twice, impatient. Gillette reached for his gun and pulled himself upright. And he spoke in a tone that carried across the night like the clapper stroke of a church bell. "Guns out, boys! Let's go!"

A challenge spat across the interval. "Who said that?"

"Rustlers die!"

"Still hunt, huh? A trap! Damn the Texans, let 'em have it!"

"Let's go! Come on, Circle G!"

The Circle G line tore up the arroyo side; and without parley the shroud of this black summer night was pricked in twenty places by mushrooming purple flame points, and the smash and the beat and roar of that crisscross fusillade twirled around the area like the funnel of a cyclone.

"Let's go!"

"No Texans wanted in Dakota! Come on, boys! Down the skids to hell!"

Gillette shoved himself directly onward and into the flickering muzzle flames; as for the rest of his men, he gave them free rein. They were old hands, they had survived border feuds, they were schooled in range war. Gun smoke rolled against his face, a thick and passionate cry beat against his ears; he was struck broadside by one of the rustlers slanting across the debated ground;, the man's horse reared and came down with its front feet hooked over his own pony's neck. The rustler rolled against him, a gun barrel slashed along his flank and as he jerked away a bullet tore into the saddle horn. The rustler's shadow was broad and fair; Gillette raised his piece and fired at that shadow. The man was down, soundless; the man was dead.

Quagmire's yell bore up from a remote quarter. Gillette sent a reply ricocheting back. He had drifted off from the Circle G men, he was barricaded from them by the rustlers, and now, hearing his yell, they closed in, twisting shapes ringing him around. A bullet's backwash fanned his cheek, and on the instant he was in the vortex of a whirlpool and men were baying like bloodhounds.

"By God, knock him down there!"

"Watch that cross fire! Crowd 'im—crowd 'im!"

He brought his horse dead about. Then he was thigh to thigh with them. An arm struck and stunned him, another arm hooked about his neck, and somebody's breath belched against his face. He let the reins go and clung to the horn, weaving and bending, fighting clear of that encircling elbow. Quagmire's boom came up as from a distance, but for Gillette there was no breath to waste. They were trying to knock him beneath the trampling hoofs.

"Drop that guy!"

"Oh, hell, pull the trigger!"

"Hold that wild talk, yuh fool!"

He shook himself free. Somewhere else was a sudden spattering of fire; a man screamed. They were crowding closer, trying to pinion him once more. Point-blank he pulled the trigger, and the spewing bullets made room for him; there was a ringing of angry oaths and the guns broke loose in fresh fury, but he was clear, and Quagmire's voice thundered near at hand. Gillette turned back.

"Come on, Circle G! The rustlers die!"

Confusion. The purple points of light flickered and faded. Saddles were empty this night, and men were down, some dead, some crying up out of the dust. And the echo of all this grim, bloody strife straggled into the sky and was lost in the cold immensity of creation. The stars were remote, remote. . . .

"Oh, for a crack o' light!"

Quagmire thundered back. "Go repo't to yo' corporation, yo' yaller dawgs! Better thank yo' Lord it ain't light!"

The gunfire crashed to a climax; somewhere was the

134

cough of a man's last breath. Once more was the shock of men and horses locked together while the very dregs of rage came spewing up. A riderless pony careened by Gillette; of a sudden the tide turned and the rustlers were in flight.

"Light?" yelled Quagmire. "Yo' light is sulphur an' brimstone! Who tol' yo' to fight a Texan, daylight or dark?"

"Come on," said Gillette. "This is a lesson for all Dakota rustlers. Pull in these flanks, boys. Let's ride."

They raced in pursuit, and now and then the stray flash of a gun showed them the way. They crept up, they lost ground. But always they kept to the trail as the night deepened and the miles dropped behind. The rustlers stopped firing altogether. At this point Gillette halted his party and heard the drum of hoofs receding.

"They's splittin' a dozen ways," advised Quagmire.

Gillette called roll, snapping at the names. Two were without answer, though he called them a second and a third time. Quagmire sighed like a man dog-tired.

"Man is mortal. It's the only lesson I learnt in forty years. Man is mortal."

"Quagmire, you take five of the boys and go back. Hunt around and see what you find. Then strike back to the ranch. I'm taking the rest with me to finish this job."

A moment's parley. Gillette renewed the pursuit, though the sound of the rustlers had dwindled and died in the distance. He veered north and after a half hour came to a ford of the river; he stopped there and went to the edge of the water, striking a match. The stream ran clear, but along the moist sand were deep prints with water standing in them. Fresh. Single file the Circle G riders crossed and held their course until the lights of Nelson glimmered up from the prairie. They swept into town and down the street. Gillette dismounted before the principal saloon and strode inside.

The place was nearly empty; but up at the bar two men stood side by side—Barron Grist and his foreman. Grist was angry and erect; the foreman's body sagged against the bar for support and his head was down on the mahogany top, rolling from side to side in evident pain. A bottle, half empty, was gripped in one fist. They were talking when Gillette entered. And then, aware of his presence, both of

135

them turned toward him, Grist in a rage that lifted him out of his negative self and put a definite character upon his smooth cheeks. The ranch boss pulled himself together, one hand whipped away a patch of blood congealed on his temple. The very sight of Gillette affected him like the presence of a ghost; he crouched.

The light played on Gillette. He was gray with dust, his face was a mask—a mask once seen not to be forgotten. He had harried the rustlers as he would have harried a pack of wolves, he had killed, and the fury of all this was settled along the rugged features. He was like his kind, slow to wrath and slow to forgive and the lees of the fight flared out of the deep eye sockets; his words sang resonantly across the dead, silent room.

"I told you, Grist, I didn't want war. You're a powerful outfit, we're just a handful. But you started it, and we'll see it to a finish. The kind you'll remember to your last day."

"Don't know what you're talking about!" was Grist's irritable answer. "You're drunk."

"You sent your men to rustle my cattle and break me. Well, some of those men are still out there. And they'll be there till you go bury 'em. Down in Texas we kill rustlers. This is a lesson for Dakota renegades, Grist."

"You're crazy," muttered Grist. "Trying to pin something on me to cover up your own dirty attacks? Don't stare at me like that, man! I resent it."

Gillette turned his attention to the ranch boss. That man swayed and his elbows straightened; a pinched gravity covered his face; his half-closed eyes clung doggedly to Gillette's right arm. "Maybe you've had your medicine, friend. Who told you a Texan wouldn't fight? We called your bluff tonight. How did you like it?"

The ranch boss was rigid from his shoulders to his hips; his head tipped. "It ain't finished yet," he grumbled.

"Shut up!" snapped Grist. "You talk too much."

But the ranch boss was beyond bridling. "It ain't finished yet! Somebody's goin' to pay. You foot the bill, you wild, blood-swillin' savage!"

His arm blurred in the light; Gillette swayed on his heels. A table crashed to the floor, chips scattered, and Barron

Grist pulled himself backward, crying: "I'm out of this—I'm out . . ." Whatever else he said was lost in the roar that ran along the space and up to the ceiling. Gillette's gun tilted upward. The ranch boss of the P. R. N. staggered and tipped against the bar, elbows hooked over it. He seemed to be nodding, and then his head sagged and he fell to his knees and for another instant tried to gather himself. It was of no use. He was dead before the gun dropped from his fingers.

"I'm out of this!" repeated Grist.

"If you've got a conscience, may God give you pity," said Gillette. "These fellows died at your orders. If you try to rustle another Circle G cow I'll come after you personally."

He passed out. In the darkness of the street he stopped and leaned against the saloon wall. The sand trickled out of him, and the cold air went through him like a knife. He was sick, physically sick, and the muscles of his arms and legs trembled. He wanted a drink, yet he hadn't the heart to go back there and see the ranch boss lying in the puddling blood. What had he done? Only what the country demanded of him, nothing more, nothing less. And as he looked towards the heavens he felt a thousand years old. He was not the man who had come out of the East with fine ideas in his head. How soon all that insecure stuff faded. All that remained now was the simple rules he had been reared in: never to go back on his word, to give all humans the right to live the way they wanted to live in return for the same right for himself. To respect rights and to see his own respected. That was all.

He drew a breath. A man got scarred in the process of passing through the world. That was inevitable, that was life. Only a fool expected to dwell in paradise; nobody had a right to dodge his chores, no matter how dirty they might be. A man paid as he went. He moved from the wall, seeing his crew patiently waiting. Boots scuffed along the walk, and a strange voice arrested his progress.

"You Gillette of the Circle G? Yeah. Was you a-lookin' for a gent by name of San Saba? Yeah. Fella built like a cotton wood an' sorrel by complexion?"

The man was old and seamed and obscured in the shadows. Gillette stared at him. "How do you know?" was his blunt reply.

"Heard you advertisin' same hereabouts some time ago. Well, be you still lookin'?"

"Where is he?"

The man's voice trailed off. "On the trail to Deadwood. Saw him four days ago. With a yaller-haired podner." And the man vanished into an alley.

Gillette mounted and rode homeward with his men. Here was another chore he had staved off as long as he could. Seemed like these things came in bunches. Oh, it was easy enough to forget them, to excuse himself from performing them. Yet if he did he would never have another moment's peace. A man had to play with the rules. On over the ford they went, and along the familiar trail to the ranch house, a light shining out to them. Quagmire already was in from the prairie, morose and subdued.

"A long ride for Nig Akers. Joe Blunt is only pinked. But Nig's done. Man is mortal. Tom, this is val'able country. Texas men is buried in it."

Gillette studied the southwestern sky. Deadwood was over there. He nodded and went into the house. Kit Ballard waited for him, framed in the bedroom door; the girl's black hair tumbled down in rippling ropes, and she held a robe around her.

"Go back to bed, girl. I can't talk to-night."

"To do what—to sleep? How can I sleep? I prayed to-night, and I never prayed before. Whatever you have done, I don't care. Wherever you choose to stay, I don't care. Tom—come here to me!"

He shook his head, the weariness pushing his shoulders down. "I'm leavin' to-night."

"For where?"

"Deadwood. San Saba's in Deadwood."

She knew the story, she knew the purpose of that journey. Her face went dead white, and when she raised her head the higher yellow light pooled in the triangle of her throat. As he looked at her all the loneliness and hunger of his solitary nature rose to torment him. No man living could miss the beauty or the allure of Christine Ballard. What was lacking in her for such a man as he was? What more could he want? The sacrifice was all hers, the surrender all hers. So he thought while the hunger grew to an obsession. A man was only flesh and blood. He pivoted on his heels and started for the door. She was in front of him instantly, throwing herself against him. He had never known what strength lay in a woman's arms once they were around a man's neck; he had never heard a woman cry in this suppressed manner. It seemed to put her on the torture rack. And all the while the incense of her hair and the warmth of her body assailed his senses.

"Kit—why couldn't this have happened a long time ago."

The crying stopped. She stepped aside, and her echo of his question rang passionately through the room. "Why couldn't it have happened, Tom? People have to live to learn, don't they? Where else will you find another woman any better?"

He stood divided. And it took a full mustering of his strength to walk to the door and let himself out.

"Quagmire—where are you?"

"Here—right in front o' yo', Tom."

"Get me the buckskin. Get it in a hurry. You're boss here. San Saba's in Deadwood."

Twenty minutes later he rode from the ranch on into the darkness lying southwest. He was running away as much as anything else, and he knew it. There would come a time when he must return and face it. But not now. He needed to break the chains Christine was forging around him. He tipped his head to the remote stars and seemed to see there the clear, grave face of Lorena Wyatt looking down at him. He felt the pressure of her hands wiping the blood from his mouth. Where was she?

12   DEADWOOD

Beyond dusk five days later Tom Gillette stopped on a ridge and studied a camp fire glimmering beside a creek below. He had ridden hard, and his own buckskin was in a strange corral away behind; the pony carrying him now was the second traded horse. Deadwood, according to his estimate, could be no more than ten miles distant, and it drew him like a magnet. Yet he was weary and hungry, for which reasons the light of the fire had pulled him off the main trail—a tortuous, rutted artery along which the freighters carried supplies into the mushrooming mining camps of the hills.

A pair of men sat beside the blaze. Others moved away the moment he topped the ridge, retreating beyond the rim of light. From this distance he saw nothing of the two in view but a blur of bearded faces beneath drooping plainsmen's hats, and for a time he debated about riding down. Out on the prairie every stranger was welcome to the chuck wagon, and hospitality was the unwritten law. A mining camp was something different; another breed of men, a hundred breeds for that matter, inhabited it, all bent on riches and all suspicious.

In the end hunger got the best of him. He quartered down the slope within hailing distance and stopped again.

"Hello, the camp."

One of the figures by the fire spoke over a shoulder. "Come on down, then."

He advanced, swung his horse so that it put him directly

toward the fire, and dismounted. He was instantly aware of a hard and prolonged scrutiny, and further aware of the others out in the shadows. It was a quick camp; horses stood a few yards off. A shotgun rested within arm's reach of the nearest man, and Gillette's questing eyes noted that each of the two wore a Colt on each hip. The ivory tip of a knife stuck from one fellow's boot. Heavy armament, even for prospectors.

"Saw your fire," explained Gillette. "I'm bound for Deadwood, from Nelson, and it's strange country to me. How much farther to town?"

"Fifteen miles."

"Straight along that road?"

"Yeah."

He squatted at the fire, warming his hands. A frying pan filled with bacon lay against a rock and a coffee pot sat beside it. Casually he turned his attention from one man to the other and out of the brief survey he received a warning. He knew his own kind, and he also knew the stamp of the border renegade, for he had been raised in a country where outlaw factions flourished their brief day and died suddenly. These men were of that type. Plainly so. The spokesman's face was heavily pitted above the line of the beard, one ear was without a lobe. The man met Gillette's inspection with a sullen, half-lidded counter glance. Of a sudden he shot a question belligerently across the small interval.

"From Nelson, huh? Travellin' almighty light, ain't yuh?"

"In a hurry," agreed Gillette. "Travelling light."

The spokesman's hand rose in signal to someone out of sight. "Look at his pony, Kid."

Spurs jingled. Faces came into the fire's glow, ill-stamped faces, the sweepings and trash of the desert. Without turning he felt himself to be covered from behind. His muscles bunched as he recognized the trap he had let himself into. A sallow youth ambled up, briefly murmuring:

"He's travelled all right. Hoss dusty." And the youth crouched in the circle, staring at Gillette with open antagonism. Gillette turned about; a giant of a man stood a pace to his rear, arms akimbo.

"In my country," said Gillette evenly, "it isn't polite to cover a man's back."

The giant shifted, but the spokesman flared. "Nobody invited you here, fella. How do we know who yuh are or where yuh come from?"

"When a man announces himself that's usually ample. As to the invitation, I'll relieve you of my presence in a hurry."

"Don't be in no rush," growled the spokesman. "Yuh came and yuh stay till we see what's inside yore coco. Sounds like another damned fishin' party to me."

Gillette held his peace. The giant barred his retreat. He understood, however, that the sooner he made his exit the better and the easier it would be. He had fallen in with an errant band of cutthroats and they were weighing him for what he was worth. Six of them, all before him, save for the giant. He heard the Kid mutter a short phrase about the time, and the spokesman, looking sidewise at Gillette, pulled a watch from his pocket and tilted it against the light. At that point the giant moved around until he stood behind this apparent leader of the crowd. "Better do somethin', Hazel."

"Do what?" snapped the leader.

"Don't bite my nose off, old-timer," rumbled the giant, "or I'll pull yuh apart."

Hazel turned to Gillette. "Lemme see yore guns."

"Not my guns," drawled Gillette. "Do I look that green?"

Hazel threw up his head, and a swift anger pulled at the corners of his mouth. "Yuh tryin' to ace me, fella? Do I see 'em or do I take 'em?"

"No powder-burning' around here and now," warned the giant, both to Gillette and to his chief. "It ain't the time."

Gillette was cross-legged; he had done this trick before, he could do it again. He swayed his torso a little forward, seeing in a glance the loose posture of each; they were confident enough of themselves. The Kid spat into the fire. "Oh, hell, let's see what he totes in his pockets an' throw him in the creek. Who's gettin' religious around here now?"

"You'll have to take 'em," snapped Gillette. His legs carried him up in one swift surge and the firelight ran along the blued barrel of his piece. All this in a single sweep of his muscles. "You damned rascals, does a traveller have to show a passport to get into Deadwood? There's where I'm goin', and all you're going to see of my gun is the front end. I'm no deputy and I'm not chasing him, understand? Now swallow it. If you want to make an argument, go ahead."

"You're a dead man," cried Hazel, swaying on his haunches.

"So are you, then," drawled Gillette. "We'll be two of the stiffest corpses around Deadwood. Keep your hand away from your belt. Kid—don't teeter like that. Have I got to argue my way to Deadwood?"

"No powder-burnin'," muttered the giant, who seemed to be more peaceably inclined. "Let 'im go—what's it matter?"

"I'm going," muttered Gillette grimly. He stepped backward, retreating foot by foot into the shadows. He had passed one point of danger, and it left him with the same satisfaction that a man has in winning a pot on a bluff. He grinned, though it was a wry grin. "If I see you in Deadwood I'll treat you to a drop of rye. But don't try to stop a Texas traveller. And I sure hope that bacon and coffee chokes you." Talk sometimes served a purpose, and apparently it bridged that parlous interval while he retreated still farther from the fire and reached his horse. He was up on the moment. The man named Hazel started to reach for his gun, but the giant, standing near, kicked his arm away; the Kid's yellow teeth glimmered in the light—the Kid was one of those adolescent white savages turned utterly bad. Tom Gillette studied the faces a moment longer, engraving them on his memory.

"Yore spotted!" cried Hazel. "I'll see the word gets out to bring back yore skelp."

"Something tells me you're a fraud," murmured Gillette. "How long has Deadwood stood for this foolishness?"

"Go on, get out of here," advised the giant. "Don't crowd your luck."

"That's advice, too," said Tom and backed his pony up the slope. The shadows closed about him and the circle, freed of threat, began to stir. The Kid whipped about, and at that moment Gillette touched his spurs and raced away, sliding to the far side of the pony. A juniper bush grazed his face and took his hat; a single explosion followed after, and then the giant's voice rose and fell like a maul. "You cussed little nipple rat, stop that or I'll tear yore lungs outen yuh! Want to spoil . . ."

The rest of it was lost to Gillette. His pony carried him up and over the ridge; the fire winked out. He regained the trail and galloped steadily onward.

"I stumbled into a convention," he mused. "They've got a piece of business on their chests and I upset 'em."

Weariness came on the heels of the let-down. It seemed he was born into a world full of treachery, full of disappointment. His mother had only thought to make a better man of him in shipping him East to school; yet it seemed to him he would have been better off in Texas, toughening himself inside and out. Four years had left him a little soft, had confused him as to the elemental facts of existence; and again he remembered a piece of his father's advice: "East is sheltered, it's a woman's country. West is for a man, my son, and don't you ever forget it."

How could he forget it? The sight of the P. R. N. ranch boss sliding forward to the saloon floor still sickened him. So thinking, he at last sighted the lights of Deadwood, forded a creek and rode down the single uneven street of this boisterous Mecca of the West.

Deadwood crouched between hill and creek, its tents and log huts and frame structures rambling along the street in a disjointed double row. There were no sidewalks, and the crowd wandering from place to place, kept out upon the pock-marked road running between. A cordwood pile and a tent nearly blocked this end of the thoroughfare; Gillette circled around and rode by the suspended sign-boards: Denver Grocery Store, City Market, The Senate, and so on past the outflung beams of lamplight. An occasional tree stood like a sentry on the street. Everywhere was a clutter of boards and timber and boxes—the roughing-in material of

144

a town on the make. Then the street ran up a scarred slope and wound around stumps into the hills. The straggling pines marched down to the very building walls of Deadwood.

He halted by a restaurant and got out of the saddle, both stiff and weary. This was a strange land, and as he met the faces of the men bobbing in and out of the patches of light he was conscious of being out of his proper environment. They dressed differently, they had a different twang to their speech, the stamp of a distinctive profession was plain upon them. A supply wagon lumbered past, eight oxen at the traces; a bull whip cracked like the explosion of a gun, and the wheels groaned in the ruts. He shouldered into the restaurant and sat up to the counter. The time of eating was past, the waitress out in the kitchen. He dropped his head and passed a hand across his face; he wanted nourishment, and he wanted a long sleep before beginning his hunt. The kitchen door opened, light steps tapped across the boards.

"Something—anything you've got to eat," muttered Gillette, head still bent. There was a swift intake of breath, and he raised his eyes.

Lorena Wyatt leaned across the counter. Her hand fell on his arm, and it seemed to him she looked through and through him.

"Why—Tom—"

It was astonishing how the depression and the grime of the long journey vanished. And because he had carried one thought and one desire in his head for so long a time, the phrase that came first to his tongue was a question. "Lorena, I—what did you run off for?"

Her hand retreated and she relaxed. "What's happened to your forehead, Tom? You've been in trouble."

He turned that aside. "What did you run away for? Is your dad here?"

"He went back to Texas. I will never see him again, Tom. Never. Here I am, making my own living."

"All by yourself—among these men?"

"Why not? Look at me. Don't you see how strong I am?" She squared her shoulders and tilted her chin, her cheeks the colour of pink roses. "Why shouldn't I work? What can

145

happen to me? Nothing can hurt me—nothing. Oh, I know what you are thinking. Men sometimes forget the bridle on their tongues—and sometimes they mistake me when I smile at them. I've quit smiling because of that. But what does it matter? All that griminess doesn't hurt me. It doesn't get into my heart, Tom. After work is done I forget it, and I'm free again for another night.''

"If I ever heard a man say—" It shook him profoundly, it woke a blind anger. What right had some of these gutter-snipes to bully her, to take advantage of their power and her helplessness? "—I'd kill him!" Men of the range, no matter how rough they might be, were trained in rigid courtesy; but the mining camps brought the dregs of the earth along with the decent.

Her small hands formed a cup on the counter. "I know. All good men feel the same toward a woman and it isn't as bad as you believe here. All I'd have to do is speak about it and there are plenty of fine gentlemen to protect me. But we can't live without getting our shoes in the mud. Only—mud doesn't scar. It can be washed away. And at night I'm free."

"Free for what?" he demanded, half angry. "Are you happy here, doing this?"

There was a piece of a smile on her lips, a small quirk at the corners that might have meant anything. She shook her head, refusing to answer. "You're hungry. But I won't let you eat here. I'm through now. Wait for me."

She went back to the kitchen. Tom Gillette moved to the outer door and looked along the street. Deadwood was on the crest of the night, and the yellow dust gutted from the hills during the day now passed across the counters and bars in commerce. A piano somewhere was being hammered, and a crowd roared the chorus of a popular song while the sharp-edged notes of a soubrette sheared through the masculine undertone. This was the dance girl's harvest and the professional man's harvest. And among these men San Saba stalked. Well, a night's rest . . . Lorena was beside him with a basket. He took it from her, and they passed out and along the street to where the hillside began to climb, Gillette leading his horse.

"Now where?"

"To my cabin. It's only a half mile along the trail and a little to one side."

"And you walk it every night alone, in this darkness? Lorena, you're crowding your luck."

"I have a gun and I've always known how to shoot. Nothing can hurt me, haven't I told you? Nothing—any more." It seemed to him there was a trace of bitterness in the last words, but she quickly covered it by a more practical explanation. "The diggings are travelling on up the cañon and farther back into the hills. Some of the old cabins have been abandoned. I use one—it's cheaper."

He shook his head. It was dark along the trees, though here and there the quarter moon shot its silver beams through the branches and created little lakes of light on the ground. The trail grew steeper, and once she slipped. Gillette caught her arm, and her body for the moment swayed against him—swayed and pulled away. "To your left, Tom," she murmured. They walked another hundred yards on a lesser trail. A cabin stood dimly before them, and Lorena opened the door and preceded him. Presently lamplight flooded the place; he went in.

"I have a home," said she, with again that wistful pressure of lips. "It's my own. I don't owe a soul for it. I said I never again would ask a favour in this world. Sit in the chair, Tom. It's a guest chair. I'm going to cook you a meal."

The cabin was old, with a hard dirt floor, a cast-iron stove, a pine bunk, and a pine board table. The chair was nothing more than a dry-goods box; there was but a single window, across which hung a square of burlap for a shade. A bare place, this cabin, yet swept clean and impressed, in the odd arrangements of her effects, by this girl's hand. She had spread an army blanket on the floor for a carpet, and somewhere in this corner of a man's world she had found white sheets and a slip for her bed. The smell of fresh paint hung over the room, a single red meadow flower decorated the table.

She built a fire, she rummaged the basket and placed the dishes with a kind of sweet formality. She was humming quite softly to herself, and from time to time she glanced toward him, and again he had the feeling that she marked his features for her memory. There was a grace to her moving hands, a sturdiness to her small shoulders.

"Say, you ought to be tired," he protested. "How about my wrangling this meal?"

"This is my party—the first party I ever gave. I was tired. I'm not tired now."

He went to the door. A small wind sighed in the treetops and eddied into the room. Away down the slope a camp fire cut an orange pattern in the night; coyotes howled along the distant ridges. What kind of a place was this for a girl like her? Things prowled these shadows. And here she was, all that was desirable in a woman, unprotected except for her own abundant courage. And that wasn't enough.

"Sit down, Tom. Supper's ready. I ate mine at the restaurant."

He closed the door. She had drawn the dry-goods box around to the far side of the table and when he sat down she dropped to the bunk and watched him.

"Well—"

"Not now. This is my party. You eat. Whatever is to come must wait. That was the best steak in the restaurant, Tom. I want you to enjoy it."

All during the solitary supper she watched him, yet when he came to return the glance her eyes fell away. So it went until he had finished and made himself a cigarette, the questions rising. She saw them come, and she staved them off with a trace of confusion.

"Now tell me what brought you here."

"San Saba's in or about Deadwood," said he.

She sat up. "Here? I haven't seen him."

"Well, he wouldn't be the one to advertise himself. It may be he turned off the trail before he got this far, but I don't think so. For a man of his kind Deadwood is too good a hunting ground to pass."

"What are you going to do, Tom?"

His shoulders rose. The girl bent forward with so intent and sober a glance that it bothered him. And she divined

148

his answer. "You don't mean to gamble on your life, do you?"

"I guess it's not much of a gamble, Lorena."

"Oh, yes, it is! He's a dangerous man, he's tricky. He doesn't fight fair, he never fought fair in his whole life. He'd throw you off guard and wait until you weren't looking. Then he'd shoot. Don't I know the man?"

"Once I see him he'll never get out of my sight," replied Gillette quietly. Somehow he felt the need of justifying himself to her. "I'm not doing this for fun, Lorena. I'm fighting against my grain all the time I hunt for him. But the score's too heavy on one end to let him go. Either I've got to hold up my end or I've got to crawl out of Dakota like a yellow dog. The hounds are yapping at my heels. It's been a bad year for Circle G all around. Last week the P. R. N. tried to rustle me poor and one of my men was killed in the scrap. They'll let me alone until they think of some other pretty scheme." His right arm stretched toward her. "Look at it. A killer's hand. The P. R. N. foreman went down before my gun. I didn't ask trouble, but I can't back out now. And San Saba's got to answer for my dad."

"You're not a killer," was her quick retort. "Don't say it of yourself. I hate to see you divided against yourself."

"What else does it amount to? I reckon I should have stayed East and learned to like tea out of a china cup."

"Don't be bitter, Tom. What good is that? You're too much of a man to be anything else than you are or to love any land but this. The East never helped you. It only hurt you."

He ran a hand across his face, and she noticed how the brown skin wrinkled about his eyes, how dogged and unyielding his features could turn. It was so now; she wanted to go over and touch his arm—anything to sweep aside for the time the troubles he carried.

"But this," he went on, indicating the room, "isn't fit for you, Lorena. It makes me cold all over to think of you here alone. You shouldn't do it."

"Nothing can hurt me, Tom."

"What's to become of you?" said he, still on the same thought. "Here you are alone. You can't live like this—

you can't travel the trail by yourself. And there's nobody fit for you in this part of the world. You're wasting the best part of your life. I'm saying it again—you don't belong here."

"I've fought that out—don't bring it back to me. I said I'd never ask another favour of anybody and I never will. I won't ever give anybody the power to hurt me again. Here I came and here I stay until—"

"Until what?"

She turned her head away, hands moving. "Oh, I don't know, Tom. This is as good a place as anywhere. Until I'm old, I guess."

"You were not meant to live alone. It's unnatural."

That brought the rose tint to her cheeks again. And still with her head averted she asked a muffled question. "Who would want me, Tom?"

He sprang up, he crossed the small space at a single stride. "I want you, Lorena! Can't you see that all over me, as plain as daylight? I want you!"

She rose, and for the moment he thought she meant to run out of the place. Such was the passing fright on her white face. It lasted only a moment, and then she was looking at him in the manner he knew so well. It took all the fight out of him, it made him humble. "That's what I've been trying to say," he went on quietly. "It's been with me ever since you ran off. What did you do that for? There's nothing behind me I'm ashamed of or afraid of. I waited a week to tell you that. There's no claims on me. Whatever you think of Kit Ballard and myself is wrong. It's wrong."

"I would never have asked you that, Tom. I wanted to hear you say it, but I'd never have asked. I'll never mention her name. That's your own affair—I've got no part in it."

"Well, you know now. I want you, Lorena"

"Tom, it's only pity you feel. And I won't have pity! I'm not the girl you'd want. I can't be. What am I—what do I know or what can I do? I can't help your name any. I see it clearer every day."

"That's wrong. Look at me and you'll know it's wrong."

She began to tremble. Gillette touched her gently, and then he was holding her, murmuring something he had no

150

memory of. All that passed in the succeeding moments was blurred. He knew he kissed her; he heard her speak once and grow still, and the silence of that small room was like the pressure of a vise. Her small hand was pushing him away.

"If it only were true, Tom! What do you suppose I ran away for? Because I couldn't stand being around you any longer! I never wanted to see anybody I ever knew. I wanted to be alone. And now you come and remind me of it again. Haven't I been hurt badly enough?"

He was helpless. He had no words at his command strong enough to convince her, he had no way of breaking through that doubt. So he stepped back, groping for a hat he didn't have. "Time's got to take care of it," he muttered. "I'm not leaving again till it's settled. And I'm not going to let you stay here without protection. I'm sleeping out under those trees."

"That's foolish."

"Let it be. You'll see me till you either get tired of me or take me."

She was a queer girl. A moment ago she had cried; now the familiar smile returned. "Well, if you must do it, there's an old shed beside the cabin with some straw in it. But you only have your saddle blanket. Take one of mine."

He refused the offer and opened the door. "I'll go into Deadwood and stable my horse. Be back right off. It sure makes my blood cold to think of you up in this desolation."

She stood by the table, and as he watched her she threw back her head and laughed. He knew he would never forget the picture she made, nor the expression of her eyes. "Tom, I've had my first party. Whatever happens, I've got that to remember."

"I wish," said he, "you'd be certain of me."

"I've been hurt, Tom."

He said nothing more. Getting into the saddle he rode to Deadwood and left his horse, immediately turning back. The town still blazed, men moved restlessly along the street, in and out of the lanes of light; and as he passed through all this glitter and empty sound he saw a face bent his way. Thirty seconds later it struck him he knew that face, and he

151

stopped dead and turned for a second glance. But the man, whoever it was, had gone. The glimpse he had of it was blurred and indistinct, yet as he wound up the slope it worried him greatly and he tried to reconstruct the features. Coming to the cabin he found the lamplight still glowing in the window. He called to the girl by way of reassurance and went around to the shed.

Lorena's voice carried through the cabin walls softly. "Good-night, Tom." The light winked out. Out of the hills came the night breeze and the distant cry of the coyotes.

13   DEATH AMONG THE PINES

San Saba came into Deadwood that night for the first time, though he and Lispenard had been camped just outside the town more than a week, watching its lights by night and edging around the hills by day. That was the ex-foreman's wary way. He didn't believe anybody in Deadwood knew him, but he had no desire to expose himself for identification. San Saba well understood his was a figure to attract a certain amount of attention. Somebody would be sure to mark and remember him.

In the back of that little nutshell head was a crafty scheme; a scheme that amounted to nothing less than a guerrilla warfare on the roving miners. There were many such men already in operation around the hills—in fact, San Saba had established a kind of informal partnership with the group led by Hazel. Yet nearly all of these renegades operated with a certain degree of openness; most of them were known and suspected, and San Saba's plan was never to reveal himself. He knew the temper a mining camp could reach, he had experienced mob justice before, and from this experience he drew his profits. So he would never have entered Deadwood if the supply of grub hadn't been exhausted and if Lispenard, an apt pupil but an unruly and sullen one, hadn't grown restless for whisky. That was the extent of his mission.

He had bought his supplies and his whisky and was on the point of leaving when he saw Tom Gillette coming out of the stable. It was only a fraction of a glance; Gillette's head swept his way and then turned about. San Saba moved like a cat, a single retreating lunge carried him out of the light; thus, when Gillette looked a second time, the ex-foreman was concealed in the shadows along the building fronts. San Saba's narrow-set red eyes watched Gillette move off. For a considerable length of time he stood absolutely still, the thoughts flashing across his brain. Had Gillette recognized him? Well, it didn't seem likely, for Gillette would have stopped and closed in. San Saba was under no illusions as to Tom Gillette's courage or to his state of mind. Only one thing could have brought the Circle G owner to this place.

"On my trail, by Judas," muttered San Saba. A party of miners filed past him, and he retreated farther into the darkness. "He's caught wind o' me somehow."

His impulse was to follow. Caution stayed him. Gillette was already out of sight, and there was a remote possibility of a trap. Time enough to handle this—to-morrow was another day. So he turned and quickly put Deadwood behind him. Up the slope and on foot—a rare thing for San Saba—he carried the gunnysack of provisions; on through the trees and to the edge of a small clearing where a fire pricked the darkness. Lispenard crouched by the blaze, a slovenly figure from all this riding and camping out. The Easterner's hair had grown down over his shoulders, and there was a thick stubble of whiskers on his gross face. San Saba paused a moment, and his lips curled in plain contempt. No matter how hard he lived or how little he valued the Commandments, San Saba possessed a measure of fastidiousness. He had a grain to him, a cold self-possession and a certain pride. Lispenard seemed without any of these elements; he grew more unkempt each day, and his appetites rode him like a scourge; he was sullen and spiteful by turns and San Saba in a very short space of time had grown disgusted with the man. Only Lispenard's possible usefulness kept him from severing the partnership. Even so the ex-foreman saw the day when Lispenard would pass a certain mark and try to kill him. When that time came he must kill Lispenard.

"All right," he drawled, as a warning of his approach.

Lispenard half rose from his seat, hand falling to gun butt. "Who's it?" he snapped.

"Me," murmured San Saba and advanced. Lispenard swore querulously. "Next time *I* go to town, old-timer. By God, I'm weary of living up here like a rat."

San Saba said nothing. Lispenard's eyes followed the ex-foreman's hand as it dropped inside the gunnysack, and he reached for the produced whisky bottle with plain greediness. San Saba watched the man gouge out the cork and tip the stuff down his throat. He drank himself, on occasion he got drunk, yet only by degrees. This avid guzzling added to his sardonic contempt.

Lispenard let the bottle fall. "That's better. Where's the rest of it?"

"Only one bottle," grunted San Saba "Figgerin' on takin' a bath in it?"

"Hell, I told you to get three or four. Have I got to go back there to-night myself?"

"Yo' won't," was San Saba's short answer.

Lispenard glowered at him. "Don't tell me what I won't do, you dam' scoundrel. I'll go if I choose."

"Yo' won't go," repeated San Saba.

Lispenard's yellow eyes rolled in a fit of uncontrollable anger. He was about to rise and start away; but there was something so cold and so grisly on San Saba's face that his rage simmered awhile and died. He nursed his bottle again, the muscles of his great throat standing out like cables.

San Saba dropped to his haunches and stared sourly into the fire. "Gillette's in Deadwood."

Down came the bottle. "What's that?"

"Yo' heard my words. He's in Deadwood."

"What for?"

"Fo' to see me, I'd reckon" murmured the ex-foreman. "But he ain't yet, I saw him first. Which suits me fine."

Lispenard swayed over the fire, half drunk. Yet he was still sober enough to feel the weight of Gillette's name and to nurse his old grievances afresh. His pendulous lips moved across his teeth. "Then let's go get him!"

"Fine," was San Saba's dry answer. "When yo' get that Dutch courage outen yo' guts maybe we will."

"I've got a score to settle, and by Godfrey I'll mark him so his own mother wouldn't recognize 'im!"

"Two gallant gentlemen see alike," murmured San Saba with the same ill-veiled contempt. His head turned slightly, and in a moment he rose and stepped away from the fire, hands dropping to his guns.

"What's that for?"

"Get away from that light yo' fool."

Saddle gear murmured up the slope, an iron hoof struck stone. A rider halted along the outer rim of the light and called brusquely. "Well?"

San Saba came into sight again, walking loosely. "Come on down, Hazel."

The renegade leader rode into the fire's circle, his pock-marked face strangely yellow above the coal-black beard. He looked only once toward Lispenard as he slipped from the saddle. To San Saba he dropped a covert wink which the ex-foreman received with a slight drop of his small head. Hazel rolled a cigarette and lighted it from the fire; Lispenard stared at him sullenly and went back to his bottle. Hazel grunted in open scorn. "What you doin' with that liver-fed trout, anyhow?"

San Saba kept his peace. Hazel swung quickly to another topic. "Missed out las' night. Stage took another trail. We ain't got the right information any more. Need a man closer to town. When you throwin' in with us right?"

"I'll play it like she runs now," droned San Saba.

"Too good to mix in the shootin', huh?" growled Hazel.

"Too wise," said San Saba. "Let it ride, Hazel. We can be useful to each other. I'm under cover. I can drag business yo' way when it's too big fo' me to swing—me an' that—" pointing toward Lispenard.

"I can plumb use another old head." muttered Hazel, "an' another good gun. I got the Kid, an' he's rattle-brained. Us two'd make a pair. Why can't you stick in Deadwood and augur out the dope for me?"

"Maybe," was San Saba's noncommittal answer. "First off, I want a man killed."

"If that's yore price for joinin', all right," acceded Hazel. "What's his name?"

"Gillette—cowman from Nelson way. He's on my track."

Hazel's face screwed into a knot. "Must be the same gent that ran into my camp. Tall, black-haired? Yeah, well, by Joe, I want his number, too. What's so big about him you can't do a pers'nal chore?"

"Why take a chance?" parried San Saba. "He's a Texas man—which maybe don't mean nothin' to yo' but it's ample to me. He's watchin' fo' me—he's slick as a lobo."

"Well get him," growled Hazel.

San Saba nodded. "Keep yo' men near town tomorrow night. I'll watch him all day an' let yo' know. We'll ketch him outside somewhere and—"

"Is that yore price for joinin'?" repeated Hazel.

"Make it that," agreed San Saba, adding a silent reservation.

Hazel pointed toward Lispenard, who was stretched full length on the ground, in a stupor. "Hell, I can't use him. It's you I want."

San Saba made a slight motion with his thumb, whereat Hazel nodded grimly. "Me an' the boys'll be jus' above the far side o' town, waitin' for yuh." He looked again toward Lispenard, and for a moment all the evil in him flashed up to the surface of those intensely black eyes. Then he turned, mounted, and rode out of the light. San Saba circled the fire and kicked the unresisting Lispenard with his boot toe.

Deadwood by daylight was half asleep, as if recovering from the carousal of the night before; the street seemed more cluttered, and the unpainted shelters more garish. Men moved sluggishly, the miners were out along the creek and back up the cañon slopes. Here and there a pack mule stood waiting; an occasional newcomer entered the town, an occasional prospector trudged up the slope that led into the heart of the hills. Tom Gillette sat inside the livery stable and watched the street closely.

All the morning he sat there, his attention roving from door to door; at noon the street grew crowded again and he drew back a little farther inside the stable, grimly waiting. If San Saba were within fifty miles of town he would sooner

157

or later appear on that street. Gillette understood this well, for Deadwood was the Mecca toward which all turned, and San Saba was the kind to be attracted by the vision of easy wealth. It was only a matter of patience, and Gillette, who had ridden five days with the fever of haste warming his blood, felt he had time enough to carry this game to its blazing conclusion; not only because the desire for retribution had been forged in him like a piece of steel, but because he played still another game that required patience. He had spoken the truth to Lorena. Until she accepted him or drove him away he would be by her; that there might be another end to the affair he never realized.

Past noon he ate at the restaurant; Lorena had little to say, nor did he try to make talk. There was something of the bulldog in Tom Gillette—once he had established himself he hung on in silence, letting his fortunes ride with the events. As for the girl, she seemed reserved, she held herself back from him, her eyes inscrutable. She understood clearly the main mission that drew him here, and as she looked upon his tall figure and the settled determination of his face something like dread took possession. She knew more about San Saba than he did; she knew the ex-foreman's uncanny power with the gun, and she had heard men of the Wyatt outfit discuss his cold and nerveless presence of mind when in a fight. What chance, then, did Tom Gillette have in an open encounter? She wanted to argue it, but she checked the impulse. She had said all she ever would to Tom; anything more would only make the struggle harder for him. This was the code Lorena had been born and bred into. Tom would never turn now.

He slipped from the stool. "I'll be ridin' up the gulch," said he. "See you to-night."

Her cherry lips pressed together; he caught a flash from her eyes as he swung out the door. Saddling his horse he left the town and cruised up the slope and through the pines while the sun went westering. The trail took him along the creek, climbing away from it until the water was but a ribbon unwinding below, flashing like silver under the sun. Men toiled down there, men picked at the hillsides, men moved in and out of the drifts they burrowed; and always

158

more men moved through the trees. Pack trains went along the trail bound still farther into the recesses of the Black Hills.

He studied all this with a shrewd eye; he made note of how watchful and taciturn were those miners he passed on the trail. And presently he turned back from his tour and returned down the grade as the sun dipped beyond the ragged hills. Twilight, then dusk with its blue shadows swirled among the trees. A halloo echoed through the woods like a trumpet, somewhere was a gunshot. Deadwood's lights winked below. A man passed him on the trail at a gallop, and he became aware of another horseman sitting silent in the saddle, twenty yards off the road. All he saw was the figure welded to the horse and a beard standing around the lighter skin. He thought the man watched him, but of this he wasn't sure. Dropping into the street he stabled his horse and went to the restaurant for supper. As before, Lorena kept aloof from him. But when he was about to leave she came near enough to say:

"There has been a man watching along the street all afternoon. I saw him directly after you left here. He's been across in the alley looking toward the restaurant and the stable."

He nodded. She added a quick warning. "Don't meet me at the restaurant to-night. Go on up the trail a quarter mile till I come. Watch yourself, Tom."

He slipped out. In the next patch of shadow he ducked back into an alley and circled the whole line of buildings, crossing to the far side of the street at one end. Once more he travelled through the cluttered boxes of débris until he stood in the alley approximately opposite the restaurant. A man stood in the mouth of the alley, and presently, as he turned and his face was silhouetted against the light from across the way, Gillette recognized the Kid, the white savage of Hazel's gang. He withdrew quietly and later emerged through another alley to the street, farther along. Here he rolled a cigarette and waited. Was Hazel trying to get him for last night's affair at the camp by the creek? If this happened to be the case, it further complicated an already tangled situation.

"The hounds are on the trail again," he murmured. His

159

life had been violently turned from its accustomed channel these last few months. Nothing came easy. At Dodge City his youth fell away from him, never to return, and he had been plunged into mystery and deceit and struggle. "Either I'm so soft I notice it too much, or else I was born to fight. Damn Hazel."

A saloon door opened. Men spewed out, brawling like strange dogs, and there was the spat of fists against flesh. Somebody went sprawling backward and fell into the street; when the door next opened to emit its momentary light a knife flashed in a weaving hand.

"Stop it or I'll gore yuh!"

"Put that stabber away, yuh yella dago! Get yore possibles and skin the camp. I'm through prospectin' with yuh."

"Gimme my half or I'll write my mark in yore fat skin, Fluger!"

"Go join Hazel's gang," was the hot retort. "It's yore style."

A cool, unexpected interjection emerged from another angle of the street. "Better handle that easy, partner. The walls have ears, an' yore apt to lose yores."

Gillette's muscles tightened at the sound of the voice. He moved backward, face turned toward the voice. A moment later he was on the other side of the street and in the deeper shadows. By and by he made out Hazel. Hazel moved across a lane of light. Gillette drew a deeper breath.

"The man keeps his promises. Has he got the camp wound around his finger?"

He travelled on, keeping abreast of Hazel and at intervals catching a sight of the renegade. Then the man dropped completely out of view. The restaurant was abreast Gillette, and he saw the place was dark. Lorena would be about ready to go; he took to the alleys once more, reached the stable, and got his horse. He rode through a path of light and arrived at the trail. Fifty yards farther up he turned in time to see a lantern rise and dip; horses drummed behind him. Out of a growing caution he drew off the trail and rested silent while they swept past and galloped on until the echo of their progress no longer rolled back through the pines. After this he travelled more discreetly, stopped to

160

mark some stray movement near by, and went on again. The night wind rustled through the boughs of the pines, the moon was shrouded, the notes of a banjo carried across the air. He halted, judging it time to wait for the girl.

But he remained still only a moment. Uneasiness gripped him so strongly that he turned and started toward town. The air was tainted to-night, there was too much traffic on the road and too many noises in the brush. No woman was safe here. The thought of the girl breasting the darkness alone, as well as living in that bleak hut alone, only added to the uneasiness. She was brave. But that wasn't enough. She judged men too leniently. In this melting pot there were always a certain number of human wolves watching.

"It won't do," he murmured. "I can't let her go on. I reckon I'll have to find some better words or some stronger words."

The wind seemed to rise and shake the scattered bushes. Shapes sprang from nothing to confront him, and a familiar voice spat through the darkness, metallic and deadly. "Let him have it!"

It was then too late—too late for him to escape. And, like the unrolling of a panoramic picture, he saw a great many scenes out of his past; foremost was San Saba's evil face studying him across the tip of the trail fire. That was San Saba's voice over there. He knew it as he knew no other. Even while his hand dropped and the whole hillside roared to the enfilading bullet he filled his lungs and shouted:

"San Saba, you dog, I've come to get you!"

Smoke belched in his face, the crack of the guns was in his ears. San Saba spoke back, but he couldn't hear then what the man said. He was firing—that he knew. How many times he didn't know, never found out. For this was to Gillette one of those blind passages in life when all things merge to a shape or a sound or a single vivid impression. He thought something fell on his head; the sap flowed out of him, and the weight of his gun became too great to manage. The saddle horn grazed his cheek, he was lying flat, both arms around the pony's neck, tasting his own blood. How had he got into such a shape as this? He should be sitting up. And still they fired. San Saba was speaking more clearly.

"Not me, yo' don't get. I'm puttin' a curse on yo' soul, Gillette. May yo' burn in hell a thousan' years. Empty those guns—empty 'em! He ain't dead yet. I want him dead! Make him fall, knock him outen that saddle! That's the last Gillette yo' trying to kill!"

He heard all this, though it sounded remote and unreal. There was a trickle of strength in him yet, but life ebbed swiftly, and his strongest desire was to get away—to defeat San Saba's vicious desire to see him stretched dead. All his will went into one arm. The horse moved downhill; he held on, the horn jarring on his temple and his feet losing the stirrups. Confusion behind and more firing. They would never quit, it seemed. Somebody yelled, Deadwood's lights were below him. He sank his teeth into his tongue to stay the advancing paralysis, he talked to himself but heard nothing of the words. One by one the wires went down and cut him off from life. He fell to the ground, rolled over and over, and brought up against a stump.

He wasn't dead yet, he wasn't out yet. This he thought with a dim pride. Of course the Gillettes were tough. They died hard. Now, where had he been hit? Maybe he could stop the blood and hold on a minute longer. Astonishing how a man clung to life. He sent an order down to his arms, but they wouldn't obey, and he knew that for him the fight was over. More he couldn't do. The gang was beating around the brush, and there was somebody still nearer calling his name in a thin and frightened voice.

"Tom—where are you?"

Lorena. Out of all this blackness she came. He framed her name in his throat with a painful care. One more effort—that was all, just one more effort.

"Where are you—where are you?"

The energy to speak that name was gone. And then in dead despair he gave up. She was forever lost to him. she was alone and he would never be able to help her. How a man missed the sun once it was gone. Nothing but blackness down this new trail, nothing but blackness. . . .

* * *

Lorena left the restaurant a moment after Tom Gillette started away from the town. She knew he was somewhere along the trail, and thus, when the burst of shots rocketed down the slope, she instantly understood what was happening up there in the shadows. She heard San Saba's voice lashing into the night, she heard him call the Gillette name. At that she dropped her basket and broke into a run. A horse galloped toward her, more shots woke the echoes; she sprang out of the trail to let the horse go by, and she heard Gillette fall to the ground directly to the rear. She wasn't exactly sure that it was Gillette lying there until the renegades started in pursuit. Then she ran back and began to call, muffling her voice.

There was no answer. She marked the spot in her mind and weaved back and forth in a narrowing circle repeating his name over and over again, while the very weight of the night smothered her and her heart pounded unbearably. She found him; found him all in a huddle on the ground just as the beams of a lantern shot along the trail. The renegades were at a halt, parleying among themselves.

"Go on—go on, Hazel. His hoss is halfway to town by now."

"Yeah, but he fell offen the brute. We got him clean. He's back there, rolled in the brush."

"I brought this lantern so's I'd look in his face and see him dead," droned San Saba. "Now, we're goin' to find the man and plant the last bullet in his neck."

"Judas, but I never saw a fella as wanted another man so bad as you. Well, let's beat around, then."

"Hustle it. Might be a posse collectin'."

Hazel's laugh exploded and echoed up to the treetops. "Nobody's goin' to be in any hurry to investigate a burst of shots. Not when they know Hazel's nighthawkin'."

All this came to the girl on successive waves of sound, rising and falling, sometimes plain, sometimes only a murmur. She was on her knees, her hands running across Gillette's body, touching his heart, passing over his face. And still again she repeated his name while the lantern dipped in and out of the trees, its outflung beams striking a little

163

nearer at each swing. They would find her in a little while. In despair she caught his shoulders and shook him. The warm blood trickled across her palm, and it took all the courage she owned to suppress the cry that caught in her throat. His horse had stopped the moment the saddle emptied and now waited on the trail; if she could only get him into the saddle once more. . . .

He was too heavy to lift. Hazel's gang swept down the incline at a faster pace, the rays of the lantern touched the ground a scant ten yards off.

"He ain't far away, bet yore hat. Shucks, man, what's the itch? I know we got him."

"I'll look in his dam' face befo' I believe it," droned San Saba. "I got to see him dead with my own eyes. Wait a bit."

The lantern bobbed; they smashed through the brush, back-tracking. Lorena's hand dropped to Gillette's heart. He still lived, and that was all.

"Oh, dear God, why can't you help me? Why *can't* you?"

She made a swift calculation. It was only a matter of yards to the creek's edge. Once she got him down there she could hide him in one of the innumerable prospectors' pits and cover him with a loose layer of gravel. She could hide until they passed. But the horse was on the trail and they would see it. After that they'd never leave until they had thoroughly covered the adjacent ground. And then it would be too late; Tom would be dead. Nevertheless, she got her arms about his chest and lifted him; dragged him across the earth five yards before stopping. He was far heavier than she supposed. She could go no farther.

They were back from the side hunt. Forward swung the lantern, forward came the trampling boots. Lorena was on her knees again, both hands stretched across his body. She thought of fighting back, but there was no gun in his holster and her own was in the basket she had dropped on the trail. Thus she crouched, a hand seeming to squeeze her heart. San Saba's voice rose and fell in a round, savage phrase. "Yo' hear me, Hazel. I'll put my heel in his dam'

164

face an' grind the sight outen him! It's the last Gillette. I'm tromplin' the breed out. . . ."

The veering beams almost touched her. Lorena shifted, and one exploring hand touched and closed about a rock. Closed about it so tightly that its jagged corners bit into her palm. She rose, stepped to the trail and threw the rock as she would have launched a lariat. It went high, carried beyond them and struck a tree. The lantern twisted and dropped; instantly it was smashed and the light extinguished by a grinding boot heel.

"Behind!"

"Yo' brash fool, what about a light now?"

"He's playin' possum behind. Stretch back there!"

The horse was a few yards removed. Lorena went toward him cautiously. She caught the reins, she swung to the saddle and in a flash she wheeled away from the trail and deeper into the trees. The noise betrayed her, as she wished it to do. San Saba was volleying words; words that were drowned by a double explosion. The bullets were low; she heard them racing toward their own horses.

All this was blind riding to her, she never had gone far from the trail or very deep into these woods; but she pushed the horse as fast as it would go, marking the town lights now and then as they appeared between the pines. These lights sank as she kept her course upward. It took time for the renegades to get a-saddle and in pursuit, and when she heard them smashing along she made a quick foray at right angles to her course, brought up by the shelter of a thicket she felt against her stirrup, and waited. They swept past her, near enough at one moment to have heard her breathing. Then they were tangled in the pockets and the underbrush of the higher ground; she waited a moment before turning back. The sound of their own progress covered hers. And they wouldn't return—not for a little while.

The horse took her back to the trail, but the exact location of Gillette was another matter, and she felt, for a little while, absolutely helpless. Then the animal's shoes crunched against the glass of the shattered lantern and instantly she was on the ground, zigzagging through the brush. The renegades were out of hearing, but a traveller came along the trail from town, his approach marked by a belled burro. That meant a prospector going into the hills; directly after hearing this new sound in the night her foot touched Gillette's body. She dropped.

"Tom—oh, my dear! I can't lift you, I can't let you stay here!"

There was a smallness to his breathing that frightened her. The belled burro neared her covert, and she rose and stepped into the trail. There was no other alternative. This man she would have to use.

"Who are you?"

The bell stopped jingling; a gruff voice answered. "Do'ee hear now? Ab's cat, is it a woman in this tarnal black night?"

"Who *are* you?"

"Ma'm, what mought be the difference? Gabe's my handle. Old Gabe. Ask ary old-timer in the Hills about me."

"You've got to help. No questions to be asked, understand? And you must never say a word to anyone. Will you do it?"

"Rags an' bottles. Mystication's what it sounds like. But if it's a lady I'll be singed if I won't."

"Come behind me. There's a man dying here in the brush."

"Better die in the brush than die in a bed," muttered the prospector. He skirted her and stooped down to run a hand across Gillette. "Dyin' be about the proper term for the sitooation."

"You've got to carry him a quarter mile for me. Hurry. He's been here too long now."

The prospector settled to a knee and expelled a great sigh as Gillette's bulk fell on his shoulders. The girl led away, up the trail, and along the lesser path to her cabin. The prospector murmured beneath his burden, and at the cabin door he let Gillette down suddenly and whistled. "A hunnerd ninety pounds solid. Nary ounce less. It'll take a big coffin, ma'm."

"Not here—inside!"

She guided the prospector through the door and to the bunk. The man swung Gillette on the blankets. "A leetle

166

light, girl. We'll see the extent o' the perforations. Old Gabe's looked at a plenty in forty years. If his lips is putty colour they ain't a speck o' use—"

"I'm grateful. You can't see him. You must forget this cabin. Never say anything about it. Do you remember?"

"Wal—"

Unwillingness trailed through the word. She shoved him back across the door sill. "Hazel tried to kill this man. I'm hiding him. If Hazel should ever find out he'd come back—"

"Oh, ay. That's a different set o' drills. Old Gabe ain't interested. Didn't hear nuthin', see nuthin', do nuthin'. Ma'm, thankee. Yore a fine girl."

"There's a horse standing on the main trail. Take him along with you."

"A hoss thief? Wal, not yet."

"Take him. Strip off the saddle and hide it somewhere before morning. Drive the horse away up along your trail and let him go."

"That's a level head. Fine girl—fine girl."

She heard him go away. Closing the door she laid the barrier into its sockets—a contrivance she herself had made since living here—and crossed to the centre of the room. The burlap curtain wasn't protection enough, so she pulled the blanket rug from the floor and impaled it on the nails serving as window rods. Thus secured she lighted the lamp and went to the bed. What she saw there undid most of the courage she had summoned this eventful night. Tom Gillette lay face upward, coated with dust and streaked with blood. It lay freshly congealed on his temples, and all along one shoulder it fashioned a crimson badge; one arm was askew, as if it were broken, and it seemed to her he had dropped down into that deep level from which the earthborn never return.

She was crying again. She had only cried twice since childhood, the other time being on the eve of her flight from her father's shelter when the memory of Christine Ballard was fresh in her mind. And as she stood there, shaken and helpless, she thought it a bitter and cruel piece of fortune that of all men he had to be the one to hurt her so badly.

So badly that she had given way to the emotion she most despised in a woman. Tom Gillette had the power to make her cry, to break through whatever armour she might put on.

She lighted a fire. While the water heated in the kettle she ripped a sheet into strips and with the butcher knife cut Gillette's shirt away from him.

14 GRIST STRIKES AGAIN

Barron Grist obeyed orders because it was profitable to do so. On his own initiative he never would have committed an overt act of wrongdoing or dared to skim along the slim line dividing legality from illegality. He wasn't robustly crooked enough to face the law on his own account. But with a corporation behind him Grist was another man. He borrowed courage from those who hired him, and he fetched and carried the corporation's dirty tools with the curious yet common philosophy of his type: he wasn't the originator, but only the agent, and therefore not bound by his conscience. After all, business was business, and if the P. R. N. could get away with so many sins of omission and commission what difference did it make? The strong survived, the weak perished, and perhaps it was just as well they did.

Whoever chose Grist for this job understood the man well. Despite his colourlessness he was persistent in pushing forward the corporation's affairs, dangerous when he had positive directions to follow. Bred to Eastern standards, he never fully realized one fact concerning the West until Gillette woke him to that fact. Out here men didn't play at life as if it were a game of chess; behind every transaction stood an alternative an Easterner seldom dreamed of using—the appeal to weapons. He had been discounting this until he saw his own foreman sag to the floor of the saloon and spit out his last breath. That both sickened and warned him as nothing ever had before. For five days he kept to the Nelson hotel, and had he been left to his own thoughts he might soon have resigned. His book of rules didn't cover such a situation and he wasn't the kind to take long chances on his own responsibility. However, he wasn't long left to himself. There arrived presently the following summary order:

> "Make haste as per instructions.
>
> "PRAGUE."

Grist tore the telegram into small squares and paced fretfully down the dusty street to the railroad office. And, still shaken by the recent experience, he dispatched an extraordinarily tart response.

> "Do you want me to shovel Dakota in apple barrels and forward to your office?"
>
> "GRIST."

"I'm sick of it," he told himself. "Dead sick. I've a notion to quit 'em. I'll pull their chestnuts out of the fire, but I won't set up as a target. Not by a jugful of cider. If they want the south bank they've got to come into the open and give me directions I can read. And directions I can show as evidence."

But his rebellion was brief, and close on the heels of the above war cry he sent a more explicit explanation.

> "One party unwilling. Final.
>
> "GRIST."

"Let them do the squirming now. I'll be hanged if I read between any more lines."

He was mistaken. Back came a telegram in the same enigmatic style, as plain as a summer sky, and as subtle as three legal minds could make it.

> "Glad to hear of your progress. Be sure everything is legal. Much confusion and conflict of titles in a new territory. Better check up on your surveys. Advise see

land office regards that. Salary raised a hundred. Use all expedition consistent with aim in view.

"RANDALL."

Had this been signed by Prague, Grist would have acted on the face value of the message forthwith. But Randall's name augured a different meaning; Randall was a miser with words, he loaded them double always. Grist settled to a closer scrutiny. "He's glad to hear of my progress. That means get busy. He wants me to be sure everything is legal. All right. If a man wanted to hit me with his left hand he'd keep calling my attention to his right one. That's a plain sign to sift the gold out of what follows. Conflict of land titles—um. I know that. He knows I know it. Check up on surveys with land office. Well, by heavens!"

He gathered the meaning. Why, this was as ancient as gilding a brick, and as crude. Grist shook his head. "They must want possession fearfully bad. How do they expect me to surround the land agent? I rise to inquire. Grist, you'll earn that extra hundred and live to spend it yet in a Federal jail."

He folded the note, mulling the situation over and over in his mind. Finally he surrendered. Every man has a dream of creating an empire. Grist had his dream; as far as that went he already possessed the empire and was its titular ruler. But the horizons spread out. More land, more power. And if he didn't do this piece of work some less soft-hearted fellow would. "Therefore, Grist, be about the business. Be about it."

He sought the land office. The agent saw him come, and before the P. R. N. man said anything the agent beckoned him to an inner room, closed the door, and went through all the motions of extreme secrecy. The fellow looked harried.

"I know what you're here for," he muttered. "I know what it is."

"You do?" was Grist's puzzled question. "Well, by Gad, you know more than I do. I'm in a state of mind."

"I got a telegram from a certain gentleman in Washington," explained the agent. "A gentleman who exerts considerable influence in some quarters."

"And so did I," grunted the P. R. N. man in eviden relief. This made the whole thing easy. How had they man aged to pull wires across all this distance? His opinion o his superiors rose.

The agent struck his knee. "Now, for God's sake, don' give me away! I owe somebody for this job, and I'm paying my debts."

"With perhaps an added consideration for the case in hand," suggested Grist, feeling himself in control of the situation.

"I swear not!" exclaimed the agent earnestly. "Do you know what would happen to me if—Well, I'd wear stripes."

"Entirely unbecoming to one of your tastes," murmured Grist. "Well, let's get to our muttons—or our beeves."

"I do it under duress," said the agent. "If the commissioner ever got wind of it I'd be crucified and hung up as a specimen."

"Protest registered. Ever read what Shakespeare said about protests? Never mind. Go on with the details."

The agent leaned across the desk. "When Gillette filed he brought the location marks, and they were inserted in the application. One of those location marks ended in a figure three. The three has been changed to an eight. I won't say when or where or how or by whom. But it's been changed. Do you understand?"

"Therefore," mused Grist, "Gillette is squatting beside water he has no right to. And that particular strip of land along the river is open to filing. Just so. But how about the responsibility of the land office? Weren't you supposed to know when he filed the location—I mean the location the application now shows—whether or not it was the place he had in mind?"

"We're not supposed to meet a man's mind," said the agent. "He gave me the figures. I registered them. As a matter of course I looked on the record to see if that location had or had not been previously filed. That's all of my responsibility."

Grist got up. "Very fine. You make out a new set of papers. I'll bring in one of my riders to sign 'em. He'll be the legal petitioner. Next in order is a writ of eviction.

Squatter's right doesn't apply on entry land, does it? Just so.''

"Gillette will contest that," muttered the agent. "There'll be a stink. But they can't prove malfeasance on me. It's his error, that's all. Not my error. I'll swear those were the figures he gave me. And what influence has he in the East, anyhow?''

"That's the essential point. You stick to your story with a steadfast heart. Virtue is not alone in receiving rewards.''

He went out, immeasurably encouraged by the turn of events. It put him in a fighting humour. There was substantial support back of him. Gillette couldn't fight Federal authority.

In the course of forty-eight hours he brought a P. R. N. puncher in to file, also got a writ of eviction, and also by use of sundry witnesses, had a warrant issued for Gillette on the charge of murdering his foreman. On the appointed hour and day he met the United States Marshal, one W. G. Hannery, and rode out of Nelson, bound toward the Circle G to see the writ executed and the warrant served.

"You tried to obtain possession of these premises?" demanded the marshal, not in love with his mission.

"No, certainly not.''

"Then what the hell about all this hocus-pocus?''

"Listen, how near that ranch do you suppose Gillette would let me approach? How long do you figure he'd listen to me?''

"Not much longer'n I'd listen to you, if it was me in the same skiff," said the marshal. "I'm telling you, frankly, I don't like to see a white man's country tied up by a bunch of Eastern highbinders, Grist.''

Grist smiled. "How Eastern? That strip is being filed on by one of my punchers. A son of the range, a product of the glorious West who never was east of the Dakota line and never owned more than a silver-mounted saddle in his life.''

"Gush," snorted the marshal. "I'm dry behind the ears. That's the old dodge. Well, if I got to do it, then I got to do it. But you want to figure a high-power rifle kicks back blamed near as hard as it shoots forward. Which applies to Gillette. And don't come running to me if you get hurt.

You're going to discover you can't hide behind the petticoats of Justice all the time."

The two of them arrived at the Circle G houses and were confronted by Quagmire and Christine Ballard. The marshal, under the influence of her smile, thawed and reached for his hat.

"I'm inquirin' for Tom Gillette."

"Deadwood," grunted Quagmire. "I'm jef here temporary. Le's have the hard news."

"Orders to get off," was the marshal's equally laconic answer. "You ain't on the place you filed on. Said place, apparently, is nearer the north pole. This fellow"—indicating Grist—"has got the drop on you boys."

Quagmire squinted at Grist until the latter shifted in the saddle. But the wizened puncher showed no surprise at the news. He dwelt in pessimism, he always expected the worst to happen. He contented himself with saying, "Something smells around here."

"I didn't ask him to come along," explained the marshal. He got down and tacked the notice to the ranchhouse wall. "Said movin' orders are meant to be promptly obeyed. But seein' as Gillette ain't here and it'd work a plain hardship to move without him on hand to superintend such I'll hold off till he gets back."

"Oh, look here," protested Grist.

"Shut up. I obey my orders. I also got a right to interpret some of 'em. I'm doin' a little interpretin' now. If you don't like it write East to them land grabbers." He remounted and started away. Then yards off he turned in the saddle and added, as an apparent afterthought, "I also hold a warrant for Gillette. Murder. Have to execute that personally. When you see him, tell him to come and get it."

Quagmire met the marshal's sober glance and held it for a long while. "Yeah. All right."

"Listen," cried Grist, suddenly aroused, "are you trying to warn Gillette away?"

"A man's got a right to know the law's after him," was the marshal's blunt answer. "Out here he has. That's another interpretation. You better be amiable, brother, or I'll

174

let you ride across Gillette range alone. And how far do you think you'd get before a bullet slapped you down?''

They went on. Quagmire waited only until the two were decently beyond talking distance before he turned to read the notice its full length. Then he ran for the bunkhouse and collected his possibles. He saddled a horse and he haltered another. He gave abrupt orders to one of the arriving punchers.

''Yo' in charge, Red. I'm lopin' fo' Deadwood to find Tom.''

Christine crossed the yard and put a detaining hand on Quagmire's arm. ''Tell him I'm still waiting.''

Quagmire ducked his solemn visage and galloped away. Presently his path was marked by a faint ball of dust to the southwest.

15 FLOOD TIDE—AND EBB

For seventy-two hours Lorena Wyatt kept her solitary vigil by the bunk, her eyes watching his face for the slightest movement, her hands now and then questing across his heart; and for seventy-two hours he lay in the self-same posture of death with only the faint rise and fall of his chest to indicate he still lived. In washing him and binding the cuts about his body she found the bruises on his temple to be only superficial, they were not bullet made, although in receiving them he must have been tremendously battered. On his flank, one long furrow cut through the outer flesh and left a path more sinister to look upon than dangerous. This she had wrapped as well as his head, knowing they would mend, but the deep hole just below and inside his arm socket was another matter. The bullet still lodged there, and whether it was seated in solid flesh or whether it touched his lungs she couldn't tell.

Time was the only mender—time and this man's splendid power of body. There was a doctor in Deadwood, but Lorena knew the medico had gone into the hills a day before to take care of some distant prospector crushed by a slide. And he wouldn't be back until the crisis came and passed with Tom Gillette. So she watched, sitting helpless on the box beside the bunk, occasionally touching him as if wishing to send some message down into the deep pit he had descended; watching him grow grayer and grayer and hearing his breathing shorten and diminish. To Lorena it was agony. She could do nothing but wait—nothing but sit by while he slipped away from her; and through her mind marched the thousand things she wanted to tell him, wanted him to know about herself. After that first cry she set her lips together and never uttered another sound; when she sat her hands locked tightly together; when she rose to replenish the fire her eyes kept straying back to where he lay. Thus the hours dragged interminably. Daylight wasn't so bad, for she could throw open the door and see the sun and let the wind strike her body. There was the sight and the sound of life by day, and it seemed to her Tom held his own during those hours. But at night there were only the blackness and the silence surrounding her little cell, only herself sitting beside him and praying passionately to herself and thinking queer unrelated thoughts . . . how the shadows fell across the strong bridge of his nose . . . how much of a man he looked . . . Christine Ballard sitting on her horse while Tom and the Blond Giant slashed and punished each other. That day Lorena saw the tiger in Tom Gillette and all his quiet reserve and all his humour had been laid aside to reveal the primitive depths. He was a man!

The first night was the longest, for at every stray gust of breeze and every sound she thought Hazel and Saba were returning to thresh the woods again; if they did so they would surely come across her cabin and break in. She put the table against the door and turned down the lamp until the room was dim and shadowy. But they didn't come that night, and at early dawn she left the cabin long enough to run along the trail and retrieve both her basket and the gun Tom had dropped. She wanted to go on to Deadwood, yet didn't dare. Anything might happen during the interval. So the day dragged and the night came once more with her perched on the box and her fists locking each other. And over and over again she tried to throw her will and her desire across the infinite chasm separating them, repeating to herself a thousand times, "You must get well—Tom! You must not die! Here I am, right beside you—waiting for you! You must not die!"

Sleep was the drug she feared, and she sat in the most cramped positions to keep herself awake. Even so the time came when she started out of what had been a sound sleep, to find herself lying on the hard floor. After that she walked the floor in a kind of shame. "I don't deserve to have him. What am I? What can I do for my part in his life? What do I know? Oh, why didn't my mother live to make me a real woman!" And then she bent over Gillette for the hundredth time, to pull the quilt higher up, to let her hands stray across the jet hair; once she kissed him and drew back startled.

That night the woods seemed full of prowling creatures. She heard something rustling the underbrush, she heard the scuff of boots at her very door. And she was swept by all the mixed fear and despair and cold anger of a trapped animal when she saw the latch slowly rise and the door give imperceptibly against the barrier. Then the latch fell back, the brush marked a retreating body, and she relaxed. The man, whoever it was, was lucky; she would have shot him before he made his entrance, for there was something of the wild in Lorena Wyatt these dreary hours. Another time that same night, well along toward morning, she heard a cavalcade gallop down the trail, stop, and go on again. Then it was day—a long-drawn day that marched into the third night. And without warning Tom Gillette turned his head toward her, his eyes clear, and a trace of colour staining the gray of his features. He spoke.

"I'm all right, Lorena girl. Get some sleep. Roll me over and turn in." That was all, he fell into a sound slumber. It was rest this time, not an unconsciousness. The crisis seemed to have come and gone. He would get well.

"Thank God!" she murmured. She dropped to the floor and was lost to the world.

She was roused by Tom's voice. "Girl—get up from the floor!"

The sun streamed in between the cracks of the cabin; she had slept the night through, Gillette moved his head slowly. "Lord, how long has this been goin' on? What day is it, Lorena?"

She rose quickly. "Thursday, Tom. You have been here three nights and two days."

"An' you watched all the time," he murmured, not quite in command of his tongue. But he saw the nod of her head,

178

and it made him fretful. "First sleep you've had, I guess. It won't do."

"I'm all right. Haven't I said nothing could hurt me? But you don't know—you never will know how I felt last night when you turned the corner."

"Me," he murmured, "I don't seem to be carin'. Feel like a wrung dish rag. Ain't dead, but I don't feel much alive. What's the extent of the damages?"

She told him, the meanwhile ripping the blanket from the window and opening the door. She told him, too, of what happened after he fell. Gillette moved one arm gingerly and started to speak, Lorena checked him. "Not now. You've said too much."

"I think I could walk," he muttered.

"No, of course you couldn't. You'll be flat on your back for a week, perhaps two or three weeks. My dear man, don't you understand what happened? They left you for dead—you almost were dead. Now sleep again."

He fell silent, eyes half closed. Something worried him, she saw. And she knew what it was before he broached the subject. "Lorena, I've got to get out of here. I can't be havin' folks—Well, put me in that shed outside."

She stopped by the bunk, her shoulders squaring. "What difference does it make, Tom?"

"Get somebody to pack me into town."

"And let San Saba know where you are? My dear, I'm going to take care of you. I don't care what happens or who may ever discover it later. Now rest."

"Thoroughbred," whispered Tom, and closed his eyes. She put the room in order, stirred the fire, and poked about the cupboard; she packed water from the spring and presently something simmered on the stove. The man moved restlessly in bed, testing himself joint by joint.

"Legs sound," he murmured. "Right hand and right side in second-hand workin' order. Shucks, it won't be any three weeks."

In a little while she had a bowl of soup for him. He ate it slowly; afterwards he seemed to expand with fresh energy. "It won't even be a week."

But she saw the danger signals on his cheeks already.

"Every word you say only adds another day to the time you stay in bed. Sleep now."

He sighed a little and shut his eyes again, instantly he was asleep. The girl watched him for a while, or until a restlessness took possession of her and she began tip-toeing about the place looking for things to do. She wanted to sing, yet dared not, she wanted to work, she wanted to do anything that would release the surcharge of emotion within her. Going outside she took up the ax and chopped boughs for fuel; then she rummaged around the shed for straw and packed enough of it inside to make her a mattress on the floor. Tom would not like it when he saw her making her bed on it, but there was no other way. Strange how simple were a man's points of honour and yet how complicated. As for herself, she looked at it with that ruthlessness and that impersonality most women possess at moments of emergency. Nothing could hurt her—and the creed protected her like a mantle. Had she been a sophisticated girl her thoughts might have travelled a different line, but all her life she had been bred to look squarely at the primary facts of existence.

It was late afternoon before he woke again. She was waiting for him with news.

"I've got to go in to Deadwood, Tom. We've nothing to eat in the place. And I wanted to see if the doctor was back from the hills. Do you think it would be all right?"

"What's the danger?"

"San Saba will be scouting around here, won't he? Supposing he should come to the cabin?"

He studied the ceiling for quite an interval. "Put my gun beside me."

She brought his revolver and laid it in his hand; his fingers closed around the butt slowly. She thought she had never seen so quick and startled a glance in any man as she marked on his face when he tried the trigger. "Judas, I can't be that weak! Trigger must've got jammed in the scrap."

She smiled at the unconscious pride he had in his strength. Even now he couldn't believe himself physically unable to walk. So she took the gun and cocked it and laid it back beside him. His eyes narrowed a little when he saw her do it, and a sigh escaped him. "I guess I'm licked. But there ain't any danger to me. You go ahead."

"I hate to, Tom. Only, we've got to have things to eat. Anything you want?"

"Go ahead. What I want is a preacher to perform a chore for us, Lorena girl, but that'll have to wait till I'm able to argue."

Her hand dropped on his forehead and skittered away. "Perhaps there won't be an argument, Tom." With that, she got her basket, closed the door to the cabin and went quickly down the trail. There had been a prowler around the cabin for she marked the boot prints in the ground; that worried her all the way to town and speeded her actions. The doctor was still away, and nobody knew when he was to return. At the restaurant she explained her absence on the ground of sickness and arranged for more or less of a vacation. She filled her basket and talked the cook out of some fresh apples and a pitcher of milk—both rarities in the camp. At the general store she bought a canvas bed tick and a pair of blue army blankets. Men were gossiping in the store, and she tarried over her bargaining to pick up the news, for she knew Gillette would like to hear something of what went on in the world. Most men did. Then she went back up the slope as the sun fell and shadows closed around the trees.

She thought she was being followed, and with a swift side-step she dropped off the trail and waited a little while; it was only a man on a horse going upward toward the diggings. A hundred yards farther she swung from the main trail to the smaller trace leading toward the cabin. Something moved out from the concealing shadows, and a man barred her way. It was Lispenard.

His bold, swollen face rolled forward, and as he got a clear view of her he stepped closer, muttering his surprise. "Well, by Godfrey, are you the girl they say lives up here alone?"

"What do you want?" Lorena snapped, muscles gathering. She had dealt with this man before, and she knew what slack and brutal impulses stirred behind his heavy-lidded eyes. Somewhat more than two weeks had elapsed between this meeting and the last; even in that short interval he had grown more slovenly, he advertised more clearly the breakdown of what once had been a will. With this type of man, disintegration was swift once it set in.

"So it's you," he muttered again; she saw the sudden dilation of his nostrils. "Our prairie spitfire. Gad, what luck!"

"Then you're the one who's been skulking around my. cabin," said Lorena. "I never knew any human being could be so rotten. If I were a man I'd be ashamed you belonged in the same—" A sudden fear stabbed her. "Have you been rummaging around while I was gone?"

"My interest," replied Lispenard, "is confined solely to you, dear girl."

"Keep those terms off your tongue. And don't come any closer! I won't stand being mauled by you again, hear me?"

"Oh, come. Virtue so high grows dev'lish wearisome. What am I to believe? Here you live alone—you've knocked around the world quite a bit, I'm bound. Lord, girl, don't be uppish. I'm no leper. I'm a man, and you'll look a long while before you find another one able to measure me. Listen, it's a dam' dreary and monotonous world, and why shouldn't we be agreeable to each other? Put it this way: I'll apologize for my last little outbreak and we'll start all over again. There's my word. Give me that luggage and I'll pack it."

"Get away from me!"

"Well," muttered Lispenard, now within arm's reach and growing angry "who is to stop me? You've got no hero hiding behind the trees this time. I'm going up to the cabin with you."

"No, you are not. Stand aside."

He was grinning. The girl stepped back a pace, her arm dropped into the basket and came up again, holding a revolver. Lispenard's head reared, and all the forced pleasantry left him. "You wouldn't have the nerve to pull the trigger," he jeered.

"Haven't I? Come another step and find out. Let's try that fine courage of yours—you filth!"

"Some day I'll punish you for all that abuse!" cried Lispenard. He stared at her for several moments. "Believe you would fire, at that. Spitfire is the right designation. But you can be tamed, my dear, and I'm the man to do it."

"Get out of the path," she insisted. "Go around me and on down the trail. Don't ever come near my cabin again. If I see you I'll shoot."

She saw a sudden widening of his bold eyes. "I smell a rat," he muttered. "I believe I've stumbled onto something. By Gad, I know I have! Who is hiding behind your petticoats? What's all those blankets for—and the grub? You'd better be a little nice to me."

"Must I stand and take all that abuse!" stormed the girl. "How brave you are to be cruel to a woman, how very brave! You are yellow clear through to the bone, Mr. Lispenard. I doubt if a dog would walk beside you!" There was a click of the gun as she cocked it. Her voice shook. "Go around me and down the trail! If ever you come again, I'll kill you!"

He said nothing for a time, but he obeyed the order, circling back of a tree and stepping some yards away. She turned, watching for trickery. His mocking voice floated through the shadows. "Don't protest your virtue too much, my dear. You can ill afford it."

She never stirred until the sound of his retreat was lost somewhere in the main trail. Then she turned up the slope with a heavy heart, came to the cabin, and let herself inside. It was growing darker, and Tom had no word of welcome for her. She dropped the barrier into its sockets with a quick rise of alarm and groped over to hang the blanket across the window again. The lamp wick flared to a match; Gillette was asleep, his hand curled around the gun.

It seemed to her that some special providence watched over this man. How could it be otherwise when Lispenard stood within a few yards of the cabin yet had not entered? And should she tell Tom of the other man's presence? She debated this silently. He needed to know it for his own safety, yet the knowledge would only add another worry to an already long list. She was strong—she could fight this

183

thing out until Tom stood ready to take it over. She wouldn't tell him until he walked again.

After Tom Gillette discovered he was a sick man and a woefully weak man he made no more attempts to force the recovery. There was a hard wisdom in him. He knew when to fight, and he knew when to ride with the current, so he mustered his patience and for better than a week he rested flat on his back, saying very little; alternately sleeping and drowsing along with his eyes half closed. During these latter hours he seemed to be in a profound study, staring straight up to the ceiling. These were sombre hours, the girl knew, and she respected his silences. That was the way he had been fashioned, he was no hand to talk; as for herself, she had little enough to say now that the crisis was past. What went on in her heart, what was stored there, would never come out, and she was content that it was to be thus. But on occasions she turned to find him looking at her so quietly and so steadily that a queer runner of emotion swept through her and the quickened tempo of her heart sent the telltale blood to her cheeks. Time and again she saw the very words trembling on his lips, yet he never spoke them. It puzzled her, as the days went on, and presently a doubt and a dread came to her. What was he thinking? A man's code was sometimes unfathomable, sometimes judgments were passed in secret by that code, and then never again were things the same. What was he thinking?

But she was soon to find out. For, one day in the second week, he turned toward her, wide awake and with an unusual intentness on his face. "Come over here, Lorena"

She came beside him. "Yes?"

"Take hold of my hand. Squeeze it as tight as you can."

She obeyed, wondering. Gillette seemed to be experimenting with himself. "Fine. Now let me see what I can do." So she let her fingers grow limp while his own slowly closed in, then relaxed. He rested a moment. "I reckon I've been a pretty good Indian—played 'possum to help old lady Nature. You go outside a minute, Lorena girl."

"Now, Tom—"

He barely smiled. "Oh, I'm not going to be foolish. But a lot depends on this."

She went out and started a few yards down the trail. Presently she heard him calling, and she whipped around and ran back inside. He was on his feet, the blanket wrapped around him, supported by nothing at all save his own strength. And he was grinning wanly, he was triumphant. "I'm sound. By Joe, I'm sound."

"Oh, Tom, that wasn't necessary yet. You mustn't overdo."

"I had to find out," said he, quite grim. Then he sat back on the bed and rolled himself in. "Didn't I tell you a lot depended on it? Listen, is there any chance for me?"

She turned away from him and walked toward the window. The width of the room was athwart them, and to the man it appeared the width of the universe stretched between. He watched her and, as always, he was immeasurably stirred by the clear oval of her face and the round sturdiness of her body. She was straightforward, she never traded with him, and sometimes he had seen a light in her eyes that left him humble. At that moment he thought he never had seen a woman so piquant, so alluring and lovely.

"I am yours, Tom."

Just that. Spoken slow and just above a whisper. Gillette gripped his fists together, his whole face tightened as if in pain. "Lorena girl, you will never want, you will never regret it. I'd sweep this land—"

"Oh, Tom, I'm not sure I'll ever be any help to you! What am I—what do I know—what can I do!"

"Stop that! There's no man fit for you. Not one! But I'll try—come over here, Lorena. I'm sound of body, anyhow. That's why I had to find out before asking you."

"What difference would that have made to me?" she cried.

"Maybe none, to you. But everything to me. By Joe, but it's a fine day outside. I'd like to be riding—I'd like to warble." He was smiling as she put her arm across his shoulder. And when they looked to each other there was a kindling and a flashing of some deep flame.

"Too much has passed between us for it to end any other way," he muttered.

"I am yours, Tom," she repeated.

It was an hour or so later before she reminded him there was no food in the cabin. There was another trip to town, and the sooner it was done the better. She got her basket and brought him his gun. This time his fingers closed about it firmly. "I can handle the blamed thing now. Lord, but I hate to see you doing all this fetch-and-carry for me."

"Why? Won't I be doing it the rest of my life?" She saw his quick frown of disavowal and a swift, rippling laugh rang across the small room. "Of course! I want to do it—every woman someday hopes to do it. And I'm strong—nothing can hurt me."

"I'll make it so you'll never have to lift as much as your little finger," he promised.

She smiled and went out and down the trail. There was a man speaking—so direct and practical in some things, so thoroughly impractical in others. She was only just across the border of womanhood, yet she saw ahead of her with that instinctive clarity of her sex. Men promised to make life easy and believed they had the power of doing it. Yet life was not that way. There would always be pain and tragedy and bitterness in the years, along with the blessings. That was life. But she was strong, and the future held no terrors. For she had the man she wanted, she had everything she wanted, and she stood ready to pay for her bargain.

The day was fresh and clear; the sun shot through the tree lanes and sparkled on the creek below. She thought she never had seen a day so wonderful, nor had the joy of living ever surged through her so powerfully as on this morning. She forgot Lispenard and San Saba and all the unravelled business yet hanging over her head. So she walked down the slope, humming an old trail song to herself, and came into Deadwood.

The town seemed unusually active for a morning, the streets were filled, and a kind of holiday air permeated the place. American flags draped the hotel, and a great banner bearing the single word "WELCOME" stretched across the thoroughfare. She saw the prominent men of the camp gathered at the far end, all dressed to the fashion and Deadwood's band stood near them, instruments slung up to play.

186

Turning into the restaurant, Lorena came across the proprietor and asked him what it was all about.

"Billy Costaine's comin'," said the proprietor, as if that were all the explanation anybody needed. The name meant nothing to Lorena, and she shrugged her shoulders, dismissing the matter. There were more important things to think about than some remote notable. The proprietor, noting her professed ignorance, was mildly scandalized.

"Great snakes, girl, Billy Costaine's a U. S. Senator. That breed o' cat don't stray into the hills very often. More than that, he happens to be chairman of the public lands committee, and he can sure help Deadwood. You bet we'll show him the sights. When you comin' back to work?"

She didn't know when, if ever, and told him as much. In the kitchen she filled her basket, chatted awhile with the cook, and reached the street just as the band struck up a tune; the harmony was a little off, but the volume was sufficient to prick the nerves of every horse on the street, and for a few moments there was an informal rodeo and bucking contest. Guns began to crack, men swept along the way yelling and down at the far end a party rode slowly into the town as if on parade. Lorena craned her neck to watch; an arm touched her, and an absymally deep and mournful voice said thrice over:

"Hey, ma'am—ma'am—doggonit, ma'am!"

It was Quagmire, his gloom-ridden, wrinkled face as near a smile as it ever came. He was travel strained, he was gaunt, and he looked to her almost with appeal. "Doggonit, ma'am, it's shore elevatin' to see yo'. Deadwood—shucks, what a town. I been here six mortal days, stepped on, pushed aside, and about stranglin' fer fresh air. Ma'am, what *you* livin' in sech a hog-waller for?"

"Why, Quagmire! Oh, but I'm glad to see you! Come back here." She pulled him toward the building walls, removed from the crowd. "Are you looking for Tom?"

"I'll announce it far an' wide I am," he muttered. "About give up hope, too."

"He's up at my cabin, Quagmire. Sixteen days ago he was shot and nearly killed. He's just able to move about now."

187

Quagmire studied her long and earnestly. Something happened inside him. "Who did it—San Saba?"

She nodded. "And several other men with him—Hazel's gang. I've been hiding him. If they knew where he was they'd kill him surely. You've come just at the right time. He'll be riding some of these days, as weak as he is. And they'll try to get him again."

He turned away, muttering to himself. When he swung about again his eyes were tinged with red. "Sorrer is the rule in this here universe, but it ain't no reason why bad luck should roost on a Gillette forever. Too much has happened to that boy. Now, by Judas, I'll play a stack in this. Lead the way"

Horsemen swept past, the band flared. Lorena looked out directly upon the distinguished visitor to Deadwood, Senator William Costaine. The Senator was a big man with an angular framework and the face of a bloodhound. There was no fellowship in the steel-tinted eyes that swept the crowd, no leaven of humour on the gray fighter's face. Here was a man who had been through the mill, who had emerged at the top of his profession with few illusions and no fear. It looked as if he was thinking, "What's the joker behind this celebration?" yet he was saved from downright cynicism by an air of intense honesty. Lorena, of course, was not aware of his reputation; but back in Washington he was the scourge of the lobbyists. He hunted them with the same ruthless pleasure he would have hunted predatory animals. His cold, legalistic brain infallibly sought for the hidden clauses, the quietly inserted riders; and when he spoke in the Senate men listened, even while some of them were being stripped of their reputations. He worked with nobody, he was a hater of compromise; and therefore the Senator was almost entirely a destructive force. But because of that very caustic quality he was a valued and respected servant.

Quagmire shook his head. "Reckon he'd be a bad man to meet out on the road. Le' go, ma'm."

As the two of them went up the slope, Quagmire leading his horse, Lorena told him all she knew of the encounter. She even mentioned her meeting with Lispenard. Quagmire grew more and more taciturn. "I reckon Tom's got yo' to thank for bein' alive," he muttered. The girl said nothing, but the puncher saw her face and nodded to himself sagely. "Yeah, I see." And still he seemed wrapped in despair until they left the main trail and progressed along the smaller pathway. The cabin appeared between the pines. Tom Gillette stood in the doorway, sunning himself. The two men came face to face, and when Lorena saw how they looked at each other and struggled to maintain a grave and casual expression, a lump rose in her throat.

"Well, Quagmire."

"Yeah, Tom."

"Ranch burn up or did you fire yourself?"

"Figgered I'd give myself a vacation an' go see the flesh-pots. What's the use o' bein' jef if yo' can't cut a caper? Been engaged in a little lead traffic, fella?"

"Some. Well, get it off your chest."

"Get what off?" mumbled Quagmire defensively. "Nothin' on it but a dirty shirt."

Tom shook his head and waited. Quagmire turned to the girl. "Ain't he a gloomy fool? Why should I have bad news? Ain't we got enough? An' if I got bad news why can't it wait? Anyhow, they's lots o' land in Dakota even if we been tol' to move from present headquarters. Never did think much of our range—let Grist an' his Eastern bosses have it if they want it so cussed bad. Of course, a writ o' eviction has got to be obeyed, but mebbe they's ways to flank it. Me, I allus thought we'd filed on the water we said we filed on, but if they's been a mistake made in figgers—like they claim—why, then whose fault is it, the surveyor's, ours, or the land agent's? I'm askin'."

"Spoken like a lawyer," muttered Tom gravely. "Come in and find a chair. Now that you're empty you might float away."

"Wait," interrupted the girl. "What are you telling us, Quagmire? That Tom is being forced off his ranch?"

"Yeah," drawled Quagmire.

"Come inside," repeated Tom. The three of them went into the house. Gillette sat on the bunk and rolled himself a cigarette, never saying a word, but the girl observed a cloud passing across his eyes, and she felt infinitely sorry for him.

"But how can they do that?" she demanded. "Haven't you filed on it? How can they take it away from you?"

"Which is what I'm wanting to know," said Gillette. Quagmire raised his two hands, palms up. "What I sorter gathered was they was a mistake in figgers, and the water yo' filed on ain't the water you're roostin' on."

"I've heard of such jugglin' before," murmured Tom. "Well, Grist said he'd get me, one way or another. Rustlin' didn't work, so he's turned to another kind of crookedness."

"Yo' better hit home right off," said Quagmire. "The marshal said he'd wait till yo' returned, but mebbe that Grist fella can force the transaction."

"I'll have to scotch it," agreed Gillette.

"Yes, but you can't travel for another week, Tom," objected Lorena. "You're not fit."

"An', by the way" put in Quagmire with marked casualness, "this Grist hombre's also got a warrant agin yo' fo' killin' his range boss."

Gillette swung his head. That seemed to touch him more than anything else. "The man's ridin' for a fall, Quagmire! By Judas, he's pressin' too far. I'll fight that outfit until something breaks—and there's gospel."

The girl, meanwhile, had gone about getting a meal. But in the midst of this chore she had a sudden idea, and she abandoned everything and entered the discussion again. "Tom, are you sure the P. R. N. is behind all this?"

"Absolutely sure."

"Well, isn't all this land in the hands of the government—doesn't the government have control of the disposal of it?"

"That's right, too."

She stood in the doorway, looking down the trail. "I have heard my father say some queer things about the P. R. N. If they are crooked, why doesn't the government stop them?"

"Because it's a long way to Washington," said Gillette. "The people behind the P. R. N. are pretty smart—and

190

evidently they've got plenty of influence. Money will go a long way, Lorena"

"It isn't right," she murmured. "I don't believe the government would allow it."

Quagmire looked at Gillette; the two of them exchanged faint smiles. "It won't do us any good to squeal, Lorena. We can't squeal loud enough. We've got to battle it out the best we can"

"It isn't right," she insisted. "I'm going outside a little while."

She hurried away from the cabin and toward Deadwood again, just a little anxious lest Gillette should divine her intention and call her back. The truth was, Lorena believed implicitly in the honesty and the pervading powerfulness of the law. She had none of a man's cynicism concerning it, and whenever she saw those two symbolic letters—U. S.— she had a picture of solemn men sitting in a row, covered by black robes and with a flag hanging above them. She knew state law could be evaded; her own father had done it. But a national law was something different, and it seemed incredible that any corporation could openly steal government land and not be prosecuted.

"It's just that nobody knows," she told herself. "If I can only see—"

She reached town and went quickly to the hotel. The lobby was crowded with men, reeking with tobacco smoke. Senator Costaine sat in a chair at a far corner, listening to some sort of a delegation. Lorena drew her nether lip between her teeth and mustered her courage. What would all these men think of her for breaking in—what would the Senator say to her for the interruption? She almost lost heart as she watched the man. He looked so grim and inaccessible, he represented something so great. And, after all, she was but a girl. Then she thought of Tom Gillette, and she squared her small shoulders and slipped through the crowd.

The Senator saw her standing in front of him. Being a man of courtesy, he rose, interrupting a flood of talk with a motion of his arm. For Lorena with her piquant features and her black eyes made a striking picture—even more striking at the moment because of a certain nervous snap-

191

ping of those eyes. She made a pleasant distraction. The Senator, as a matter of literal fact, was tired of the smoke and the heavy jests and the dingdong of figures and facts and the representations and the pleadings. All this was an old story. It never varied. He smiled at the girl, whereat his features became almost pleasant.

"Senator Costaine," said the girl, conscious of a hundred eyes watching her, "I—I would like a word with you."

"Certainly," agreed the Senator. He took her by the arm and moved away to a more secluded angle of the room. "You must not be flustered by men in the mass," he reassured her. "They have no more power to hurt you than singly."

"But they have," said Lorena, turning. "That's why I've come to see you. Senator, could you spare an hour and walk a half mile up the hillside to see a man?"

"My dear lady, if I tried to escape from these gentlemen my life would be worth nothing. Perhaps if you could state, more or less briefly, what the occasion was—"

"I know you are very busy," she apologized. "But there is a man up the slope just recovering from an attempt made on his life. He isn't able to come here, and even if he were able, I don't believe he would. I do this on my own responsibility. He has a ranch over near Nelson. Several Texans migrated there this year. All were bought out by a certain corporation, except Tom—except this man. He refused to bargain. The corporation has tried to run him away, they have tried to rustle his stock. And now they are tampering with his water right through the local land office. Senator Costaine, why doesn't the government stop such things?"

The question brought a remote smile to his fighter's face. "If I could answer that question I would be a great man. The government is composed of human beings, and it is human to err."

An immaculately dressed young man drew near the Senator, speaking urgently. "You've only a half hour for lunch, Senator. We are due to ride into the hills directly after."

"Yes—yes," muttered the Senator. He looked to the girl. "As to this gentleman's affairs, that is a matter for court

192

action. If there is fraud—provable fraud—then I'm sure it will be taken care of.''

She saw he was about to slip away. "Can you always prove the unjust things that happen? You know you can't.''

"True. But how can you expect the United States government to do much better? I should like to help you, but I'm certain I couldn't do much good. It's a matter for the district attorney over there. And now, if you'll excuse me—''

"Senator, do you know of the P. R. N. Land Company?''

His attention had wandered; at the question it came back to her and his steel-coloured eyes seemed to narrow and focus. It was as if a powerful light flashed on her face. What little pleasantry his features held up until then vanished. "Was that the corporation involved?" he asked sharply.

"Yes.''

"I shall be extremely interested in meeting your man,'' he said, and motioned to the immaculate secretary hovering anxiously at hand. "Nicholas, I'm going out for an hour. No—no. I don't give a rap if lunch does get cold. Ward off these fellows for me—keep 'em humoured. And now,'' turning to Lorena, "I shall be pleased to follow you.''

Lorena led him into the street and toward the trail. Three or four prominent citizens came along in hot pursuit; Costaine waved them back, and thus the two of them struck up the slope, saying not a word. Lorena had fought a battle, she had nothing more to offer. And the Senator seemed buried in his own thoughts. They cut off the main trail and went up the short little pathway to the cabin. The Senator looked to her inquiringly, and she motioned him inside. Tom and Quagmire apparently had seen them come, for they were standing in the centre of the room.

"Tom, this is Senator Costaine. I have told him about your trouble with the ranch. I know he can help you if you'll explain.''

With that she turned about and left, hearing the dry, rasping voice of Costaine carry an abrupt question over the interval. It was almost as if the man cross-examined a witness. Lorena sat on a stump and waited. A half hour, an hour; the immaculate secretary came panting up among the trees. "Where in God's name is the Senator? What have you done with him?"

Costaine ducked out of the door, grimmer than before. The secretary spread his arms. "They're waiting for us—and you've had no lunch. It will be an all-afternoon trip into the hills. I can't allow you to neglect yourself like this, Senator!"

Costaine seemed not to hear the man. He stood a moment in front of Lorena. "My dear girl, you have rendered me a favour. I think we have got wind of something that will scorch as big a scoundrel as ever lived." Then he swung down the trail with the secretary, and she heard him giving the younger man abrupt orders. "Never mind, Nicholas, never mind. What's a meal missed? I've discovered something about Ignacius Invering's pet Christmas tree. He's a gone goose, Nicholas. As for the trip into the hills, that must be postponed. We start for Nelson immediately."

With Quagmire on hand to keep watch and with Tom mending swiftly—and becoming more and more impatient at each wasted hour—Lorena was relieved of her long vigil. The men slept out in the shed and took their meals in the cabin; and during the following five days she often saw them loitering in the trees, out of earshot, talking earnestly. She never intruded on these councils; rather she drew back within herself and went about those innumerable chores a woman never fails to find. If she had her worries—and she understood that as far as San Saba and Lispenard were concerned there was yet to be a day of reckoning—she kept them hidden. No matter what the future held, it could never by any stretch of the imagination deal with her as harshly as had the past month. And so she was content.

One day Quagmire went to Deadwood and returned with a horse and saddle for Tom; and for an hour the latter rode around the hills, testing himself. When he came back, he slid down with a kind of tight-lipped triumph. Still he said nothing, but she observed that Quagmire made a second trip to town for supplies. And that night at supper the puncher sent a mysterious glance at Gillette and murmured, "Well, I got it."

At breakfast the next morning Gillette seemed unusually preoccupied. Quagmire left the cabin and disappeared in the thicket; and as if that were a signal Gillette came directly to the issue. "We can't stay put any longer, Lorena. I came here to get San Saba, and instead he about got me. Well, it's just a score I'll have to leave unsettled. If I don't hustle back to the ranch I'm apt not to have one. So we've got to pull out."

She was of a sudden busy at a dozen odd things, and each of those things seemed to keep her face turned from the man.

"Lorena—it still goes, doesn't it?"

"I don't change overnight, Tom."

"Well, I didn't think so, but a man like me can't expect too much good luck, so I figured I'd better make sure. But— but look here.

She turned. Gillette stood with his back to the wall, looking harried. "You've got to know something. Quagmire only told me last night, and if it makes any difference to you— The fact is, Kit Ballard is still there at the ranch, and she told Quagmire she was waiting. I want you to know I'm free. What's past is past—and cold as ashes. I didn't ask her to come, I didn't want her to come, and I'm under no obligations. You know where my heart is, Lorena."

"That is your own affair, Tom. I told you once I'd never pry into it."

"Well, you've got a right to know what you're jumping into. Fifteen minutes after we get home she'll have to pack her trunk—but I wouldn't want you to come up against that situation without knowing of it."

She walked over to him, and one hand dropped lightly on his shoulder. She went up a-tiptoe better to meet his eyes. "Whatever happens, I will never doubt you. Never! And I want you to believe the same about me. Oh, Tom, sometimes the whole thing frightens me—it seems as if it can't be true!"

He gathered her into his arms. "By Judas, what right have I got of doubting? You bet it's true. Quagmire and I

195

are riding into town now to settle our affairs. I'll be bringing back a preacher—and a spring bed wagon and team for you to ride in.''

"That's not necessary. I can ride the saddle, it will bring us home quicker.''

"Nothing's good enough for my wife,'' said he gaily. He kissed her and turned out of the door, red-faced. Lorena's silver laugh followed him down the slope and from the distance he turned to grin at her. "You've got to remember I'm not used to this sort of thing yet.''

"Some day it will be so old a story you'll forget.''

"Not while sun shines or grass grows!''

Quagmire came out of the trees and joined Tom. Together the two of them followed the trail to town. Quagmire already had dickered for a wagon and a team, and Tom verified the bargain, paid for it, and went rummaging around the stores for accessories. He bought a light tent, a patented oven, and sundry dishes. He bought this and he bought that while Quagmire made relays from store to wagon, gloomy and skeptical. When all the purchasing was done and Gillette returned to the wagon he was somewhat staggered at the burden it made. Quagmire only spat on the ground and echoed a scant phrase.

"Yo' figgerin' to enter the freight business? Better hire six more hosses''

"Hush,'' grinned Gillette. "On a day like this I'm apt to do 'most anything. Quagmire, nothing's good enough for that girl. Now where's a preacher?''

No more than an hour elapsed from the time they entered Deadwood to the time they crawled upward through the trees. The smaller trail would not admit the wagon, and they were forced around in and out of the occasional alleyways. Gillette hallooed at the cabin and jammed on the brakes impatiently. Quagmire kept his seat, and the parson gingerly slid down and combed his whiskers with his fingers. Gillette walked toward the open door.

"Lorena—all right, Lorena''

She had no answer for him. When he looked into the cabin all the humour and the anticipation were swept from his face. She was not there. And that was only a part of the

196

story, for every movable piece of furniture in the room was overturned, dishes were shattered, and his questing eyes saw a piece of her dress as big as his hand and ripped on all sides lying on the floor. That room had seen a tremendous struggle. Lorena had been kidnapped!

16 A DUEL

San Saba was no fool; he had all of an animal's perceptions, he almost instinctively knew when to avoid danger and when to crowd his luck. In no other way could the man have survived so long his doubtful and shaded existence. Sometimes those perceptions prompted him to do queer things; more than once, when in the full tide of fortune, he had quietly taken to his horse and left the scene of his victories behind him, apparently impelled by no other motive than that of plain cowardice. And there had also been occasions when San Saba stuck to his course when every indication would have warned an even less cautious man. The ex-foreman was full of seeming contradictions. He had absolutely no scruples, and it must be said of him that he had an abundance of a certain kind of courage; for all of that he was no firebrand, and he seldom took an open course when a secret one served him as well. What made so dangerous a figure was that uncanny ability to sense the thoughts of others and to feel and to interpret the cross-currents sweeping around him.

Thus he knew that Lispenard harboured some secret design. It took no great amount of perception to fathom this sullen and changeable figure, but it did augur uncommon wisdom that San Saba forbore forcing the issue. He waited as the days passed along and Lispenard grew more and more restless and more and more given over to fitful periods of brooding. The man rode out into the hills a great deal and always came back with a smouldering fire in his eyes, and after these excursions he always affected a casualness that only the more plainly warned San Saba. Still the ex-foreman bided his time. Then one morning Lispenard saddled his horse earlier than usual and started away without comment, San Saba's small eyes narrowed, and he called after the man.

"We got a chore with Hazel to-night. Don't forget it."

Lispenard turned fretfully. "To hell with Hazel. What's he done for us? Oh, I'll be around when the time comes."

San Saba squatted on the ground, listening to the horse's hoofs crunch across the fallen twigs. The sound scarcely had died out before he was up and over to his own mount in one swift dive; and as he started in pursuit of the Blond Giant his arm dropped toward the gun at his belt. Every feature grew cramped and bleak, the telltale film of crimson spread around the white of his eyes. "The dawg—the rotten-livered houn'! He ain't fitten to know what he does know—he's too rotten to live. Gillette's up there—he's traffickin' with the man. Sho'. He can't play that game with me."

He quickened his pace, then stopped as he saw Lispenard crossing a distant alley of the forest; then he went on again with all the stealthy intentness of a cat.

As for Lispenard, he had no caution about him this day; he was ridden by a solitary desire, and the farther he advanced the greater it became. Earlier, when he first discovered Lorena, he had been at some pains to conceal the nature of his expeditions, to double back and watch for pursuit. But San Saba had never followed, and in time Lispenard grew careless in this maze of trickery. He suspected Gillette's presence in the cabin, and he lay cached day after day among the bushes until he saw the man step uncertainly out into the sunlight. At that point he had a fair target. He could have killed Gillette from ambush, or he could have set San Saba afresh on the trail, neither of which acts was he above doing. Instead, he kept his own counsel and waited.

Before he got within sight of the cabin he heard Gillette calling back to the girl, and later he saw both Gillette and Quagmire swing down toward Deadwood. This was the situation for which he had long waited; directly they were out of sight he slipped off his horse, crept around on the blind side of the cabin, and circled until he stood by the door. She was singing to herself, crossing and recrossing the room. He marked her step until it came quite near the door, then he slid up to the entrance, traversed it at a stride and came face to face with her.

She drew back, she started to turn. His arms caught her like a trap, and all the pent-up sullen rage broke across the few flimsy barriers left of his decency. He struck her with his closed fist, and when she cried out and the echo of that cry trembled through the still, hot air he struck her again and shook her with all his strength.

"Shut up—you spitfire! I won't be bilked any more. By Godfrey, you'll pay your bill to me and you'll pay it in a neat lump sum!"

Her gun lay on the bunk, only a yard removed; and as she saw the taint in his bold eyes and the swollen flabbiness of his face every fibre in her revolted, every ounce of strength went into a great effort at freedom. He was a little off guard, and she wrenched an arm free and struck him across the mouth; her nails tore twin furrows in his slack lips, laid open the skin about his eyes. He let go of her then, and she sprang back; the table was between her and the bunk, and before she could circle around he came raging over the interval. She tried to make the table serve as a bulwark. His thick arms took it up and smashed it against the room wall as if it were only a toy. After that, and for all her courage, everything seemed to grow dim. She felt herself throwing things at him, she felt her back near to breaking as he caught her. His fist dropped on her shoulder with all the effect of a sledge; and when she next knew anything clearly she was in front of him, on his horse, going swiftly up the hillside and deeper into the trees.

All her instincts summoned her to keep up the struggle. Yet when she tried to pull away and drop to the ground she found herself pitifully weak, and all she succeeded in doing was to arouse his unbalanced anger so much more. His circling arm cut into her waist.

"Now stop it—stop it! I'm done with using words on you, my dear. Quite unmannerly of a gentleman to strike a lady. But I'm no gentleman and you're no lady. And you've had this coming to you for a long, long time. You laid open my scalp with that sharp tongue of yours more than once. I suppose you think your sex protects you. Well, it doesn't. Stop that moving about or I'll squeeze you purple."

"Where are you taking me?"

"Don't you wish you knew?" was his mocking retort. "You will never see Deadwood again, you will never see your charming hero again. My great regret is that I had to watch him day after day and couldn't shoot."

"Put me down!"

"You had better save your breath. There is one great lesson in my life, my dear girl, I wish to impress upon you. Never judge a man by appearances. I may have looked simple . . ."

The horse carried them upward and on. Once Lispenard dragged harshly at the reins and set the horse on its haunches. The man was muttering to himself and staring around at the trees. "Where's that rustling?" Then he went on, sinking his spurs deep into the animal's flesh. They fell over a rise and started down a pocket. The courage was out of the girl, she felt cold, pulseless; somewhere, deep down, hope was dying and all her fine dreams shrivelled and scattered. There was no good in this man—not an honest impulse, not a single saving grace. He represented the most debased point to which a human being could fall, he was the most brutal and degenerate specimen upon the earth— a man trained to be civilized, reared in the graces and knowing right from wrong, yet deliberately throwing all this overboard and reverting to the jungle. There was no element in Lispenard to which she could appeal, she was utterly defenseless. Even the animals had a code of a kind; this creature with the wild, bulging eyes, racked by passion and swayed by sullen angers and petty spites and raging thirsts, had no code.

They swept out of the depression and smashed through the brush, Lispenard never ceasing his mutter of talk and his weaving inspection of the forest around him. Something was on his mind, and the farther they travelled the harder he gripped her and the more he punished his horse, raking his spurs all along the animal's flanks, sawing at the reins. As badly as she herself was placed she felt sorry for the beast; the man was killing it with his temper. And presently she began to feel ashamed of her own lack of spirit.

"Let me down! You can't go on with this. You'll be caught sooner or later."

"Ha—you think so? Well, I'm not the tender Easterner any more, girl. I've studied under good heads. D'you think your blessed Tom Gillette will ever catch up? He can't do more than sit in a saddle. By Godfrey, I wish he would follow! There's a debt I'd like to pay. Oh, but I'll pay it! I'll leave him in torment the rest of his life!"

"Let me down!"

"Stop that screeching, or I'll give you something to cry about!"

"You'll never get away, you swine!"

"Don't believe all you read in the story books," he jeered. "I've got a nice little retreat picked up here. And you'll wash and mend and cook for me while they search till the very pit freezes over. You'll see 'em within hand's reach, too, but I'll have you whipped then! You won't have enough spirit to raise your head!"

They swept into another small depression, ringed around by the pines. The horse swerved, and Lispenard sat back in his saddle to curb the animal, his grip on the girl relaxing. She had been watching for such a moment; her whole body gathered into one last effort, she wrenched the encircling arm free and flung herself outward and down, landing asprawl on the uneven ground. Lispenard's cry of rage broke like a bomb in the glade, the horse came to a swirling halt, and the man sprang from the saddle. Lorena rose and ran. If she only could reach the shelter of the trees and just for a moment put him off the trail . . . She heard his heavy body pounding in pursuit, she heard his laboured breathing nearer and nearer; she knew she had no right to look around, but the fear she had of him was stronger than her reason. So she turned her head just as his great arm came swinging outward. It struck her on the temple and she collapsed, crying like a child with a broken heart.

Lispenard stood over her, watching her face. But for the moment she was done, she had no tricks left in her. The brush rattled behind him, and he whirled about, yanking the gun from his belt and challenging.

"Who's that?"

There was no answer. Lispenard's rolling eyes passed around the circle; a patch of sun came through the aperture of the trees and sparkled along his sweatbeaded face. In the hard light he seemed more gross, more frenzied than before; the great muscles of his neck stood out sharply, and his immense chest rose and fell to his laboured breathing. Presently he became aware that he made a fair target, and the thought sent him tramping around the edge of the glade, knees springing at each step and his gun veering from side to side. Down went his yellow head, like that of an enraged and trapped bull. Near the girl he stopped.

"Get up!"

He saw her tremble; it seemed only to rouse the last vile dregs of his temper. "Get up, you spitfire! Don't sham with me! I've got you and I'll keep you! Next time your try that I'll break bones! Get up!"

The brush stirred behind him; he swung on his heels, every flabby muscle of his face cutting a seam across the white flesh. Lorena rose to her knees and turned her head. Across, on the opposite side from Lispenard, San Saba stood framed between two small pines; the ex-foreman's little red eyes were affixed to Lispenard's back and his thin features were set and drained of emotion. Even as she looked, his arms dropped and rose, and there was a gun levelled in his palm.

"Turn aroun', yella-belly."

Lispenard revolved, the breath blasting out of his mouth. "By Godfrey!"

"Drop that gun."

Lispenard appeared rooted; his eyes rolled and flashed. "No by a—"

"Drop it or yo' die this minute."

The gun fell. San Saba stood straighter, and there was an unperceptible flickering of emotion across his gray lips. "Yo' been deceivin' me right along, man," said he, droning out the words. "Yo' knew Gillette was in that cabin. Yo' tricked me to he'p yo' own plans."

"Well," snapped Lispenard, "he's still there. Go back and get him if you want him. Don't interfere with me."

"Trash. Yo' jest trash. I don't traffic with women, and I got no use fo' a man as does."

"Don't be pious! Get out of my affairs!"

"No, suh. I'm a dam' rascal, like I once told you. But I don't sleep with snakes. Well, yo' had yo' minute of grace. I'm wipin' yo' out now."

Lispenard saw death across the interval and his whole face twisted into lines of agony. "Here—let me get my gun. You tricked me out of it. Fair fight."

"I don't fight fair," said San Saba, each word falling sharp and rhythmically across the space, "unless I've got to."

The girl averted her head from the ex-foreman. She felt the movement of Lispenard's body; there was a single smashing echo, and the Blond Giant was on the ground, threshing his life away. She had never heard a cry wrung out of any creature half so shrill or so despairing; San Saba's boots advanced, quite slowly, each slap and squeal of leather cutting a deeper furrow into her nerves. He passed behind her, he stopped. The fallen man's breath came in tremendous gulps. There was one more shot, and then utter silence descended upon the glade, and the girl sat on her knees, hands over her face as if she was praying. Out of that silence, as long as a century, came San Saba's brittle words.

"Yo' have nothin' to fear from me, ma'm. I don't traffic in women."

She thought she heard a shuttering sound away down the slope. San Saba spoke a little more quickly. "Ma'm, yo' got nothin' to fear. Stand up. Did the dawg do an—"

There was a break to the sentence. She looked up to see the man facing north, slightly bent, and his little eyes running back and forth over the trees. The drumming became plainer, more insistent, brush broke and crackled. San Saba shook his head at her. "Keep still. No sound from yo'." He retreated and presently was in the thicket. Lorena got to her feet, meaning to run over and meet the oncoming horsemen; before she could move Gillette swept into the clearing, hatless, and a streak of crimson fresh on his face. Lorena flung up her arms, crying.

"Tom—look out—watch the bushes!"

She saw him sway. A shot blasted the glade. Gillette was pat against his saddle, gun speaking along the far side of his horse. There was a rumbling yell, and Quagmire spurred on across the opening. More shots ran into each other, and a swift exchange of words rumbled and died out there beyond sight. The brush smashed, Quagmire sounded again, farther off; at this Tom slipped from his saddle and gathered the girl toward him, saying not a word.

Quagmire returned, wrath simmering on his morose face. "San Saba. Pullin' consid'ble leather. Waitin' to take a bite at yo', Tom. Looks like he got a stray skunk befo' he lit out, though. Durnedest fella ever I met. One shot an' run. Shucks, I couldn't ketch him with this hay burner"

"Let's turn back," said Gillette. He stepped around the girl, shielding her from the sight of the dead Lispenard; he put her into his own saddle and took the dead man's horse. The three of them rode down the slope single file.

"One chore done, another to do," murmured Quagmire. "Allus a little bit o' scandal left over. It ain't creation's pu'pose ever to let mortal man get a square deal. All we do from cradle to grave is play a rigged game. Ain't it foolish?"

17 ALL TRAILS CROSS

They came back to the cabin. The horses and wagon stood in the clearing, the preacher sat on a stump trimming himself a switch; and when Lorena saw him her tired, troubled face turned to Tom in a mute appeal. He helped her to the ground, murmuring:

"I know it's been a mighty hard day. Can't blame you for not wanting to be married after all this water's gone under the bridge. If you'd rather postpone it until tomorrow—"

She shook her head slightly and motioned toward the cabin. Once inside she closed the door and faced him. "It's not so much that, Tom. I know I should be sorry for the man, but after all's happened I can't bring myself to feel much sympathy. It had to happen, he was doomed to die; all I regret is that San Saba was so cruel about it—so cruel, Tom!" She stopped a moment, and he saw her fighting for control. He was about to support her; she shook her head again. "I'm strong—nothing can hurt me. It isn't that, but—"

"You've changed your mind?" he asked, the words running together.

"Tom, I can't ever change my mind as far as I'm concerned with you! What's in me will always be there. But why do other people live so securely while with us everything goes wrong? The very moment I saw you, Tom, trouble started for you and everyone near you. I know it.

Treachery and bloodshed and bitter feeling—and now you are about to lose all that you own."

"You've had nothing to do with it," he interrupted almost roughly. "What's to be is to be. All this is in the cards. A man's got to fight to live. What you saw to-day is on your mind—it'll die out."

"I'm not sure. Sometimes I think it's a warning for me not to marry you. What can I bring you, Tom? The other girl, she's more of your kind—she's beautiful and she's educated. She can talk of the things you know, she's been a part of your life. What am I? Oh, Tom, I don't know—"

"I won't hear any more of that," muttered Gillette. "There's more in your little finger than in her whole body. I know who I want, don't I? By George, I reckon I've got to marry you by force before you let these queer notions get the best of you."

She seemed not to hear him. There was a set to her chin and a remote light in her eyes. She had come to a decision. "I'll not marry you here, Tom. I'm going back with you. I'm going to see that girl. Call it queer if you want, but I can't disobey my instincts. I'd—I'd feel almost unclean—"

"Look here, Lorena—"

"It's settled. Now let's go, Tom."

There was nothing more to be said; he saw that nothing on earth would move that subborn ruling. Lorena Wyatt was no half-heart; every fibre in her was steel true; she owned a courage and a will, and now she used them, no matter how it hurt her. Gillette dropped his head, unable to meet her eyes. She was whispering something to him that he didn't hear, her arm touched him and slid away. Then he swung on his heel and went out.

"Let's go," he told Quagmire. And to the preacher he added a short phrase. "Reckon we won't be needin' your help to-day."

Lorena's effects went into the wagon, she climbed to the seat beside Tom. He turned the team and wound down-hill through the trees. Quagmire followed a-saddle, leading Gillette's horse. And the caravan dropped through Deadwood's rutty street and on out into the swelling land that stretched northeast.

It was a long and tedious trip, the blazing sun pouring out of the cloudless sky by day and the sharp winds slicing across the prairie by night. Ahead of them was uncertainty, behind was nothing but the memory of disaster, of a dead man and of a man who deserved to die yet still lived. What none of the three knew was that this man followed them like a stalking beast all across the leagues of sand; and at night he closed up the interval and lay on the crest of a swell or in the shelter of an arroyo, watching their camp fire with his round, unblinking eyes. He might have come within revolver shot, he might have made his attempt at Gillette's life in the darkness, but he never so much as harboured the idea; for San Saba had tried to kill Tom Gillette on four different occasions by stealth, each time failing. He was a hard-headed renegade, yet there was in him a trace of that mysticism known as the gambler's hunch. The hunch told him he never would master Gillette by that method; therefore he would try another—he would wait, and he would face Gillette, and he would match guns openly. Thus he kept to the shadows, and at day waited until the wagon had dropped out of sight before taking up the pursuit.

Ordinarily San Saba was a cautious man; he loved to look upon the world from a place of shelter, to be slightly withdrawn from the light. He had infinite patience, and up to this point in his life he had never let his hatred obscure the cold reason dwelling in his little nutshell head. Sometimes the scales tipped against him, and rather than even the score he had turned and ridden away to other places. With him it was usually a matter of fresher and farther pastures. The very fact that he disobeyed this life-long habit now augured a powerful and upsetting change. San Saba had arrived at that point in his checkered career where personal satisfaction outweighed every other consideration. He hated Gillette as he had never hated another man; it was a matter of pride, of instinct, and of a dozen other unfathomable reasons. Whichever way the man turned he saw Gillette standing before him, seeming to mock and threaten him out of those deeply set eyes. Gillette was a challenge. He would never rest until he settled the affair. So the poison spread through San Saba's thin, malarial body and constricted his temper until the red signals spread around his lids, like a cobra raising its hood.

The little party climbed at last the slope beyond which lay the Circle G ranch houses. Quagmire spurred ahead. When Tom Gillette drew the horses in and wrapped the reins around the brake handle, the crew was mustered before him. The eviction notice still clung to the house wall; nothing had been touched, no other move had as yet been made. Quagmire announced it with a tight satisfaction. Gillette studied the horizon a moment, and Lorena saw the muscles snapping up along his cheeks.

"Then we'll push right on to Nelson and battle this through," he decided. His eyes wandered toward the closed house door; he stared at Quagmire. "Is that all the news?"

Quagmire squinted up to the heavens. "Yeah," he mumbled.

Gillette got down and came around to give Lorena a hand. "You're sure you've got to go on with this?"

She nodded her head, and of a sudden her attention rose above him. The house door had opened. Christine Ballard stood there, a splendid picture in the sunlight, as self-contained and enigmatic as he had ever seen her. She was smiling at him, waiting for him to come up; and the familiar cadence of her voice reached him.

"Welcome home, Tom. We have kept the fort."

Lorena dropped to the ground, going directly toward the other girl. Half across the interval she looked around, and it seemed to Tom Gillette he saw a touch of fear in those sombre gray eyes. She nodded and went on. There was a murmur between the women; Christine Ballard threw back her head, then the two of them passed inside and the door was closed. Gillette swept the circle with an irritable glance. "Snake out a couple fresh horses. Hustle it—hustle it. Quagmire, you're riding to Nelson with me."

And five minutes later he and the puncher were heading away on the last leg of their journey. Quagmire raised a skinny arm to the sky. "Ask no favours o' this world an' yo' won't never be disappointed."

"Quagmire, she won't get away from me again."

"Women has got ten times the cold nerve of a man,"

209

reflected Quagmire. And he shook his head. "If that girl figgers to go through with a thing, yo' better save yore breath."

Senator William Costaine had a nickname that sometimes was spoken around the corridors and committee rooms of the Capitol. It was bestowed humorously, yet as in most nicknames it contained a measure of significance. They called him the "wrath of God," and many a man who had felt the force of his outthrust jaw, his rapierlike questioning, as well as the devastating sarcasm of his speeches, went away from that ordeal with the firm conviction that the term was nothing less than appropriate. When the Senator got on the trail of corruption he seemed to generate volcanic fumes, he had all the overwhelming energy of a steam roller.

In this humour he struck Nelson a full week before Gillette returned; and within one hour of his arrival his room at the hotel became a chamber of inquisition. He summoned a notary and installed the man beside him and then in turn he sent out a series of brief invitations—to ranchers and surveyors, to the United States Marshal and allied officials, to Grist and to the land-office agent. The Senator asked questions, he listened to statements, and he asked more questions while the heavy boots tramped up the stairway and the room grew clouded with smoke. The depositions thickened to a respectable pile on the notary's table and into the Senator's frigid eyes there came a gleam that anyone back in Washington instantly would have recognized. It was the light of battle, the flickering of an ironic pleasure; the Senator was establishing a case, and presently there would be men scurrying for shelter while the halls of Congress heard his husky lawyer's voice piling up evidence and laying the mark of Judas across the names of certain gentlemen he long had suspected. Costaine was no pettifogger, nor did he ever raise the cry of "turn the rascals out" just to hear himself talk. When he had no evidence he kept silent and went on with his interminable digging. Therein lay his authority and his manifest power.

Presently the room was cleared. He lighted himself another cigar and tilted back his chair, nodding at the secretary.

"Nicholas, we've got Invering scorched. He'll wear no more purple, and he'll run for his hole like a scared rabbit. I detest and I suspect a man who continually and publicly wraps the flag around him and bares his breast to the arrows of iniquity. Oh, yes, Ignacius is scorched. The gentleman's dream of royal robes is sadly blasted. Nicholas, we leave for Washington by the next train. Arrange it." And presently, after shuffling through his depositions he raised his iron-gray head. "That fellow Grist didn't come, did he? Nor the land agent. Well, we'll pay 'em a visit. Come on."

Down to the land office he went. The agent knew very well who Costaine was, but he affected ignorance, only asking "What can I do for you?"

The Senator laid his card on the counter. "I want to see the records of this office, sir. Want to see 'em all."

"Not open for inspection," said the agent, inclined to be surly.

Costaine bent over the counter, frigidly polite. "Oh, yes, they are. Don't tell me what the regulations are. And you had better drop that public-be-condemned manner, sir. I want to see every dot and comma in this office."

"You can't come out here and tell me what to do!" snapped the agent. "I take my orders from the department! You senators think you run the government, but you don't run the land office. My books are all in order, and I'll open 'em to the proper authorities."

"So," mused the Senator. "Either I see those books or your head will be chopped off in the next forty-eight hours. And moreover, you will find yourself answering certain distinct charges. Nicholas, find me a chair in this rattletrap of an office."

The land agent capitulated. The Senator put on his steel spectacles and started down the pages in a kind of flat-footed patience; all of his life he had done just exactly this sort of thing, and there was no man in America more experienced in smelling out discrepancies. Better than two hours later he left the office, turned back to the hotel, and from thence went to the station and got aboard the train. But Costaine was no hand for delay, and a long telegram preceded him to Washington.

"It will be interesting to discover," he confided to the ever-present Nicholas, "by what extraordinary circumlocution those fine gentlemen got around the plain intent of the law."

In the course of the Senator's investigation he had failed to interview one man. Christopher Grist was in town all during the day; he had been told that Costaine wanted to see him, and later, from his office, he saw the Senator pass along the street to the land agent's. But Grist avoided a meeting; as quietly as possible he left the back door of his office and as quietly disappeared, not to appear again until night. But when he did return he found the land-office man waiting for him uneasy and uncertain.

"Look here—did you meet the Senator?"

Grist smiled. "I made it a point not to, my dear fellow. I'm doing no explaining. Let the bosses stand inspection."

"I know his reputation, the dam' muckraker," growled the agent. "It's his kind that cause all the trouble in America. Well, he looked at my records, but he never found anything. They've got nothing to pin on me, Grist! I'll face 'em!"

"That's right," assented Grist cheerfully.

The agent pointed angrily at him. "It's your cursed outfit that's got me in trouble! You've got to take some of the blame, I'll not be the goat."

"Thought you said there was nothing to pin on you," replied Grist.

"Oh, well, don't be a fool. That man means to manufacture trouble."

Grist touched a match to his cigar. "Let me tell you something, old fellow. The Senator doesn't need to manufacture anything. If he looks he will find—and from the bird's-eye view I had of the gentleman I'd judge he was one hell of a good bloodhound."

"That's a fine way for you to talk," grumbled the agent.

"It's not my land, not my cattle. I'm only working for folks. If you want to know the truth about it, I've acquired an extraordinary detached point of view about the P. R. N.

212

in the last few hours. What that outfit can't stand is daylight. Public attention will kill 'em quick as a shot. And I forecast much attention in the next few weeks. Watch out for it. Those fellows are the world's best evaders of responsibility. That's why I've got a detached point of view—and stand quite ready to detach myself from their employ."

"Say, you don't figure they'd be so low as to try to hook us small fry, do you?" the agent demanded, more and more disturbed.

"Don't you doubt it. A rich man's hide is no thicker than a poor man's. What on earth's the matter with your face? Got yellow jaundice?"

"Well, I'm clear, anyhow," muttered the agent, ducking out of the office.

"The poor fool," murmured Grist. He smoked alone in the darkness, turning over all his own transactions, examining his career with the P. R. N. for flaws. As far as he could reason the thing out they could pin nothing on his name. He obeyed orders, he didn't give them. If those orders happened to be ill-founded in law, what fault was that of his? He wasn't a lawyer. Of course, he had used his power criminally more than once—as in the effort to rustle Gillette's cattle. But there was no proof of this, and his own crew wouldn't ever testify against him.

"I happen to have all their instructions to me neatly filed for reference. And yet those instructions, when you come right down to it, are as innocent as a new-born cat. Ha—it would appear I was in the hole, after all. They'd be just the gentlemen to say I horribly violated their orders to be legal. Now who's foolish?"

He stirred in the chair and threw away his cigar. "I'd be wise if I drifted now. Still, it might blow over. Anyhow, the Senator isn't in Washington yet and won't be for a few days. So, why not wait? I'd hate to duck out of a good job and then find out nothing happened. We'll hang on a week."

Grist, however, was a little short on his time calculation. He overlooked the telegraph wires, and Senator Costaine kept those wires busy all along the route to the capital city. The effect of those messages was to throw a certain clique into high alarm, and forty-eight hours after his departure from Nelson the repercussion of that alarm returned to Nelson and struck both Grist and the land-office agent almost at the same moment. Grist received the following short query:

"What have you done in violation of instructions?"

Grist pondered over this a full day before sending back his answer, which was almost equally terse though a great deal more flippant.

"Have washed some dirty shirts, as per instructions."

The land agent came down to Grist's office in very much of a hurry. He looked older, and there was a furtive expression on his face. "I told you—I told you! Now the department is on my heels. There's an inspector coming out here. My God, this is what a man gets for trying to pay his debts! Look at me!"

"I see you distinctly. What are you worrying about? You're on solid ground. No proof of a forgery or anything like that, is there? Stand fast and get hold of yourself. This battle isn't lost yet."

"All right for you to say," muttered the agent. "You don't know what kind of a mess I'm in." He turned about the office two or three times before going out. On the threshold he threw a last word back. "I'm taking a little ride to clear my head."

Grist saw him go to the stable and presently come out with a horse and rig. The tail of the rig was filled with luggage; and as the man dipped beyond the street end and struck across the tracks into the open prairie Grist nodded. "That's the last of him. Well, he's wise. I should be doing it right this minute. But we'll wait and see what the next mail brings forth."

He rode back to the P. R. N. home ranch and stayed two days, in the course of which he let off no less than ten of his punchers; among these being the man who had filed on the Gillette water right. His instructions to them were pointed. "This country's getting pretty hot. It's a rotten climate.

214

Were I you I believe I'd travel west until I found the exact spot where the sun went into a hole." With that done he returned to Nelson and found a pair of telegrams waiting for him. He read them in the order of their date.

"Dislike tenor of last wire. Innuendo insulting. We hear from reliable sources you have overstepped your authority. Do you understand any unlawful act on your part implicates us? If such is case you must take consequences."

And the other telegram:

"Keep within your explicit instructions. Who told you to extend range south of river? Withdraw all cattle from that section, drop all business connected with it. Your lack of judgment and discretion astounding. Involves us with government. Get your books in order and render us a full account of your acts. Letter follows."

"In other words they're putting themselves on record as disavowing me," mused Grist. "They've tucked tails, the fat yellow scoundrels. Overboard goes the furniture to save a leaky boat. It won't do. They'll lose the beef contract, and they'll lose every inch of land they've had me steal. I'm through."

He saw the handwriting on the wall. Methodically he set about bringing up his account, and during the ensuing four days he brought together all the odds and ends of company business, even leaving a list of instructions for his unknown successor. And then, with all that behind him, he closed down the desk top, locked the office door, and crossed to the hotel. He was through.

"Just so. All it took to knock over an empire was one little puff of air and a single beam of daylight. Grist, my boy, let that be a lesson in high morality for you. There's always one honest man among a hundred fools. Now we shall eat the feast of Nero, salute this town, and depart. One more day and I'm apt to find myself in the lock-up. They're desperate for a victim."

He gave the office key to the hotel man with instructions to transfer it when his successor came; he started for the dining room, hungry and moved to a kind of flippant amusement. Half in his chair he heard the hotel man say:

"That's Tom Gillette ridin' in, ain't it? Sure. Somebody told me he went to Deadwood. Well, he'll be on somebody's trail."

A startled expression skittered over Grist's face. He did not touch the chair's bottom; pivoting he went out the back door and on down the back alley.

Gillette's first visit, once in Nelson, was to the United States Marshal. "Well, you invited me to come get a warrant, Hannery. Here I am."

The marshal tilted back his chair. "I wasn't in any hurry about that, Gillette. Why in thunder are you?"

"Because I don't want it hanging over me," said Gillette soberly. "That's some of friend Grist's work, isn't it?"

"That's right. So is the eviction proceedings, if you want the opinion of a private citizen."

"All right, serve your warrant. If there's twelve men in Dakota who'll convict me on that charge then they're a new brand of settlers to me. I'll go that one better—if there's six men, outside of the P. R. N. crew, who'll convict me I'll pay for my own funeral."

"I know that as well as you do," drawled Hannery. "Don't you figure I'm familiar with public opinion in this district? Hell, it's so flat a case the U. S. Attorney won't clutter up his docket with it. He told me so."

"Well, I don't want it hanging over," said Gillette. "Let's clear the matter up. Let's go through with it."

Hannery shook his head. He was a florid man, and he owned a rough sense of humour that now and then snapped to his eyes. It appeared now. "Reckon I've got to disappoint you, Gillette. Fact is, I filed that warrant somewhere and I've lost it. All my papers get throwed around so dog-gone carelessly. If you want to be served you'll have to wait

216

till I find it. Meanwhile you go about your business. My opinion is it got into the waste basket by mistake. Come to think of it, I'm almost sure somebody cleared my desk the other day.''

Gillette rolled a cigarette, frowning over the operation. Presently he looked up. "Hannery, you're a white man."

"The country used to be nothing but white men," was the marshal's gruff answer.

"Grist'll bring it up again, though."

"Like hell he will. Haven't you heard any of the news? Grist resigned his job three days ago. He's still around town, but he's got nothing to do with the P. R. N. any more. What are you worrying about?"

"A fact?" murmured Gillette, plainly surprised. "What jarred him loose?"

"I don't know for sure. But Senator Billy Costaine stormed into town some ten days back and took enough depositions to fill a wagon. Right after that the land-office fellow skipped. Next, Grist filled in his ticket. You can guess for yourself." He leaned forward, a stubby finger tapping the table. "Speakin' privately, that Eastern bunch was ridin' awful high, and they stood to make a million out of this land-grabbin' deal. They'd of made it, too. Nobody around here could shout loud enough to make Washington hear anything. Most of us didn't know enough to register a kick, and some of us knew but weren't in any position to make any very big noise. How Costaine came into the wind I don't know. But he did, and when that fellow gets on the trail something drops. I'm bettin' you solid silver against a hackamore there won't be any P. R. N. Land Company in these parts when the year rolls around."

"That's why I didn't see any cattle south of the river, then?"

"Grist told me he was ordered to draw everything back from that side and quit bothering with it."

Gillette got up and tilted his hat. He was smiling. "Any time you want to evict me, Hannery, just go ahead. I'm going to move anyhow. To-morrow morning I'll be squatting where Wyatt used to be. I'd like to see anybody take that from me."

"I was going to drop that bug down your collar myself,"
replied Hannery. "P. R. N. can't hold it—they won't dare
to go through with the schedule. And nobody else's got wind
of the situation. You bet it's going to be a white man's
country yet. Say, you look kind of peaked. Deadwood trouble you some?"

"I went after a party and he saw me first," was Gillette's
sombre answer.

Hannery's eyes swept down Gillette's loose frame. "You
don't carry that gun low enough by two inches."

"I'm no killer, Hannery. I've had enough to last me. All
I want is to be let alone. Well, thanks."

He walked out and joined Quagmire who crouched in a
patch of shade. The sun went westering, and at the moment
Nelson was aflame under its slanting beams. The tide of life
ran along the street in a sluggish trickle; down at the station
a train stood ready to pull eastward, smoke pouring out of
the engine's funnel stack. A bell clanged resonantly and
Quagmire stirred, rubbing his knee joints with a slow, uneasy motion.

"Come on, Quagmire, let's get something to eat. It's a
long ride home."

"Ain't hungry," murmured the puncher. "I don't feel
right. I don't fer a fact. They's somethin' wrong. You go
ahead."

Gillette went on and into the hotel dining room. Only a
matter of habit put him there—habit and the need for something to occupy his mind. He was tired, supremely tired,
and his muscles served him none too well. The long trip
from Deadwood had been a pretty hard strain, even though
he rode the wagon seat. It seemed to him that he was growing old; here a month was gone since the night San Saba
and Hazel's gang had ambushed him, and still he was weak.
Where was his vitality? There was no snap to him, no re-
siliency, and he observed with a detached and critical dis-
approval that even for so simple an operation as reaching
for the salt shaker it took a distinct order from his brain and
a conscious pull of will to extend and withdraw his arm. He
was dull, dead on his feet.

"Wherever she goes," he told himself "I'll follow. Clear to the jump-off."

It seemed mighty queer to him he didn't feel elated at the sudden change in his affairs. As far as his range and his water right were concerned there wasn't even a struggle to be made. Lorena was to be thanked for that. Lorena! Her name echoed like a pleasant melody in his head. He remembered when he saw her spurring over the swelling land, a pert and boyish figure mounted on a horse she called Mister Jefferson Davis. And she had swept around him like an Indian to reach out of her saddle for a prairie blossom. He had never forgotten the picture she made with that crimson flower stuck in her black hair and her white teeth set into her lower lip.

Well, water had flowed under the bridge since. That sturdy slip of a girl on the vague border of girlhood had risen to be a woman.

"By Godfrey this man's world has bruised her! And after all that does she think I'll let her go? It's got to be the other way!"

Nothing mattered with a man. He was supposed to stand up and be licked and stand up again. Else he wasn't a man. No crying for the breaks of luck. But it did matter with a woman—and Lorena, at the very worst of it, still had smiled at him out of her dark eyes while she kept telling him nothing could hurt her. He never observed that his fists were clenched about his plate, nor that the food on it grew cold. Somebody was beside him, muttering. He looked up to find Quagmire.

"Say—well, Judas, what's happened to you, Tom?"

"Nothing."

"Say, I haven't ever horned in on yore business now, have I?" demanded Quagmire. "No, you bet not. Only yo' got a chore to do yet, an' I figgered mebbe you'd ease yo'se'f an' lemme take care of it while yo' et. That all right?"

"What chore?"

"Jus' a fragment of unfinished business," said Quagmire evasively. "That's all right, ain't it? Yeh. See yo' later, then."

"No, come back here. Come back here, you confounded

fool! I'm not delegating anything I don't know about. Spread it.''

Quagmire swung around, his pale eyes squinting. There was a hot personal anger in them—Quagmire was roused against his own boss. "Listen, Gillette, if yo' don't know enough to come in outen the rain I'll take my spurs and go!''

"You've got that privilege any day," snapped Gillette, and thereupon cursed himself for the tag-end collection of nerves he had become. "Oh, swallow it. What's on your mind?''

Quagmire moved his arm sheepishly. "If yo' got to know—San Saba's in town. He's down by the stable, standin' in the middle o' the street.''

"Then I reckon he wants to see me." Tom got up from the table, laid down his half dollar, and walked through the lobby. At the door he stopped and turned again to Quagmire. "Old-timer, let that last remark wash down the creek.''

"It goes twice," muttered Quagmire. "I'm a galoot for tryn' to butt my mug in another gent's personal affairs.''

"Well, here's the end of the train ride," said Tom. There was something the matter with his ears, for he heard himself as from a distance; and his arms were heavy.

"I know the gent's habits," Quagmire broke in. "In a pinch he don't use that belt gun. It's another under his arm yo' got to watch.''

Gillette nodded, not hearing the words. The street was half shade and half sunlight. Over in the shade he observed men standing near to the walls and moving not at all. A spotted dog padded across his vision leaving a trail of dust behind. "I wish I knew her answer now," murmured Gillette and walked out into the sunlight. San Saba's lank frame was in the shade, fifty yards along. There were a great many men against the building walls; Gillette saw the blur of their faces, and he heard some faint voice calling his name. And then all this died out of his attention; he swung and walked to meet the renegade ex-foreman.

He thought at first the man meant to wait for him; but a moment later San Saba stepped sidewise into the sun and

220

came forward. Gillette marked how the man's long legs buckled at each step and how the dragging spurs fluffed the dust. San Saba's arms swung with his tread, in a short arc, and the palm of his gun hand seemed to brush holster leather at each passing. He was marked by hard travel, his clothes were an alkali gray, his butternut shirt was open at the neck, and Gillette saw the two front cords of his neck taut against the sunburned skin.

Nothing was said between them; that time had come when there were no words to carry any meaning either would understand. They were, the both of them, thrown back on instinct, back to the stark and ancient promptings. So they closed the interval, and for all the emotion they displayed they were as men coming up to shake hands. San Saba's body swayed a little forward of his feet, and his little nut-round head nodded. Gillette advanced erect, watching how the ex-foreman's eyes grew narrower at each pace. Time dissolved into space and, save for the sound of his own boots striking, he would never have known himself to be moving. Somewhere a spectator coughed, the sunlight grew dim, the spotted dog ran between them. And then all his range of vision was cut off and he saw only San Saba. San Saba had stopped. His arm rose slowly away from his belt; a bull whip snapped twice, sounding to Gillette strangely like guns exploding. The spotted dog raced back, barking, and men ran out into the street and made a circle around a San Saba who had disappeared. Gillette stood alone, wondering. His arm felt unusually heavy, and he looked down to find a gun swinging from his fist; the taste of powder smoke was in his throat.

"Yo' got him. Come away an' let Nelson bury its own carrion."

Quagmire stood at his elbow, face seamed with great wrinkles. Gillette drew a breath and holstered his gun. He said something to Quagmire, whereat the puncher stared queerly. The marshal came along at an unhurried gait, still smoking; and the marshal threw out a warning as he walked. "Better lower your belt two inches, Gillette. It's too high."

Gillette headed for the hotel. The last idea in his head was that he hadn't finished his meal and that he'd better go

221

back and drink the coffee even if he wasn't hungry. Directly at that point the whole significance of the scene broke across his mind. "Then it wasn't a bull whip after all, but the guns. The man's dead. Another chore done. I can see the end of the trail."

He was at the hotel door, facing Lorena Wyatt. Where she came from he didn't know. But she was there, support-ing herself against the wall, eyes aflood with strange mists.

"Settled?" he asked. The memory of the gun play was wiped out; all else for the moment ceased to matter. He drove directly at the thing he wanted to know. "Settled? I'll follow, no matter where you go. It can't be any other way."

"She's gone, Tom. One of the men brought us to town in the buckboard. I'm going back with you."

His head dropped. "Well—"

"Never ask me any questions about it. There is the one thing I'll hide from you. The rest of me is yours."

He took her by the arm, throwing a swift glance at Quag-mire. "Go get a preacher."

A half hour later they were travelling away from Nelson and back to the ranch, while from a second-story window of the hotel Christine Ballard watched them fade into the dusk of the prairie; she was dry-eyed, her training wouldn't let her cry now. But when the last vague outline of Gillette drooped into the swirling shadows and was lost it was to her as if the light of the world had been extinguished. She crouched down, her head resting on the window ledge. And long after Nelson had sunk to rest she was still in that same position.

Quagmire rode through the night with the silhouette of the buckboard ahead of him. The stars were scattered in the sky, shimmering like diamond dust; the wind bore up the cry of a coyote on some distant ridge. The loneliness of the ages was in that solitary chant, and Quagmire, hearing it, drooped a little lower in the saddle, cigarette tip making a criss-cross pattern in the velvet shadows. "Yestiday I was a kid an' my mammy sung songs to me soundin' like that. To-morrow I'm dead. It's jes' a day between sleeps. There's a couple which neither asked nothin' from the universe an' accidental they busted through the crooked game for a win— temporary. Well, somebody's got to win temporary. A minute to smile and an hour to cry—then we sleeps, an' them stars keep on shinin' like that an' some other ki-ote howls out on the same old ridge. Man is mortal. Go along, pony. Wish I had as little to think about as yo' did. Yeah, man is mortal.''